One
of the
Family

SADIE PEARSE

sphere

SPHERE

First published in Great Britain in 2020 by Sphere

1 3 5 7 9 10 8 6 4 2

Copyright © Sadie Pearse 2020

The moral right of the author has been asserted.

A CIP catalogue record for this book
is available from the British Library.

ISBN 978-0-7515-7703-7

Typeset in Baskerville by M Rules
Printed and bound in Great Britain by
Clays Ltd, Elcograf S.p.A.

Papers used by Sphere are from well-managed forests
and other responsible sources.

Sphere
An imprint of
Little, Brown Book Group
Carmelite House
50 Victoria Embankment
London EC4Y 0DZ

An Hachette UK Company
www.hachette.co.uk

www.littlebrown.co.uk

For my daughter, Marlie

Part One

Part One

Prologue

29 August 2001, Dorset

Seventeen years of living in Fern Bay. I've seen all there is to see, in this place that is sure it knows the whole of me. This curve of sand on the Jurassic coast, with its high cliffs and small minds, has a way of locking you in. I've had enough of being locked in.

Past midnight. It's dark, it's quiet. It's time to go. In the hallway I put on my denim jacket and lace up my DMs on the bottom step of the stairs. It's the same place Freya and I used to put on our shoes when we were kids getting ready for school – Dad starting up the car, and Mum calling out from the kitchen – orders, or, when she was in a better mood, that she loved us. I'd sometimes hide one of Freya's shoes to wind her up. It was pretty easy to wind her up. She'd hit me with it when she found it, and we'd end up laughing.

I push those thoughts away. They're the kind of thing that stops me moving on. I don't want to be held back any more. I want to be me. I want for it to be OK to be me, and I feel like this time it will be.

I put on my backpack. It's heavy, heavier than it was the other times. I've planned it out better: I've got all the clothes I'll need, and enough money to get out of town.

I draw back the chain and unlatch the front door as quietly as I can. Mum

3

and Dad are away, so it's not them I'm worried about. It's Freya – she's a light sleeper. I don't hear anything from upstairs, and as I close the door behind me I let out the breath I've been holding. I go from the silence of the house to the silence of the summer night outside. Inside, outside. Captive, free. I look at the bluebird tattoo on my forearm, and get a warm feeling inside.

I'm walking down the front path and out on to the pavement, the slabs of concrete lit by the moon; it's a fat white moon and it's low in the sky tonight. My heart speeds up as I reach the end of our road, Beech Close. Excitement and fear mingle in my stomach. I'm walking out in the direction of the A-road and I feel this rush inside me, as though all the energy I have finally has a place to go.

I've been here before. More times than I can count on both hands. But a day or two on I've always turned around, gone back too soon, back to those relieved faces, but feeling like I've let myself down. Not this time. This time I won't be on my own.

I look back and I see the light go on in Freya's bedroom on the second floor. I walk faster down the road. Instinctively I put a hand on the wallet in my pocket. A fat roll of twenties, some mine, some not. Just keep going . . .

I glance back. I see Freya silhouetted in the window.

Damn.

For a minute seeing her makes me want to go back. Then her light goes off. One day, Freya. One day, I'll see you again.

Chapter 1

April 2019, Fern Bay, Dorset

Freya opened her post at the dining-room table, making a pile of admin to go through. The radio was on, a play that she was half-listening to, as she sat down with her laptop and a mug of tea. She twisted her hair up into a bun and glanced out of the window, distracted by thoughts of Jessie, her six-year-old daughter. You could see most of Fern Bay from their living room, the sandy sweep of beach and the jagged cliffs, the paths that filled with tourists in the summer and emptied out as the days grew colder. Dark clouds had gathered through the morning, and it was raining heavily now. Jessie and her dad would be soaked.

Louisa was in the adjoining room, lying on the sofa with her feet up. She had headphones on, and was nodding to a beat Freya couldn't hear, surrounded by open textbooks and revision notes. She'd been studying since nine that morning, preparing for the GCSEs she'd start in a couple of weeks. Louisa had inherited her mother's tendency to want to get things right, and Freya sometimes wondered if she might be pushing herself too much at school. She couldn't be sure – Louisa's world was a more private place these days, and Freya was still adjusting to the way the doors had closed. It wasn't only her school work. When her daughter was sitting down in the evenings, her thumb running over her phone screen, her eyebrows drawn in towards one another, Freya would wonder where those messages were going, and what was coming back. But usually, just at the point Freya felt a prickle of concern, Louisa would laugh, look up from her phone screen and maybe even relay a line or two of the conversation. They'd chat together, Louisa's cheeks flushed and her eyes shining. She was more independent these days, and that was how it should be, Freya reminded herself. It was just hard, sometimes, to let her go.

Anyway, she had Jessie, her ball of sunshine, who still told her everything – from the questionable plotline of every *Shopkins* episode to just how wobbly her teeth were. Jessie had Freya firmly at the centre of her world. At times her demands for attention were exhausting, especially on the days Freya came home after long hours at work. Her job, as a location scout, took her along the coast and through the West Country – finding places that would come to life on TV, and making arrangements for the film crew to use them. She got a buzz from the travel, but when she was away a lot she felt torn sometimes, aware of Jessie's need for her to be closer. Freya reminded herself that one day soon, like Louisa, Jessie too would slip more firmly into her friendships and away from her mother, and then she would miss this time.

Louisa took off her headphones. 'Test me on these ones, Mum?' she said, showing her mother a revision card. 'The pink-highlighted bits.'

History. Not Freya's strongest subject, but better her than Joe. Joe ... well, Joe was Joe – by all accounts, he'd spent most of his schooldays bending the rules when he could, breaking them when he couldn't. Louisa, though, seemed to absorb facts and details effortlessly.

'OK – so, the English Civil War—' Freya started.

'No, sorry, not that one, the twentieth-century stuff.' Louisa switched the cards around. 'This one.'

'Right, so in 1918—'

The kitchen door opened, cutting her short. Joe and Jessie bundled into the room noisily, Jessie taking off her wellies and raincoat and dumping them on the kitchen floor.

'Hey!' Freya said. 'There are hooks for those.'

Jessie shrugged. 'In a minute.'

Freya looked at her pointedly.

'Now, Jess,' Joe said, taking her over to the hook. 'Christ, it's really coming down hard out there.'

'There's thunder and lightning!' Jessie said. 'I told Dad I didn't mind, but he said we had to come home.'

Freya got Jessie a towel to dry herself with, but she batted it away, running over to Louisa and hugging her. 'Hey, Louisa!'

Louisa pushed her away. 'Urgh, Jess!' she protested. 'You're soaking.'

Jessie shook her head, letting the wet strands whip her sister's face, like a dog fresh from swimming.

'MUM! DAD! Get her OFF me,' Louisa cried. Giggling, she lifted Jessie up and carried her into the living room, where they got down on the carpet and pelted each other with cushions.

'Everything go OK?' Freya asked Joe.

'Good, yes,' he said. 'Jess and I had fun today. We went down to the rock pools for a while before the rain got bad. Then we ducked into a café.'

'You mean you filled her up with waffles and ice cream?' Freya asked, with a raised eyebrow.

'Yep. I filled her up with waffles and ice cream. Right before lunch. Sorry,' he said, smiling. 'Sorry, not sorry.'

She pushed him gently, wrinkling her nose. 'Be off with you, then.'

'Bye, girls,' he called out. Jessie and Louisa waved back. Joe and Freya walked together to the front door.

'I'll pick Jess up on Monday for school,' he said.

'OK, sure,' Freya agreed.

'Louisa getting on OK?'

'Yes, I think so. She's been studying hard today, but there's so much for them to learn. And if she's really serious about going to medical school she's going to have to get the results this summer. A lot of her friends seem to have tutors—'

'She doesn't need that, Frey. She's smart. She's been working hard, like you say.'

'I know. It's just, since she got her mind set on becoming a doctor, it really matters.'

'She'll be fine,' Joe said. 'She's an intellectual powerhouse. Gets it from you.' He smiled, and his eyes crinkled a little at the edges.

She saw it then, what she used to see. Joe. The Joe she loved, the one she had a thousand memories with. They had been so close, once – it pulled at her heart to think how close, because things were different now.

He turned and walked down the path, then along the street that led to his flat. Joe. Still her husband, but not her partner. Two people. Two daughters. Two homes. It was as simple, and as complicated, as that.

Freya went back into the kitchen, and returned to her papers as the girls played. She looked over at them. It came naturally now, parenting like this, and she tried not to think too much about where things would go from here.

Freya had met Joe in her first year at university – her only year, as it turned out. She remembered how it had been, leaving her family and arriving in Bristol knowing no one. She'd known about Freshers' Week – she'd been handed flyer after flyer for club nights as soon as she arrived – and her thoughts had immediately kicked in to work out how she could avoid it completely. The thought of socialising with complete strangers made her twitch. All she wanted was to get hold of all the books and articles on her Film Studies reading list, and get to work.

In that first week, she'd busied herself hanging photos in her bedroom and buying the things she needed – pans, crockery, bed linen from town. In the evenings she sat in her room watching films, while her flatmates made cocktails in the shared kitchen. They'd invited her out, but she'd said there were things she needed to do. She could hear them getting ready, laughing, the volume increasing. By Friday they'd heard all her excuses and the invitations became more insistent. She saw that her shyness was starting to look like rudeness. She thought of Sam – how easy she would find all of this, the chat about music and travel, the talk about boys they'd met or wanted to. Freya had friends back in Fern Bay. She'd cultivated them carefully over years at school. But she didn't know how to do this – dive into a social whirl with strangers, and find something to say. Even the thought of joining her flatmates around the kitchen table over tea made her cheeks burn.

A text came through from Sam. *How's Freshers' Week? PLEASE DON'T TELL ME YOU'RE NOT GOING OUT.*

She bit her lip, then typed back: *Sam, I'm not finding this easy. Everyone is going out all the time.*

Stop being a plank, Frey. Just go – get a couple of beers down you. Dance. You can do this. I'd be killing it if I was there with you.

I know you would be. I'm not you, Sam.

Just do it. Someone's got to like you, right?

Freya smiled. Could picture her sister's face as she'd teased her. *How about you? How's sixth form?*

Boring.

9

Really?

Yep. BUT. I went out on Saturday to a gig, and met a bunch of cool people.

OK. Interesting. Freya smiled to herself. *There's someone you like, right?*

There might be.

Go on then, what's his name? Freya asked.

The reply was a while coming.

Eliot.

I knew it, Freya said. *Update me.*

It wouldn't take long, Freya thought, for her sister to get into this guy's head. When you looked like Sam, willowy with long, wavy hair, skin that glowed and a laugh that rang out – it wasn't hard. Men noticed her wherever she went, even when she seemed not to notice them.

I will.

Freya's concentration was interrupted by a knock. Her flatmate Cathy put her head around her door. 'We're going to Gino's for pizza, then on to the pub. Tell me I can convince you to join us this time?'

Freya smiled, and slipped her phone back into her bag. She felt buoyed up by the conversation with Sam. She was going to do this. 'Yes. Thanks. Give me two minutes to get changed and I'm with you.'

That was the night that Freya met Joe. After the pizza, she and her three flatmates went to a pub in town where he was working behind the bar. She tipped her pint of beer all over the bar, and him, and felt mortified about it, but he laughed and they cleared it up together. Joe was easy company, and easy on the eye, heavy-set with a certain softness to him, the sort of body that invited hugs. When he asked her to go for coffee with him the next day, she agreed. The bar job was just a stopgap, he said, but he wasn't going anywhere in a hurry; he liked the people he worked with.

He hadn't done that well at school, but he'd train one day, maybe become a teacher. He liked working with kids, and would do boxing training with them at the weekend.

Their friendship grew, and she found she was spending more time with Joe than anyone else. It stayed just that, a friendship – they played table football in his shared house, went on hikes, and watched films together. He liked hearing about her course and the things going on at university; she enjoyed being at his place, with none of the pressure of academic life. They'd hug, and sit together on the sofa, and she'd wonder, sometimes. But what they had stayed just as it was. He met Sam, once, during the Easter holidays, and asked her about herself, about college. He didn't get much of a response. Freya apologised afterwards – that was how Sam could be sometimes. She could seem cold. She wasn't always polite.

Then, at the end of summer that same year, Sam disappeared. Freya called Joe the next day, and he got the coach down to Dorset to be with her. When he arrived, he saw Freya's shock and upset, and held her. She told him about the searches, and together they went out. He was there by her side, day after day, as she made phone calls, knocked on doors, walked through fields and along the beaches and, when it grew dark, searched the internet for traces of Sam.

As autumn turned to winter, she knew she couldn't let things continue as they were. She could tell Joe wanted to be with her, and it was natural, and fair, that things would progress in that way. After all that had happened that summer, being with Joe felt like putting down an anchor. He'd always wanted kids. Louisa wasn't planned, but it felt to Freya as if the pregnancy had happened so quickly for a reason. She didn't go back to finish her degree. It didn't feel right any more. Joe came to live in Fern Bay, they found the house around the corner from Freya's parents, and Louisa was born.

11

For Freya and Joe, having Louisa, and becoming a family, had brought them closer together, and given them both the direction they needed. They made their own way, and the baby had given Freya's parents a focus too. When Harry, Freya and Sam's dad, died two years later, being a grandmother became even more important to Jilly. At the funeral, she had held Louisa's small hand, and showed her off proudly to her friends and family. It felt right. And Freya had known it was easier than her mum having time to think about how it felt to have Harry die. How it had been devastating, and deeply sad, but also – the whispered words Freya's own subconscious delivered – ultimately, a release. Sam's disappearance had brought out Harry's negative personality traits until they'd almost overwhelmed the good in him. He'd been broken by Sam's disappearance, and raged about what she was putting them through. Then he had started to grow furious at all the irritations in life that he felt had been placed there to make his life harder. He was seventy-three when he had the heart attack, at the gym. They'd all told him to slow down, but he wouldn't. He'd never listened.

Freya had stayed at home with Louisa at the start, while Joe worked odd jobs locally, but the money didn't stretch to cover what they needed. She'd started to feel restless at home, too. She'd begun working as a location scout for a film company, and, while the hours were long and unpredictable, and it wasn't always easy fulfilling the writer and director's vision, she'd found something she loved doing. It sometimes felt like being a researcher, other times a magician. She left home early in the mornings, talked with and convinced locals, and found ways of squeezing the most out of limited budgets and time. The work kept coming, and Freya had begun to make a name for herself in the industry.

It had worked well at first: she would work, and Joe would look after Louisa at home. He'd said he wanted to do it, and over time any talk of him training to be a teacher fell away. Louisa had started school, and things had continued – he'd said he was fine, but something in him had started to fade. She wondered if he missed Bristol, his hobbies, the friends he left behind, but he said he didn't.

He said what he'd loved most of all had been having a baby, and that he wanted them to have another. Freya hadn't consciously thought of it as a way to bring them back together, make them complete again, but maybe that had been part of the reason. Another baby to bring back the feelings about each other that they'd had the first time. And once Jessie arrived they both fell in love with her, and she was all that mattered.

Freya had gone back to work, and Joe had taken over the care of Jessie, but the drawing together as a couple that they'd hoped for hadn't happened. Joe had seemed lost, and the more Freya tried to help him, the more he withdrew. He said he supported her in her career, but it didn't always feel that way, and he seemed resentful of the long hours she sometimes had to work. She loved him, but that love began to feel like a habit, something she did because she couldn't remember how to do anything else. As he became more depressed, she had picked up more of the domestic load, organising things for the kids, and rising before dawn to get their packed lunches and things ready for school. Joe would sit up until the early hours gaming, and Freya lost patience with it, and with him.

They did what they could to build bridges. They went to counselling. But the change seemed slow, if it was coming at all. Joe couldn't understand why Freya was exhausted and stressed out – he said her standards were too high, that she should relax, things would work themselves out. She'd felt that if they stayed as they were he would never be nudged out of the slump that he'd fallen into – he needed to wake up to the fact that things

13

weren't working. In the end they had decided that, while they worked things out, they would live apart. Joe had admitted that he needed time to decide what he really wanted to do in life.

Joe had rented a flat nearby, and they'd made a slow transition from family unit to a family that was based in two homes. They had found their own way. The girls were at the centre of their lives, and nothing there had changed – but other things had, in a positive sense. They treated each other more kindly and respectfully now than they had before. They saw that the best way forward – and the best chance they had at making things work for their family – was to give each other room to breathe. And weeks had turned into almost a year.

It wasn't how either them had pictured their family life turning out, but the girls had taken things well, and that mattered far more to Freya – to both of them – than anything else. In the past months, something seemed to have shifted. Joe had started teacher-training, and, while he found the workload challenging, Freya could see that the light had come back into his eyes.

She didn't know what would come next – neither of them did. But she was proud that they had done something, that they were making their own choices and doing what felt right to them, rather than giving in to the pressure from friends and family to stay together. Without a model to look to, they were making this work. She and Joe were taking their time and doing things their way. The girls – happily, crucially – had accepted the set-up, slowly, and seemed to be thriving.

Life wasn't always easy, and it certainly wasn't perfect. If Sam's leaving had taught Freya anything, it was that. This bump in the road of their marriage seemed natural to Freya somehow. They were getting by. And it was OK. It was more than OK. This was the shape of them.

Freya looked at her elder daughter, who had put her textbooks aside and was sitting with Jessie, chatting on the sofa. Louisa laughed, and in that big wide smile, the moment of open-hearted abandon, Freya saw a flash of Sam. Genes were curious things, the way they brought features to play in and out of your children, she thought. There'd be a reminder of Jilly in Jessie's eyes, and the girls had Joe's sandy hair, not her own dark brown. So when traces of her sister had started to appear in Louisa around her fifteenth birthday it had seemed natural, really. There were features and gestures that Freya hadn't seen in years – the sharp chin, the dark, arched eyebrows, the hair flick – it was as if Sam were there again.

'Mum,' Louisa called out, nudging Freya out of her reverie. 'You OK?'

Freya nodded, smiled. She encouraged her daughters to get back to what they were doing.

The girls asked about their aunt, sometimes, and Freya would give them as much of an answer as they needed. They knew the outline of it – that Sam had walked out one summer's night and no one had ever seen her again. Freya focused on the positive when she talked to them. One day Sam might come back. They'd asked what she was like, and Freya had told them. She'd tell them about the way Sam would share her headphones when she had a good tune on. How she'd dance barefoot in the dew in the garden. How she used to filter through the Haribo and pull out the cola bottles, eating only those. The way she'd find any reason good enough to laugh. That she was difficult, sometimes, and they hadn't always got along.

She'd tell them the truth: that she knew nothing at all about where Sam was. That maybe, after years living a different life, their aunt might walk right back into her old one and have a chance to meet her nieces, whom she would adore. Or it might be different – they could hear of her life in a faraway place, and be told she never wanted to come back. That way, at least, they'd be able to let go, knowing that that was her choice.

But the pain of it? Freya kept that to herself, or talked about it with Joe. After so many years, she had needed to accept the darkness inside, and let it live alongside the hope. It had been eighteen years, and no one had ever found a trace of Sam. When a light goes out, and you have no means of putting it back on, sometimes it's easier to sit there in the dark, rather than forcing yourself to remember what the room looked like when it was lit. Her sister had never used her bank cards, or her phone, after that night. The police had looked for her for months, interviewed everyone they could. The whole community had searched Fern Bay. There had been a suspected sighting once, in London, but nothing had come of it. Those were the facts. They sat with Freya, heavily, and there were times they left her feeling desolate. She couldn't lie to herself – her sister might not have been found because she was dead. That, in itself, wasn't a fact – and she hoped it never would be – but it was one of a dozen possibilities.

Freya had never let it define her, the fact that her sister had walked out of their house and never come back. Back then, neighbours had fallen into two camps: those who'd rallied round, brought food and support, and those, like Adriana who lived on the corner, who had retreated from the family as though they had something contagious. Those people who distanced themselves saw Freya as the girl from the family where something had gone wrong. That was the feeling Freya got, anyway.

She looked at Louisa – the light, the smile that was part of Sam, had crept back in unexpectedly. It was as if Sam was coming back into Freya's life, and Freya's home, piece by tiny piece.

*

16

Margate, Kent, 2019

The lights from Dreamland flicker across our bedroom wall. Like a little show all of our own. Dino loves it. You can see it in his eyes, tracking the lights beneath those long lashes.

Yellow. Flash. Red. Orange. Dino follows the lights with his bare foot, tracing the path of them with his toes. He's not saying much tonight, but he's good company for me all the same, and his face is relaxed, calm. He's OK.

People say Dino's quiet. His teachers at parents' evening, shopkeepers, grannies in the street. But I don't see him that way. To me he's an open book, whether he says anything or not. You can see what he's feeling if you look at him properly. People don't take the time to look closely, that's all.

Some nights we'll sit here and chat, and it's like he'll never stop. He'll talk about tadpoles and frogs, or how a clock works, or the Spanish Armada, things he's learned at school. Tonight I feel like a spliff, so I wait it out, until his eyelids lower, and his bare foot falls on to the mattress, and at last he's asleep on the bed next to me. I roll it and smoke it in the other room with the window propped open. You can hear the noise of the fairground from our flat, the shouts of kids on the rollercoasters.

It's like being on holiday here, that's what people say. The hipsters who flood the old town at the weekend, with their beards and pale skin and their estate agent's leaflets. I've been here a long while and seen it change a lot. Margate didn't feel like a holiday when I arrived, and it still doesn't now. But sometimes, when I look at those bright lights, I can squint and imagine. What it might be like to be here for a day, get dizzy on rides and candyfloss, get some postcards and then go back home.

Home. I take a deep drag, and it helps a bit.

Dino's my home now. He's the reason I get up. The reason I try and find work, even though those suits take one look at me, at the tattoo on my forearm, and they've already made up their mind that it's a no. It's because of Dino that I don't give up. Because you can't, can you – when you have a kid? I can watch those cars go by. I can watch the trains. There's no jumping on them. Under them.

Because of Dino. Because I've got him now.

Chapter 2

Freya approached her childhood home on Beech Close, a cul-de-sac five minutes' walk from where she lived with the girls. She felt a slow churn in her stomach. She'd dropped Jessie at school that morning, then got back in her car and driven over to her mother's house. Normally she might have lingered at the school gates, chatted with the other parents if she had time, but today wasn't like other days. She didn't want to make small talk today. She couldn't.

As she approached the house where she grew up, memories flooded back. She felt the rawness of Sam's disappearance all again.

April 30th. Sam's birthday. Thirty-five.

Freya glanced up at her old bedroom window. She could half-remember waking the night that Sam left, putting on the light and going over to the window. She could recall it two ways: one where she looked out and thought she saw Sam walking away, and another, where she saw nothing but the roads and fields lit by a big white moon. She didn't even know which memory was true any more. To keep going, she did what she could to block out thoughts of Sam – it was her way of getting on with life. She tried to be strong. But there were still days when she felt as if she was slipping into the costume of someone who was coping, pretending to be a woman who didn't have a piece of herself missing.

She'd fallen back to sleep briefly that night, then woken again at three, certain then that something was wrong. She had gone into Sam's room and found it empty. She'd run away again. The worry then the panic was familiar for Freya. But this time was different. Sam usually left after an argument with their dad, but their dad hadn't been there this time.

She'd called Sam on her mobile, again and again. Then she had called her parents, who'd driven through the night, back home. They'd searched, and they'd searched, and the police had searched. And they'd found nothing at all.

Today Jilly was in the front garden, pulling up weeds, her hair in a ponytail. Her hair was jet-black, too black for her age really, but it was one thing her mum wasn't willing to let go of. She'd let it lapse, for a short time. But on the eve of Harry's funeral Freya had helped her to dye it again. They'd been silent that night, united in sadness, in grief, for the man they'd loved and had lost suddenly.

Freya was pretty sure they'd both been wondering the same thing that night – whether Sam would come. Whether she would – somehow – have heard about her dad's death and return for the funeral. She hadn't.

Jilly was immersed in her task, creating a pile of dandelions and leaves, and for a moment she didn't notice her daughter at all. Freya called out to her.

'Oh, hi, love,' she said, squinting into the sun. She smiled. The smile didn't quite reach her eyes. In truth, it was a long time since it had, for any amount of time. Jilly would have noted the date in the calendar that morning, just as Freya herself had.

'How are you, Mum?'

19

'I'm OK.' She got up, pulled off her gardening gloves, and laid them down on the wall, signalling that she was ready to take a break.

'Thirty-five,' Freya said.

'Thirty-five.'

'You really OK?'

Jilly nodded. 'Listen, I know you worry about me. Especially since your dad died. But this day each year – it's not a sad time for me. It's one of the things that helps me feel close to her.'

Jilly had been a strong woman once – swum in the sea most days, never shied away from racing or games with Freya and Sam when they were kids – but since Sam had left, and then even more so when her husband had died, she'd diminished – become a slight, frail figure whom Freya could barely connect with her childhood memories, or the photos on the mantelpiece.

'Let's go in for tea,' Jilly said. They went into the house together, and Jilly put the kettle on. 'I got a phone call this morning,' she said. 'Claire, she said her name was.'

Psychics, Freya thought. They'd spotted the fragility in her mother years ago. They'd come as close as she'd let them, offering their toxic mix of hope, misinformation and false promises. The first weeks after Sam's disappearance had been the worst. They'd come to the house, with clues and insights. Preying on her parents when they were at their weakest. Her dad had got rid of them, back then. Freya would have thought they'd have got weary by now, but instead it looked as though they were still finding their way to her mother. When Freya could, she'd speak to them herself, get them on their own and warn them off – but they still seemed to slither back in through the cracks.

'Claire travels around, and she's here for a few days. She said she has something to tell me.'

'I'm sure she did,' Freya said, cynicism creeping into her voice.

'She knew things, Freya. She knew it was Sam's birthday today.'

'Of course she did,' Freya said. She bristled. That, or she'd checked a Missing Persons website for the date, as all the others did.

'Don't roll your eyes, Freya. I can see you. She said she'd had a sign. Had some ideas about where Sam might be.'

'Well, I hope you told her where to stick her sign.'

Jilly turned her back, busied herself getting boxes of tea out of the cupboards. 'Earl Grey? Lemon and ginger? Some nice ones here from Fortnum's—'

'Mum, I said I hope you told her where to stick her sign,' Freya said, more firmly.

Jilly shrugged. 'One meeting, that's all. She might genuinely know something. It might be important.'

Freya sighed. 'And how much is she charging?'

'Oh, don't be crass. We didn't talk about money.'

'I'm not being crass, Mum,' Freya said, annoyed at the idea that her mum was being taken advantage of. 'I'm just trying to protect you.'

'I don't need protecting,' Jilly said. 'I'm stronger than you think, Freya. And I've got money of my own, as well as from your dad. It's up to me how I choose to spend it.'

'But don't you think, Mum, that if finding Sam was easy the police would've discovered something by now?'

'She said Sam was living somewhere far away.'

'OK,' Freya said, trying to keep her patience.

'Near a beach. Which makes sense, doesn't it, Frey? Sam always talked about Thailand, didn't she? And she took her passport with her.'

'Yes, she talked about Thailand, and yes, she took her passport, but there's been no sign of her ever using it. I'm sure a lot of teenagers talk about beaches, and Thailand. I'm sorry to be blunt, Mum, but this woman doesn't have unique powers, any more than I do. She's trying the most obvious tricks in the book.'

'I just choose to try and be positive,' Jilly said. 'Don't get at me for that. I don't think it's that far-fetched to imagine that she might be living on a warm beach somewhere. It happens.'

'I'm not getting at you, Mum. Don't you think I want to believe it too? I'm just realistic about who can actually help.'

There was no point continuing the conversation. Freya and her mum had fallen out over this before, when Freya had first suggested that maybe they should both be open to considering that Sam might never come back. On that point they'd never be able to meet in the middle. There *was* no middle.

Jilly brought out the tea, sat down. 'Let's change the subject. Please.' She rubbed her temples. 'How are the girls doing?'

'They're doing well,' Freya said. 'Jessie's training for her gymnastics competition, and Louisa's been revising a lot. Keeping her head down, which is good, because there's a lot for her to do.'

'That's good,' Jilly said. She paused for a moment, as if considering what to say. 'And Joe?'

'Joe's fine. He was out with Jessie yesterday.'

Jilly's eyebrows lifted a fraction, in interest. 'How's his teacher-training going?'

'I didn't ask – but well, I think. He seems happier lately.'

'I'm glad. And—'

'Please don't, Mum. Not today.'

'What? It's a natural question to ask, isn't it? You wanted him to get back on his feet, and now it's starting to look like he's done that.'

'It's not that simple,' Freya said. It was definitely positive, that Joe was taking more control of his life again. But he'd done this before – picked things up and put them down. She needed more time to see how things would play out. She needed to see if she

22

could feel differently, because, at the moment, it seemed as if too much of the past was still weighing them down.

'You still love each other, though, don't you?' Jilly persisted. 'You make each other laugh. I've seen that.'

'We get on better now we're living apart, that's for certain,' Freya said. 'But you remember how we were arguing, this time a year ago?'

'Every couple argues,' Jilly said, flatly.

'I *know* that, Mum,' Freya said.

She thought about how it had been in their house growing up. Her dad had always been proud of them, and he'd been a loving man, but he hadn't been perfect. It was as if he short-circuited sometimes. He would lose control, shout, assign blame where it didn't necessarily belong. They didn't talk about it, just each found their way to live alongside it. Her mum would argue back, if she felt she needed to, and then retreat to her bedroom when she didn't get anywhere. You could never get anywhere. Sam would fight back until she had nothing left to give. Then, as she got older, she would run away. Freya would stay calm, and try to support him. Her dad just needed to be understood, accepted. He wasn't a bad person; he just hadn't had an easy start in life. He loved them all. He couldn't help it, the outbursts, it was just the way he was. You simply had to wait for the storm to pass, that was all. When it passed, Freya was the one there, still with him.

She thought of Joe, and felt sadness again, that things hadn't been easier. 'We didn't separate lightly.'

'He's a good man,' Jilly said. 'A good dad.'

'I know that,' Freya said. 'I don't need to be with him to value it. I appreciate it every single day.'

'Is he seeing anyone else?' Jilly said.

'I don't know. I don't think so. And I'm certainly not. I don't think that's what this is about ... It's about giving each other space: about Joe finding himself, working out what he really wants. I feel like we were so – I don't know – *smothering* for each other, I guess. And now I feel like I can breathe again. I can be solid, and strong for the kids. I'm not in a hurry to change that.'

'I respect your decision, and I'm trying to understand it,' Jilly said. 'I just think it's important, you know, for the children. For them to see their parents together. It's hard for me to get past that, but I *am* trying.'

'The girls are doing fine, Mum,' Freya said. 'Doing things this way is giving us all the best chance we're going to have.'

Freya remembered the police coming to their house the next morning, sitting in the kitchen, her mum insisting on everyone having tea, restlessly moving about the room.

'Samantha Jackson,' the policeman said, making a note in his book. 'Well, we'll look into it, of course – a missing person is always going to be a priority for us – but we have to take into account that there's a history here.'

He wasn't a stranger to them, no one in this town was – and he'd been here over a dozen times, sat in this same room, with their mother fussing over him in the same way. They'd say sometimes that Sam had been missing as much as she'd been found. They'd say it like a joke, but there was always too much truth in it for that. She would run away when she fell out with her dad – it had happened for the first time when she was eight, and she'd got as far as the end of the road before a neighbour brought her home. She'd left again at thirteen, when their dad had told her she couldn't go for a sleepover at her friend's house, because he was a boy. When their exchanges got heated, she would walk. Her dad would never admit that he regretted losing his temper with Sam, but Freya could see, etched in the lines on his brow, that part of him, beneath the pride, did.

Sam left, and left, and left. Freya stayed, and waited, and searched.

'I know,' Jilly said, putting the tea down and finally settling in a chair. 'She'll be back. She always comes back.'

'Has anything happened lately?' the policeman asked all of them. 'Anything that could have upset her and caused her to want to run this time?'

Freya couldn't bring herself to say it. Not here. Not now. She settled for part of the truth.

'She and I haven't been getting on that well lately.'

The police officer glanced up at the wall clock, impatient to be somewhere else. 'Have you contacted her friends?'

'Yes – the ones I have the numbers for – they haven't seen her.'

'Boyfriend?'

'No,' Freya said. She thought of Eliot. She'd sent him a message this morning. 'No one's seen her ... She's ... been different lately.' She said it reluctantly, feeling the hypocrisy. She had been different too.

'They're not a great crowd, the ones she's been hanging out with,' Jilly said.

'Can you tell me the names of some of them?' he asked, taking out his notepad.

'There's Echo ... her real name's Nicola Blake. She lives on the other side of town.'

He nodded, 'Chris Blake's daughter. I know the family.'

'Then ...' She searched her mind for the surnames. 'Anya Rierdon, Mel West, Eliot James.'

'And what are they like? When you say "not a great crowd" ...'

Jilly shook her head. 'They're not our kind of people. They weren't good for Samantha.'

*

25

On Sam's birthday every year, Freya had developed her own rituals. They were habits now, and each time she'd revive the hope that they might yield different results. She'd do it monthly, sometimes, but certainly and without fail on Sam's birthday, and the anniversary of the night she disappeared. She'd search the internet for Sam's name, along with some of the places she might have gone to – along with Thailand, she used to talk of Amsterdam, or Budapest, or Berlin. Freya would keep going until she'd covered all the combinations and permutations she could think of.

She felt compelled to repeat the same search, again and again. There had been a pull that summer, strong enough to make her go. But, with the passing of years, whatever it was would surely fade. She told herself that. Again and again.

She picked up her phone and went on to Facebook. Sam had disappeared a few years before social networking had started up, and she'd never had a profile. Freya had checked from time to time and one had never appeared, at least not in her own name. She clicked through, finding some of Sam's friends, some now with babies in the profile shot, others in wedding dresses or graduation gowns. One page Freya lingered on for a while.

She went to Messenger. She sent a note to Echo first, Sam's best friend at the time she'd left. A girl Freya had never warmed to, or figured out, but one her sister had seemed to like spending time with. Then she messaged Anya, then Eliot, then another couple of friends she knew the names of. It was the same message as always, to all of them.

Hi, It's Freya, Sam's sister. Today is her 35th birthday. Have you heard anything from her, or about her? If you have we'd really appreciate it if you could let us know. We're still thinking of her every day, and searching. Thanks.

She got up, poured herself a gin and tonic. She went over to the window and made herself wait. She messaged them, again, and again and they were decent enough to reply, but they never gave her the news she needed.

The gin did barely anything to take the edge off. She finished her glass and then went back to her phone to check it. Anya's reply came first.

> I never heard from her – still nothing. I'm sorry for you and your family. Anya

Then, a few minutes later, Eliot's.

> I wish I had a different answer for you, but no. I'm sorry. You know I haven't stopped looking.

The punch of disappointment in Freya's stomach, once, twice. So familiar. Too familiar.

There was no reply from Echo. There rarely was.

Was there a day when Freya didn't think about her sister? She couldn't remember one. Sometimes it was the child-Sam, a flash of her smile as she ran off through the park towards the slide. She'd always been fast on her feet and impossible to stop once she'd started. Other times it was Sam at seventeen – her dyed hair, dark at the roots, pale pink at the ends, up in a top-knot. The Nirvana T-shirt over grey jeans. That was what she'd been wearing that night. The last one. Freya had played and replayed the memory in her head so many times that it had worn a groove. She could return there any time she liked; the years had barely faded it.

Freya could still hear her sister's voice really clearly. The determination. The frustration. She had always been like that. As if she was talking to people who never got it, and who weren't able to see things the way she did. It was a source of frustration for her. Freya had seen something building in her sister that summer. Something that was making her too big for their house. They'd got used to her leaving, after arguing with Harry – but that night, when she'd gone and not come back, Freya had known it was different. She'd sensed, deep down, that this was more serious, and it hadn't surprised her when Sam didn't come back.

Freya had tried to explain to Joe what Sam was like – the fieriness of her. They'd only met that once, so briefly, and Sam hadn't taken more than a couple of minutes to talk to him. She didn't think he really got it, what she was like. He hadn't had a chance to see the good parts of her.

She put her phone down, deciding to call it a night and go to bed. It was nearly midnight. As she was washing up her glass, another message pinged through. Once her heart would have leapt. She used to think – this could be it, the lead she was looking for. Her heart would once have raced. But she'd learned to manage her expectations.

She picked up her phone and tapped on Messenger.

Eliot.

I think about that summer a lot. How things could have turned out differently.

Chapter 3

I give Dino his Weetabix, watch him pour the milk, and you know I can already feel it rising up in me. The rush. All I need to do is get him to school and then I'll be free to be with it – this feeling. It's like all the colour is coming back in at once. The days I've just gone through, slow and sludgy, just making it from the start to the end and now whoa – it's like I'm coming alive again.

'It's PE today, Mum,' Dino says, as he crunches the dry bits of cereal up, pushing them into the milk.

'OK,' I say. 'That's cool.' I know this means I need to do something but I'm feeling this bubbling up inside me.

'My trainers—'

I don't have room for it this morning. I don't need to be feeling bad about his stuff, the stuff that I can't afford to replace. I need space for me. I need to run a bit wild today, that's all.

'Sure, love, sure,' I say. 'Next week, I'll sort you out for then.'

'It's just, it's today. And last time . . . '

I go over and give him a big hug. That'll make it better. 'Yep. I'll sort it out, don't worry.'

Let's just go, let's just go. Get to the school gates and then I can drop him and then I've got the day – the day with this feeling, the day running free and

29

it's OK. It'll be OK. There's a drive burning in me and I know – however much I don't want it to be there – that I can't ignore it.

I get the key from the mantelpiece and give it to him. 'Here, take this,' I say. A world opens up to me then.

'So you're not . . . '

'You can walk back after school by yourself just this once, can't you, love?' I say. He's done it before. I did it as a kid, all the time. There's no harm in it – a bit of independence.

'When will you be back?' he says.

Always the questions. I don't mind them from him, but always from someone, the questions.

'I won't be long, love. Not long.'

There's some bread in the bread bin, some noodles in the fridge. He's independent, this one. I raised him to be strong like that. He'll be OK.

Freya checked on Jessie, and found that instead of being dressed and ready for school she was standing next to a pile of her clothes.

'What's happened in here?'

'I couldn't find any school T-shirts,' Jessie said, with a shrug. 'I got all my other things out, but I still can't find one.'

'Are you sure?' Freya said. She went over to the pile, and rifled through it. She pulled out a pale blue T-shirt almost immediately. 'Isn't this one?'

'Oh. Yeah. That's one,' Jessie said brightly, taking off her pyjama top and slipping on the T-Shirt.

'Thanks, Mum?' Freya nudged.

'Thanks, Mum,' Jessie said, smiling.

Louisa put her head around the door. 'See you later, you two,' she said.

Freya noticed she was wearing more make-up than usual, and had on lipstick, which she didn't usually use. 'You sure? You don't want a lift? I can drop you at the corner if—'

30

'No, it's fine. A friend's picking me up. '

'OK,' Freya said, hesitantly. This didn't happen. Not normally. They had their routine, and it had been the same for years. 'I didn't know any of your friends had their licences yet.'

'It's a new friend.'

Friend, like female friend? Freya thought. Or male friend? She bit her tongue. 'OK, then, love. Just be careful.'

'I will be.'

She watched her elder daughter go down the stairs, carrying her school bag. She'd noticed a difference in Louisa lately – she was sure of it. It wasn't something that could be attributed to changes at school, exam pressure or anything else. Louisa was becoming . . . visible.

For years Louisa had stepped lightly around the town unseen. While her friends had bloomed, at thirteen or fourteen – Louisa had retreated into herself, becoming shy and withdrawn, and immersing herself in her schoolwork. But now something had changed. When they'd walked down the street together in recent weeks, people had noticed her – young men looked, older men looked, women looked.

Freya glanced over at the window.

'What are you looking at, Mum?' Jessie asked.

'Nothing, sweetheart,' she said, walking closer, so she could look out.

'You're *snooping*,' Jessie said, laughing.

'I am not,' Freya said, shortly. She looked out of the window. There was a blue Ford parked outside. Louisa opened the passenger side door and got inside.

'You *are*!' Jessie said.

'I just want to be sure she's OK, that's all,' Freya said. 'That's my job.'

She squinted, but couldn't make out the driver. Jessie got

up on her tiptoes beside her and followed her gaze. 'It's a *boy*,' she said.

'Is it?' Freya said, trying again to look.

'Yes,' Jessie said, giggling. 'It definitely is. And I was right – you *were* snooping.'

After dropping Jessie at school, Freya drove up the coast towards Lyme Regis, and turned the music up loud as she went. She tried to make sense of this morning. This morning was the first time Louisa had made any mention of having a new friend, and she'd done so without giving much information at all. Now Freya thought about it, she had been quieter lately. She thought of Sam. One moment her sister had been there in their home, in their lives, and the next she was gone. She didn't want to miss anything, not this time. Freya had put Louisa's quietness down to revision, but now she was starting to wonder.

She tried to focus on the day ahead. That morning, she was meeting with the director of a TV drama she was about to work with. Sian was a director Freya had admired from afar for years, and a few months ago, hearing of the plans for a new series and that it was going to be partly based in Dorset, Freya had contacted her. They'd met for coffee and Freya had told the director that even though she'd never done a job quite like this one before, she wanted to do it, do it well, and give it her all. Last month, Sian had called her, and told her she was taking a leap of faith and wanted to make her location manager.

Getting this role was a big deal for Freya. She'd always enjoyed her work, the travel, the people she got to meet, the way no two days were ever the same – but the end products were limited: a tourist information trailer here, an advert there. This wasn't just a step up in her career, it was potentially a whole new direction. Getting to build colour into a story like this one, find the perfect spaces to support a 1950s period drama – this was the sort of project she'd dreamed of for years.

She spent the morning walking with Sian around coastal locations, bright white cliffs and quiet village halls, and hearing more about Sian's plans for the series. They worked out the logistics of the filming, and then found a local café to put down the schedule.

'You're good,' Sian said. 'You've got vision. I'm glad I trusted my gut with you, Freya. I'm really happy to be working with you on this.'

Freya thanked her, then went back to putting the details in on the paperwork. But quietly, inside, she was spilling over. She felt like printing those words out, putting them on her fridge and looking at them every single morning, a reminder that she could be more. And that she would be.

That night, when Freya got home, Louisa was sitting on the sofa, painting her toenails. 'Hey, Mum,' she said. 'How was it today?'

'Good,' Freya said, sitting beside her, a smile on her face.

'You look like you've won something,' Louisa said, laughing.

'No,' Freya said. 'Although it almost feels like that. I'm excited about this new project.'

'What's it about?'

'It's a period thing, 1950s; we found a church hall over in Lyme Regis that I think is going to be great for one of the scenes. And then there's the beach huts, this stunning old hotel ...'

'Your eyes have gone all shiny.' Louisa smiled.

'Have they? I guess I am a bit excited. This is something I've wanted for a while.'

'Like Dad becoming a teacher.'

Freya thought of Joe, and how he finally seemed to have found something he felt really passionate about. 'Yes. A bit like that.'

'And me becoming a doctor.'

'Yes,' Freya said. She felt so proud of her daughter's ambition, but nervous for her at the same time. It was great to know what you wanted. But at the same time the stakes were so high. In knowing what you wanted, you had something to lose. She gave Louisa a hug. 'Revision going well? Nice work on the nails, by the way.'

'Thanks. Yep. I'm a multi-tasker.' Louisa laughed.

Freya took a breath. She didn't want to disrupt the moment, but at the same time she knew she had to ask about the car.

'This morning, Lou. I noticed you got a lift—'

'You were watching me out of the window, weren't you?' Louisa said, with an exasperated look on her face. 'Can't I get any privacy around here?'

'Well, yes, and no, Lou. You're only sixteen – I'm allowed to care whose car you're getting into. That's my job.'

'OK, OK. Yes, I got a lift this morning.'

'Who with?'

Her cheeks flushed. 'His name's Matt.'

'You've not mentioned him before,' Freya said.

'I only met him a couple of months ago.'

'And now, what, you're going out?'

Louisa nodded shyly. 'He asked me to be his girlfriend last week.'

Freya had always known this moment would come – but this didn't feel like the right time. Not remotely.

'Does he go to your school?'

'No.'

'So how did you meet him?'

'In town. He's friends with Carly's brother.'

Freya processed the information. Carly she knew, but not well. Carly's brother, she'd never met. This boy was pretty much an unknown, and she didn't like that.

'Which school does he go to?'

34

'He's left school now. He works at a sports shop in town.'

Freya's heart started to race. 'How old is he?'

'He's nineteen.'

Nineteen. Ouch. That she hadn't been ready for. Louisa wasn't a grown-up sixteen, like some of her friends were. She was a young sixteen. A pretty vulnerable, trusting sixteen.

'When were you planning on telling us?'

'I don't know,' Louisa said, shifting slightly in her seat. 'Soon, I guess.'

Freya steeled herself. She knew this wasn't going to go down well. 'Louisa, I don't know about this. It seems very quick.'

'But it feels right,' Louisa said.

Freya shook her head. She couldn't ignore her gut feeling. 'You're going into an important exam period – and this could really disrupt things. I don't want that for you, Lou. I don't want you to miss this chance for your future.'

I know this isn't good. It's Sunday night, or at least I'm pretty sure it's Sunday night. When I realised I couldn't remember for sure, I knew I had to go home.

I'm walking down our street, concentrating on putting one foot in front of the other – just getting there, to the front door. It's been a long stretch this time, that much I can tell you. But I couldn't tell you exactly how long. It wasn't an hour, or an afternoon. I think I left on Friday.

I rode the wave, and it felt good. I needed it. The release.

But I didn't need for Dino to be seeing it. I needed to be with Cassie, with the girl in my life who can understand what it is to chase that high. There used to be Neil too – I think of him, and it hurts a bit in my chest. Having the time to be free with Cassie means I'm stronger to stay away from all that. I can rely on Cassie for that. She's got my back. She always has had that. She was the one holding my sweat-drenched self when Dino came. Not every baby is born with a dad all happy to see them. I don't think mine ever

35

was, really. He'd say things that cut really deep. I can't see that as love. It felt like the opposite of love. Those things he said got right into my heart. I kept trying to make it right with him, to help him be better. I kept trying and each time I did, it was like he hated me more. That summer, I felt what it was to be stronger, and I left. But I wasn't about to let my own kid's life play out that same way. Dino's dad doesn't even know that he exists. It's better for all of us.

But being on your own isn't easy either. I woke up this morning on Cassie's floor, on that carpet, the thin, scratchy kind, and I felt the sun hot on my face through the window, and just thought— oh, God. I've done it again. It's been too long.

So I'm putting one foot in front of the other, getting home to my boy. I get the keys from my handbag, relieved they're still there. The time at Cassie's is a blur – of laughter, of drifting in and out of consciousness, of thinking we'd worked out the answers. I find the right key and put it in the lock. I'm trying to get in but at the same time I don't want to. I don't want to go in and see his hurt face and the mess I've made – what I've left and what he's had to work out for himself while I was gone.

I told myself it was better to leave him than have him see me like that, but what if something's happened to him while I was gone? My hands start to shake. The lock clicks, but before the door can open I'm aware that tears are falling, hot and fast, down my cheeks. I'm rubbing at them, but can't seem to do it quickly enough. This sound comes from inside me and it takes a moment for me to realise it's come from me. It's sort of a sob. I don't want my son to see me like this – but I can't leave him on his own any longer. I force myself to go inside, up the narrow staircase that leads past the downstairs flat, and on to the landing and our front door. He'll be in there. He wouldn't go out. He wouldn't leave. I've done this enough times – there again, the wash of shame, it's intense, I hate it – to know that he would never go out without me. Because he trusts me.

When I go in he's sitting on the orange chair in the middle of the room. It's one of those hard ones; I found it on the street and brought it home. It's *one of the only bits of furniture we have. He's sitting on it, and he has the iPad in his hand, the one with the cracked screen. It's not even working – the screen's black.*

The words come out of me in a rush. 'I'm so sorry,' I say.

He looks at me and I want to disappear. I need to disappear in one way or another. I don't deserve to be here.

I go over to him and hold him, hug him close to me. 'I'm sorry, D,' I say. Usually what happens is that he leans into me and his body softens, and it's quiet and eventually he smiles, and we find our way back to how and where we were.

This time it's different. He's stiff, he doesn't reach out for me. I hug him closer, but he still doesn't say it. I wait for the words, for the way they make me feel better. It's OK, Mum. But all there is is silence. Cold, dark silence. And what's ringing in my ears is the wrongness, the badness of what I've done. I can't fix it this time.

'Dino, I'm sorry.' But there's nothing. I guess I was wanting him to forgive me, to wash me clean of all this. And he can't. This time he won't.

'I'm really sorry. I messed up this time.'

Damn, the tears, they're back, and they're coming even faster now, plopping down on to his head. My tears are coming, but his are all inside, in there – it's all tight shut.

He's a kid. And I'm a grown-up. That's how it should be, anyway. I feel it in my throat, raw, harsh, and in the way my chest tightens.

This sweet soul I've held in my hands, and loved so much. I just went right ahead and crushed it.

That evening, when the girls were asleep, Freya poured herself a glass of wine and phoned Joe.

She thought of Louisa, and the conversation she'd had with her earlier. Finding out about Matt had come as a shock, and she was still working it out in her mind.

'Hi, you,' he said, warmly.

She always liked hearing his voice, one of the constants in her life. 'Hi,' she said. 'I have news.'

'Intriguing.'

'Kind of. Also, well – I don't know what.'

'OK. Less intrigued now, Frey. More just scared.'

'Louisa's got a boyfriend.'

'She has?'

'Yes. He's been driving her to school in the morning.'

'Driving her? How old is he?'

'Nineteen.'

'Whoa,' Joe said.

'Yep. Whoa, right?' Joe was with her on this one, and that was a relief.

'She's gone from zero to seventy there pretty quick, hasn't she?'

'That's what I thought. I mean she's never even mentioned a boy to me before.'

'So, what do you think? I mean it's a good sign, isn't it – that she's found someone she likes?' Joe asked.

'I don't know. My gut feeling is that this is too much too soon. She's a month away from her exams. I think we should put a stop to this for now.'

'I can see your point . . . ' Joe said. He seemed hesitant.

'But?'

'She's not a kid, and she's always been pretty sensible. Are you sure that's what this is about. Her exams?'

A prickle of defensiveness set in. 'What are you getting at?'

'I mean – if we're going to stop her seeing someone, we need to be sure that it's really about Louisa.'

'And not about Sam?' Freya snapped.

'Yes,' Joe said.

*

Dino's asleep now, next to me. Tonight it was me, not him, who suggested he curl up with me in my bed. He didn't even seem to want to this time, and that cut deep. Because I get it. Of course I do, I'm not stupid. I've let him down so many times that he's growing hard edges. But you know something? Even now, as I cherish the feeling of him next to me, safe, I can't say I won't do it again. I'm not even going to make him that promise, because then it's even worse when I break it. I'm not going to lie.

I can't say I won't do it. Because I need it – the release. I need a release, some days. I need to let go. I know I should be sacrificing everything for him – that it should come to me, naturally, to do that. But I don't work that way. There's something inside me that's broken. Once I start to let go, I can't rein it back in – it's like there's no stopping me. Another drink, another whatever it is that lets me let loose.

It wasn't always like this. I don't like to track back. I try to look forward, because I have to. But when I was younger, it was better. I was better. When I felt in control, and I didn't feel I had to get myself right all the time. I'm not going to go there. I don't want to go there.

Chapter 4

Freya caught Louisa as she came out of the shower the next morn-ing, her hair wound up in a white towel. 'You got five minutes?'

'Sure,' she said, coming to sit on the edge of her mum's bed. 'Is this about Matt?'

Freya steeled herself for the conversation. 'I spoke to your dad last night. I'm sorry, Louisa. I just don't think this is the right time for you to be starting a new relationship.'

Louisa's face fell. 'No way. You can't do this.'

'You've got your exams in a month. And you've worked so hard to get this far.'

'But Mum—'

'I know it's not what you want to hear. But this is a really important time. These few weeks could make a difference to the rest of your life.'

'Matt knows I have to study,' Louisa said, desperation in her voice. 'He's supportive of that. You don't know him, you don't know—'

'I know he's three years older than you, and that gap ... it's quite a lot at your age. He's at a different stage in life; he's got all of this behind him.'

'I'm meant to be seeing him this Friday,' Louisa said. 'He's got tickets for a film.'

Freya told herself to stay firm, be clear. 'If he really likes you, he'll be there for you in July, when your exams are all done.'

'You're telling me I have to ask him to wait until then?' She looked panic-stricken.

'Yes. I am.'

'What about talking to each other, messaging?'

'Let's just press pause on all of it,' Freya said. 'It's not for ever. Just for a few weeks. And I know you might hate me for it, but in the long run I hope you'll understand.'

'I'll never understand,' Louisa said, tears in her voice. 'I can't believe you're doing this to me. What about Dad, what did he say? He's always saying he wants me to be more independent – he said he wanted me to find someone I really like. Well, I have – Matt's a really good person – and now you're saying I have to let him go.'

'I'm really sorry,' Freya said. She felt split, but she couldn't let it show. 'But your dad and I have agreed that this all needs to wait.'

It's been a couple of days since Mum came back, and things feel normal again now. Tomorrow we are going to pretend it's Mum's birthday. It was actually a while ago, but I forgot, and Cassie did too, and Mum never said anything about it. Cassie picks me up from school because Mum's not feeling well, she says. Cassie gave me two pounds last week, for cleaning her bike for her – and I found 50p down the back of the bed. It's enough to get her something. When Cassie comes to walk me home she has new rags tied into her hair, blue ones. I like them. I tell her I want to go to the Pound Shop to get something for Mum, and she says that's a nice idea. She gives me another pound, as she says I've been really good, so now I've really got enough for a proper thing. I get Mum a basket with flowers in it. They're not real but Cassie says that doesn't matter, they'll last longer that way – and I know she's right, because we've never had a plant stay alive in our flat for more than a week, I don't think. It makes me and Mum laugh because we get them, and we try, but then we both forget to water them and we end up with empty pots.

I'm not sure how much Mum likes flowers but I think she'll like these. I get her a card too, with a tiger on the front, because those are her favourite. She says they are her spirit animal. Sometimes that makes me laugh because how can you be a tiger when you do things like go to Aldi or hang up laundry or go to the Jobcentre and she says that's not how she's always been. That's not what her spirit is. She doesn't really talk about how it was before but I know she came from another place, another place with a beach, and that she had a family before she came here.

I think I have a grandma or a grandad somewhere, because I've heard Cassie and my mum talk about it, when they are in the kitchen and they think I'm not listening. I asked once but Mum just says we are bigger than that, we don't need other family. We've got each other. She squeezes me extra hard when she says that. But sometimes when the other kids talk about their grandparents I get an empty feeling. It would be nice having someone to take me fishing or whatever. Like Neil used to say he would, but we didn't do it because when the day came he was too busy. He had this other side to him that I didn't like and I don't think Mum much liked either. He'd shout, and bang things. Anyway, we never went fishing.

Cassie gets her cigarettes out and I give her a look because I know it's not good for her but she says she can't help it. She says I must never do it, ever, and she says, 'Look at how it's given me a cat's bum mouth,' and she screws up her face and it's kind of true and it makes me giggle.

We walk home together. She says she'll stay over with us tonight and we can make a cake to surprise Mum with.

Tomorrow Mum will be feeling better, and tomorrow I will give her the presents and it'll make her happy.

I wake up. It's dark. There's an alarm going off, really, really loudly.

My plan was to wake Mum up in the morning and sing her Happy

Birthday and show her the cake I made with Cassie, but instead it's the middle of the night.

I can hear shouting. Mum. Cassie.

Cassie comes in. She's shouting that I need to get up.

My heart is beating super-fast. I get up and out of bed.

'We need to get out of here,' she says to me.

Mum's shouting from the living room, saying that it's full of smoke.

I'm in my Moshi Monsters pyjamas and Mum's only got a nightie on but she says we have to run. She tells me to put my hand over my mouth and try not to breathe and we run through the hall, where she grabs her phone, and out of the front door.

On the stairs I remember about Cassie and Mum does a swear and then, just as we turn around, Cassie comes out, with her face all stressy.

We're outside. I breathe in the air, cold, clean. It feels good.

I want to know is it Mum's pretend birthday yet, or not, because I'm not sure about the time. Because even though it doesn't matter any more, it still does, to me.

Outside, the pavement is full of people who live in our block. The woman from next door passes me a blanket and wraps me in it. Mum gives her a look like she's annoyed but glad at the same time. The woman says they think everyone is out. Mum gets on the phone and calls 999. Someone shouts out that the fire brigade is already on their way. I am shivery even with the blanket. My heart's going really fast still.

The fire engine arrives, siren going, like in a film. The firemen come out and rush into our building. Some kids at school like Billy would say this was exciting but I don't think it is because this sort of thing happens to us a lot. Not exactly this, but things like this. I like it better when it's calm and quiet.

One fireman comes out and he says they've made sure the block's clear and no one's in there. Mum says she doesn't know how it happened and something faulty in the kitchen maybe? Mum's said before that Cassie mustn't smoke in our flat but last night when I went to bed she was still smoking in her chair and she seemed really sleepy. They say our stuff is all black and we'll need to

43

go somewhere else for a while. Then the fireman takes Mum aside and says something that I don't hear.

I won't be giving Mum her things today after all. Because they've gone. And we need to go somewhere else. It makes me feel so sad deep down because I wanted to do that right. I wanted to make her happy, for her birthday. Mum's crying really hard, and there's nothing I can do to make it stop.

*

We're at Cassie's flat tonight. Dino's asleep in her bed, curled up. He looks younger when he's asleep, more like the little boy he was once. Shit, what a mess. I was out of it. So out of it. It was Cassie who shook me awake when the fire started.

The fireman's words are in my head still. Repeating, going around and round. He was an older guy, grey in his hair, tired-looking, like he'd been doing the job for too long. He took me to one side, away from Dino. He had a hand on my arm, but it wasn't to reassure me, more to make sure I was listening. He looked right at me, with those steely grey eyes, like he could see inside me, see through to the darkness in there. 'I know you're using,' he said. 'I've seen the stuff up there in the flat.'

Tears came to my eyes and I rubbed them away, I didn't want to be weak with this guy. 'They're my friend's,' I said. 'She's been staying—'

'I don't care whose it is – you've got a kid in your home. This isn't OK.'

'Please don't—' My mind ran through the scenarios, like it has a hundred times before – them coming to take Dino away from me.

'You've got a good kid there,' he said. He glanced over at Dino, who was standing barefoot in those pyjamas Cassie got him for Christmas, watching me, his eyes wide. 'He needs to come first. You need to sort yourself out.'

It wasn't kindness in his voice now. It was frustration, anger. Like he'd seen it all before.

'I'm a good mum to him,' I said. I said it like I meant it, like I was sure.

'I want to believe you,' he said, but he was shaking his head. 'But I don't. Your son could have died in there tonight.'

He walked away then, rejoined his colleagues and loaded the stuff back on to the fire engine.

I'm stuck with this sick feeling that he's right.

1990

Freya and Sam had a den at the back of the garden, that their dad had helped them to build one summer, when they were still small. This year, with Freya at eight and Sam six, they were getting big for it, but they'd taken blankets, and doughnuts, and reading books, and torches, and told their parents they would see them in the morning.

Their parents had laughed, and Sam had insisted. 'We'll be back for breakfast – you won't see us before then.'

They'd put the lead on Hancock, their fox terrier, and taken him down into the dark at the end of the garden too.

Freya was shining the torch at the top of the den, reassuring herself that there were no spiders up there. Hancock nestled down into the blanket with them, and sniffed out the bag of doughnuts before they could hide it.

'Stop it, Hancock,' Sam said, batting him away. 'Here you go, Frey.' She passed her one with white icing.

'Thanks,' Freya said, taking a sugary mouthful.

'Shall we pretend to be married?' Sam said.

'What do you mean?' Freya said, laughing. 'We can't be married.'

'This could be our house, and Hancock's our dog. And this is our proper bed. And we'll always live together, for ever and ever.'

Freya smiled. 'No, Sam.'

'Why not?'

'I don't know why not. But it doesn't happen,' she said. 'Sisters don't get married. You'll find a man, fall in love, and marry him.'

Sam went quiet, and twirled sections of Hancock's fur between her fingers.

'What's up?' Freya asked gently.

'What if I don't want to?'

I need to do the right thing, for Dino.

I'm going to get myself clean. That's it. I'm done. And I'm going to do it myself. I can't go the other route – telling my GP, Social Services – that's not going to happen. The minute I do that they'll be on Dino and then I won't have an option – they'll take him away from me, and I might never get him back. Especially if they find out what happened with the fire. But if I do this myself – just make a bit of time to get myself straight – then it'll be OK.

But I can't do it with him here. I can't let him see me through the hard parts. I have to do it on my own. Cassie has helped me out before, but this is different – I can't give him over to her for as long as I'll need, she's almost as messed up as me.

He needs looking after, so I can get myself back on track.

There are people out there who could give him more, who could care for him better. They might never love him as much as I do – no one could – but they could help him learn and grow. They're not here, though. Not Cassie, not Al, and not Neil. Definitely not Neil.

I think back to Fern Bay and of the one place I felt safe – in Beech Close. I remember the house, with its big rooms and soft beds, the garden that stretched out towards the sea. I felt good there. I felt loved there. I know things didn't turn out right, but I also know that love was real. It won't be the same, I know that, but maybe there would be enough in that part of Fern Bay, and in that family, for Dino to feel that way too.

I think of Freya, and making this connection again seems like climbing a mountain. I wasn't always kind to her. Her life can't have been easy. There are things I haven't said, things I haven't told her, things I could have done to make it easier. If I'm going to open this door, talk to her and persuade her to help me, I have to be careful how I do it.

But getting straight, whatever it takes, isn't a choice any more. I have to do this. I have to make it happen, and, while I do, Dino needs a safe place to be.

I pick up my phone. I don't feel good doing this, but it needs to happen. I'm at the end of the road, and I can't see another way forward. I find Freya's details. This feels weird, really weird, and I try not to think too much about whether it makes me a bad person. The end is going to justify the means. I write her a message.

Before getting into bed, Freya checked her phone. A new email had come in, from an address she didn't recognise: blackbird-singing@gmail.com.

She clicked to open it.

> Freya.
> It's Sam.
> Your sister, Sam.

Freya's heart thudded in her chest, and the palms of her hands grew damp.

This couldn't be. This wasn't real.

Why now?

This moment she'd hoped for so many days and nights. The day she'd dreamed of – it was here. Here, in her hands, was the proof. Sam was back.

47

Chapter 5

I know this is going to be a lot to take in.

It was happening.

Only it didn't feel the way Freya had always thought it would.

Sam was back. She was here. This was what she wanted, had always been searching for. But it churned the earth up. Freya felt raw, and confused.

Sam. Where have you been?

The years she'd been gone flashed through Freya's mind.

Why have you been gone so long?

Freya's children. She'd done it all without Sam, and yet Sam had been there at every single moment. In the hospital delivery room Freya had wished her sister could be there with her. She'd imagined Louisa, that tiny, squalling newborn she'd once been, cradled in her sister's arms. When they'd gone away on holiday she'd see sisters together, drinking wine on balconies in the early evening, laughing by the pool. Her sister's face had been there in her dreams, and her daydreams. She thought of their dad's death, and how alone she'd felt in that grief. Sam had chosen not to be there for any of it.

Sam. You're back. And I want to be happy, Freya thought, but I'm not. Because you did this to us, and you didn't have to.

You're back, and part of me really hates you so much for being gone.

When Freya woke the next day, she felt for a moment as if she'd dreamed the message. She checked her phone, and saw it there. Read the lines over, so that they sank in again. She called Joe, and told him about it.

'Whoa,' Joe said. 'You must be . . . '

'I don't know what I am,' Freya said. Her stomach still flipped with it all – the excitement, the hurt, the shock, the relief. The impossibility of knowing what would come next.

'Where is she – what did she say?' Joe had been there at the time, been side by side with her during the search. He'd been there for every month and year that followed. He knew how much it had turned Freya's life upside-down.

'She says she needs my help.'

Joe drew his eyebrows together. 'Help – is she in trouble? Did she say anything more than that?'

Freya shook her head.

'Have you replied yet?' Joe asked.

She nodded. 'I wrote right back. Said whatever it was, I was here.' Tears came to her eyes and she rubbed them away roughly. 'I just hope she writes back.'

'You'll hear back,' Joe said, confidently.

'I hope so. Because it hurts a lot, what she's done to us, all of these years. But at the same time . . . Joe, I can't bear the thought of losing her now.'

Freya walked on the beach at Fern Bay, the words from Sam still on her mind. Her sister was out there, living, breathing, in touch.

Freya felt as if she was regaining sensation in a limb that had been numb for years. She'd almost resigned herself to being an only child for ever, only to find this – part of her had returned. It changed the colour of the sea, the sky, the sand, just knowing that her sister could take the same steps that she was taking. Sam had chosen to seek Freya out. Surely that meant that what had got broken that summer, they could fix.

Their mum had held her breath for so many years in anticipation of this news, and now Freya would be able to pass it on. The rupture in their family had been so sudden and brutal. So very, very deep. And now – in a single moment – she had been reminded that you couldn't always predict what would happen next in life. Yes, her feelings were mixed – there was frustration and resentment and unanswered questions. But she'd also remembered what hope could feel like.

She'd been wrong to expect Sam coming back to feel simple. It didn't. In some ways it felt messy, and confusing. But in there was light. Such bright light. She'd been given this promise bud, and she would nurture it – even when that wasn't easy. Nothing, nothing on earth would get in the way of her seeing it bloom.

When she got back to the house, she checked her phone and saw that a reply had come.

From: blackbirdsinging

I know this is coming out of the blue.

I mentioned that I need your help.

I'm a mess, sis. I need to straighten myself out. I need to go away for a while.

What did she mean – drugs? Drink? Freya's mind raced through the scenarios. She didn't want that to fit, but, in a way, it did. Sam had always done everything in life fully, with no half measures. It might have led her to all sorts of places.

She could be the person Sam needed – and she would be.

I have a little boy, your nephew. He's called Dino, he's seven. He's a great kid. He's my whole world.
    I'm not the mum he needs at the moment, I'm letting him down. But I will be, I can be — with your help. Could you take him, Freya — look after him over the summer?

Freya took it all in. A boy. Dino. A boy she'd never met – a nephew she'd never had the chance to be an aunt to. Her mixed feelings were swept away in a tidal wave of excitement at the prospect of seeing her sister again, and meeting her child.

You're a mum! Freya typed back. Yes. Yes, of course.

Chapter 6

Freya was sitting with her mum. Her chest was tight. Seventeen years. Seventeen years without a single word. Sam's getting in touch had shaken her, and now she tried to settle her nerves so that she could tell her mum what had happened.

'I've heard from Sam,' she said.

Her mum's face paled. 'From our Sam?' she said, her voice a whisper.

'Yes. Our Sam.'

Jilly was bewildered. 'But how? What did she say? Is she OK?' The words came out in a rush, as if her mother was in a hurry to know it all, to join Freya in knowing every detail.

'She sent me an email,' Freya said. 'She didn't tell me anything about where she was, what was going on – where she'd been. Just that she needs to go away for a while, and she needs help—'

'What kind of help?'

'She's got a son, Mum.'

Her mother's face lit up.

'A seven-year-old. Dino. A boy.'

'Really?' Jilly smiled.

'Yes.'

'So now what – when can we see them?'

'Not quite yet, Mum. At the start of the summer holidays. She needs us to look after Dino for her.'

'So we'll see her? When she brings him?'

'I expect so. She seems sort of . . . ' Freya searched her mind for how best to phrase it. 'She says she needs to straighten herself out. I don't know exactly what's going on with her.'

'Did she say anything else?'

'Like sorry, you mean?' Freya said. 'Or anything about where she is, or what she's doing? No.'

'I suppose we just have to take this for what it is,' Jilly said. 'She's back in our lives. I can't really believe this is happening.'

'I know,' Freya said. 'It's a lot to take in, isn't it? Sam. And a grandchild you didn't even know you had.'

'And Dino, her boy – will he stay with you?'

'Yes. Don't worry, Mum. I know you can't take this on on your own. He'll arrive here, so you can meet him, then come to ours to live with me and the girls. But I will need your help while I'm working.'

'OK,' Jilly said. 'Well, we'll just have to wait until then, won't we? Sam – back in our lives, and me with a grandson I haven't even met.'

A look passed between them.

'I wish Dad were still here.'

'I know, love,' Jilly said, gently. 'I know. Me too.'

A new message arrived that afternoon.

I wouldn't blame you and Mum for being angry.

Freya paused. Sam was right – about her at least. Freya *was* angry, in a way she hadn't fully anticipated. Then it hit her – 'you

53

and Mum'. Sam hadn't said 'Dad'. She must have known, then, about him dying. She'd known . . . and she hadn't come back for the funeral. Freya cast her mind back – was it possible that her sister had been there somewhere, lurking in the shadows? No. She was sure of it. It seemed now that Sam had chosen not to be there.

I get that you would be upset with me – *I'd* be upset with me. But there was a reason I had to leave Fern Bay. I wasn't ready to tell you about it back then, but when I see you, I will. I owe you both that much, I know. That and a lot more.

Freya's head was spinning, trying to process the new informa- tion flooding in.

I know I'm asking a lot. But I need you to just trust me on this one. I can't be there for Dino like I want to be. If you could look after him for me over the summer, then it'd give me a chance to get back on my feet again. I'll be back to make this all right. With you. With Mum. I'll explain. But for now this needs to be just between us, Freya. I don't want the police on my case, or social services. This is about our family, and I need it to stay that way.

Freya and Louisa were alone in the kitchen, getting dinner ready – chopping vegetables, standing side by side. The radio was on quietly, a jazz station that Freya liked. The music did very little to mask the tension between them.

'Lou,' Freya said, 'I know you're still cross with me.'

'Yep,' Louisa said, bringing her knife down into a courgette.

'Come on, you can't punish me for ever.'

'I won't,' Louisa said. Her eyes were narrowed, cold. 'Just until you let me see Matt again.'

'Lou . . . ' Freya said.

'What?' Louisa said. 'I really like him, Mum. I've never liked anyone before. Not in this way. And now you and Dad have done this – and in a few weeks he'll have found someone else.'

'If he has, then you'll know he wasn't worth it.'

Louisa sighed, and went back to the chopping.

'We're letting you go on holiday with Ava, aren't we?'

Louisa shrugged her shoulders. 'I guess.'

'A week over in France, with Ava's family. That's a big deal, Louisa – it's not like me and your dad don't give you freedom. We do.'

'I know,' Louisa said. 'But I'd give that up, if I could see Matt again. Talk to him, even.'

'I know it feels long, love. But it isn't – not in the grand scheme of things. One day—'

'I'll thank you?' Louisa snapped. 'No. I won't.'

They fell into a stony silence. Freya steeled herself. She needed to tell Louisa about Dino, and now was as good a time as any.

'There's something else I need to talk to you about.'

'Yep?' Louisa glanced at her mum and her expression changed. 'You've got your serious face on.'

'Something has happened, and it's kind of big.'

Kind of big. That didn't really cover it. Freya felt as if her entire world had been turned on its head. Over seventeen years had passed and in that time she had given birth to Louisa and Jessie and watched them grow, and her sister had also become a mother without her. Her mind was filled with questions and she wondered if she'd ever get the answers to them.

'I heard from my sister,' she said.

Louisa's jaw dropped. 'Sam?'

'Yes.'

'Christ.'

55

'I know.'

'Mum.' Louisa searched her mother's face for a reaction. 'Are you OK? What did she say? Where is she? Where's she been?'

Freya shrugged. 'She didn't say. I don't know. There's still so much I don't know.'

Her daughter looked bewildered. 'How could she not—'

'She's not like other people, Louisa. She's amazing, and I love her, but she's never been easy. She was always running away. I told you, she and Dad used to fight like cat and dog. This time she ran away for longer.'

'And now she's coming back?'

'I don't know. I hope so. But it's not just that. There's something else you need to know. Sam's got a son.'

'We've got a cousin?' Louisa's eyes lit up. 'How old is he? What's he called?'

'He's called Dino. He's seven – just a bit older than Jessie.'

'Can we meet him?'

'Yes.' Freya thought of how to phrase it. 'More than that, actually. He's coming to stay for the summer.'

'Staying – what – here?'

'Yes. For a few weeks, maybe more, while Sam gets on her feet again.'

'What's up with her?'

'I don't know. She didn't say. I didn't ask.'

Louisa looked confused, and Freya couldn't blame her – saying it all out loud made it sound even stranger. This reunion that wasn't how she'd really ever imagined a reunion being.

'You don't seem that happy, Mum.'

'I am,' said Freya. But maybe there was something in what Louisa had said. It wasn't happiness, not really. It was something closer to a sense of breathing out. Of letting go of the worst-case scenarios that had haunted her for years. Of knowing that even if she didn't know everything – she, finally, knew something. Sam might not be OK, but she was still here.

'Are you OK with it – Dino coming to stay?' Freya said. 'Your exams will be over by then – I wouldn't let anything disrupt those, you know that.'

Louisa shrugged. 'Course. Why wouldn't I be?'

Freya smiled, and squeezed Louisa's hand. Her daughter, so cold and unforgiving just a few minutes before, had softened, just a little.

1992

Sam passed Freya a razor-clam shell, and Freya put it in the bucket she was carrying. The sun was directly above them in the sky over Fern Bay.

It was Freya's tenth birthday. Their parents were a few metres away: their dad was asleep, his face under a newspaper, and their mum was sitting up reading a paperback. This was what Freya had wanted for her tenth birthday, nothing more, nothing less. To be with her parents, and her sister, and to have birthday cake on the beach. When they'd eaten it with their picnic lunch it had been grainy with sand, like the rest of the food, but still, in the sun, with the wind whipping them gently, it had tasted like heaven.

'I still don't get why you didn't want a proper party,' Sam said, placing a few more shells into the bucket. 'We could have gone to Monkey World at least.'

'You can always do that for *your* birthday,' Freya said. 'But I don't like all the noise of parties. I wanted to do this. And I'm happy.'

'Is it because you don't have any real friends?'

The words stung. She did have friends. There was Rebecca,

57

and Annie … although, well, they had started to hang out with each other a lot more than with her lately. It was probably just a phase. Anyway, it wasn't to do with that. She just didn't like the fuss.

'No,' Freya said. 'I just like spending time like this, as a family.' She glanced back at her mum, who seemed to sense her looking and gave a smile from under her wide-brimmed hat. When her mum looked at her like that, Freya felt OK. Whatever it was she was doing.

'I don't. I don't like being just us.'

Freya looked her sister in the eye. 'You're not being very kind.'

Sam shrugged.

'I don't get it, Sam. Why are you being mean?'

'I dunno.' She scuffed her bare toes in the sand.

'Are you jealous because it's my birthday?'

'No!' Sam said. 'Why would I be jealous of you?'

Freya looked at her sister's face, the bright green eyes, the gathering of freckles on her nose.

Sam looked over at where their parents were, her gaze resting on their dad's sleeping form.

'Sam?'

'I'm just not like you,' Sam said. 'That's all.'

I'm lying in bed. We're still at Cassie's, so the bed isn't really a bed, it's a mat on the floor. It's one with Indian gold patterns and elephants on it. It's comfy but not quite long enough, so the bottom part of my legs is on the floor.

Mum says it's going to be OK. The landlord will get the flat sorted again and she'll get more furniture to replace the things that got damaged in the fire. She needs to go away for a few weeks and she's found somewhere else for me to go. It'll be during the summer holidays so I don't need to worry about missing school. She says I'm going to another seaside place, and it'll be good for me.

She says all this but the thing is, it doesn't make me feel any better. I don't want to go away from her.

Freya checked her phone over her morning coffee, and found a new email. Hey, Freya. Thanks again for what you are doing. I've told Dino. As soon as school breaks up, we'll come over.

Freya replied. We're looking forward to having him. I can't believe I'm going to see you again, Sam.

She waited, and a message finally came through.

I know. Me too.

Only a couple of words, but to Freya they were everything. The weeks stretched out in front of her – she wanted to race through each one of the days so she could arrive at the one where she would see Sam and meet her nephew. How would it be, after all these years? Would she still look the same? Would they hug and the time disappear completely?

Freya would be complete again.

It was finally going to happen.

Part Two

Chapter 7

Freya picked out a pair of indigo jeans and a red flowery blouse. She brushed her hair so that the dark fringe fell straight. She was used to thinking about what she wore, for work, but this – dressing to see Sam after seventeen years apart? This was different.

She put on eyeliner, and lipstick, and a simple silver necklace. She didn't look the way she had when Sam had disappeared. But she couldn't change that – her harder edges – that couldn't be undone.

She remembered Sam so vividly – the dance of her smile, her bright eyes, the way she'd move constantly, restlessly. That endless energy her sister had as she drank up the whole of the world, greedy for it. I don't want her to be perfect, Freya thought. I've never needed that. I just need her to be Sam.

She slipped on her shoes. Was she ready? If this was something she could ever really be ready for, then yes.

Freya walked up the path towards her mum's house, trying to calm her breathing. This was it. After all these years, she was about to see her sister again, and to meet her nephew. This was really happening. She felt shaky with the adrenaline, but made herself keep going, keep putting one foot in front of the other until she reached the door.

She rang the bell, and Jilly answered it. Her face was blotchy and her eyes were red, as if she'd been crying.

'Mum – what's wrong?' Freya said. 'What's happened?'

'Sam isn't here,' she said.

Freya felt as if she'd been hit in the stomach. 'I've missed her?'

'No,' Jilly said. She pressed her lips together, keeping in the tears, and nodded in the direction of the living room. 'Dino is here. But a friend of Sam's brought him. Sam never came.'

'How—?' Freya started. 'Why—?' She'd pictured her reunion with her sister a hundred times, run through different versions of it, warm, painful, awkward. She'd felt within touching distance of it this time, and now it had been taken away.

The memories of all the times Sam had run away. The way she'd run away that last time and left them with nothing. How she'd given them nothing at all for so many years – not even a phone call – until now, when she needed something. Why had she expected anything else? Of course Sam would do this.

'Her friend, Cassie, said Sam sent her apologies. She had to be somewhere else.'

Apologies. The word rang hollow. It sounded as if this were a business meeting Sam had had to miss – not seeing her mum and sister for the first time in nearly twenty years. It seemed cowardly and weak that Sam wasn't able to do this, wasn't able to face meeting them and explaining herself. Freya felt herself bristle – she was angry with Sam, and with herself for ever having expected more. She shouldn't have let herself hope. She'd been stupid to think it would be this easy.

'Did this friend say anything else?' Freya asked.

'She said Sam would be in touch,' Jilly said. 'She left a list – a note with some things about what Dino needs and likes. But that's it.'

Freya took a breath. She took her mum's hand and her rage fell away, letting through a sadness that Freya feared would engulf her. A grief for what she'd hoped for and what was newly lost. She put her arm around her mum's shoulder and brought her into a hug. She just needed a minute, a moment to get her breath back, to put this pain away.

'I suppose she's just not ready,' Jilly said.

Freya drew on all her strength. 'I'd like to meet Dino.'

This couldn't be all about Sam. She had to let all of that go. She would meet her nephew, and be there for him. He was what mattered now.

Jilly led her through to the front room, and Freya saw the boy sitting cross-legged on the carpet. He was bent over, looking at a book. She didn't know what she'd expected, but he didn't look like she'd thought he would. He was mixed-race with dark hair, close-cropped, and his build was slight.

'Hi,' Freya said, softly, getting down to his level and sitting beside him.

He raised his head. His eyes, framed by dark curled eyelashes, were green, like her sister's. There was something there of Sam, she thought. It felt bittersweet.

He looked so vulnerable. As his eyes met hers, her hurt and frustration at Sam became irrelevant. This was about her nephew now. About him meeting her, and the rest of their family.

'I'm Freya,' she said. 'I know we haven't met, but I'm your auntie. And I'm going to be taking care of you.'

Dino didn't react. He didn't smile, but he didn't move away either.

'I'm going home soon,' he said, quietly. 'Back to my mum.'

'That's right,' Freya said. She thought of Sam, and wondered what she was doing now. 'This is just for a while. But you're here now – and you're part of our family.'

It wasn't easy. No matter what they might think. I couldn't go on the way things were – it wasn't fair on him or me. I need to get myself right. Because God knows I haven't always been. He's a good kid, mostly, but I can't take much of the credit for that. I was there for him when he was a baby, a toddler, but once he was able to dress himself I guess I felt like he could get on with it. I started going out more, slipped back into old habits. I don't want to do that any more, but that's the thing with habits. You get stuck. All of a sudden, that's the pattern of your life, whether you like it or not.

I tried pills once. The kind you get from your doctor, I mean, for the bipolar. That's what they said is wrong with me. But I don't know. How can just one label be enough to say why you are the person you are? Because there are good parts of it too. But I couldn't stick with them. The truth was, I didn't even want to – I never liked them, and I just stopped taking them. Felt like they were stripping me back to nothing.

I wanted to be there for Dino, but how was I supposed to do that, if I couldn't be me? I didn't want to stop being me, and that's what they did. Made my moods flat. Took the real me away.

So I take the other pills instead. And I drink more than I should. Those things don't fix anything, I know that. But they help me enough to get me through.

Dino was silent in the car. As she drove the short distance home, Freya stole a glance in the rear-view mirror. There he was – Sam's son. The boy her sister had been raising. She tried to imagine the mother Sam would be – warm, loving. A little chaotic. She would've been good to him, though, Freya was sure about that. Sam wouldn't have come easily to this point of asking for help. She must have really needed it.

Dino's gaze was turned towards the window, trailing the horizon. Their eyes met for a brief moment in the mirror.

'Do you like the sea, Dino?' Freya asked.

He nods. There's a sadness in his eyes.

'Have you been to the seaside before?' she asked, tentatively.

'Yes. We live there too.'

He gave the information up so easily, just like that. As if it were nothing.

To Freya it was everything. She could ask him for more – and she felt compelled to. The disappointment of Sam not having been there to meet her was crushing. She couldn't let it stay this heavy.

She wanted to know where Sam was, and where they had been living. She felt an inch closer to knowing the truth about her sister, and it was the most anything had moved in years.

'The girls are looking forward to meeting you,' she said. Jessie had arranged soft toys on the bed in the spare room, and put some of her Lego out for Dino to play with. Louisa had arranged to be in that afternoon, which, in her own way, was as generous an act. She'd finished her GCSEs a couple of days ago.

Dino spoke, but his voice was low and quiet, and Freya could barely hear him. He said something about girls. Maybe that he didn't know any, or he didn't like them. Freya couldn't be sure.

'You'll like these two,' she said.

She pulled up outside their house, and got out of the car. He didn't move.

'Do you need any help?' she asked. She checked that he knew how to undo his seatbelt.

He shook his head, and remained rooted where he was.

'Let me ...' she said, reaching to take his hand. She didn't know if he would take it.

Gingerly, he did, and he got out of the car. The two of them walked together up to the door of the house.

Jessie and Louisa came to the door. Jessie's eyes went straight to Dino, observing, gently interrogating. 'Welcome to our house,' she said.

'Hi,' Louisa said, giving Dino a welcoming smile.

He looked down at the ground.

'Don't you have any bags?' Jessie said, her little brow furrowed.

'Yeah. I do.'

'It's in the car,' Freya said, thinking of the bag her mum had passed her. It didn't seem enough – she hoped she hadn't left anything back at the house. 'I'll get it out in a minute.'

He entered the house tentatively. Jessie showed him to the bottom step of the stairs and explained that that was where they all sat to take their shoes off.

He sat down and stared at his trainers as he undid the Velcro. He took his time over it, and put his shoes away tidily next to Jessie's black school shoes. When he'd finished, he looked up at Freya, seeking some guidance about what to do next. She wanted so much for him to feel at home in the house, but he looked as if he had landed on the moon.

'Let me show you your room,' Jessie said. When Dino hesitated, she took him by the hand and led him up. He followed her.

Freya went up after them. She stepped lightly and spoke positively, as if she were a cheery B&B hostess, pointing out the bathroom, and where the towels were kept, where her own room was, and which bedrooms belonged to the girls.

'I put animals on the bed,' Jessie said, pointing out the well-loved Tigger and a polar bear that were half-tucked under the duvet. Dino sat on the bed and tested it, bouncing gently.

'You can bounce on it properly if you want,' Jessie said, in a stage-whisper. 'I do it all the time.'

'Jessie,' Freya said, sighing. She looked at Dino, expecting to see a smile. His face was blank. His eyes shone as if he was on the verge of tears. She saw it in his eyes, there was no mistaking it for anything else – he was scared of them.

'I'll go and get your things from the car,' Freya said. 'Jessie, you show Dino where you put the Lego for him.'

Freya took Dino's bag out of the boot of the car. As she lifted it up, she again thought that it was surprisingly light. Dino was inside with Jessie. He wouldn't be able to see her. She paused for a minute, and then with a pang of guilt bent to open it. As she slid the zip open a fraction, she could already see it was practically empty. There was a T-shirt, some pants, one pair of pyjamas, a toothbrush and a book, but nothing else. She checked in the back seat and the front footwell, in case she might have missed something else, another bag that he might have carried in himself without her realising. But there was nothing.

What was her sister thinking, sending him here with hardly more than the clothes he was standing in – and without letting her know he'd need more? She closed the zip on the bag, and took a deep breath. She couldn't judge. She couldn't presume to know what was going on in her sister's life. Her heart still burned, though, with the disappointment of not getting to see Sam that day, and of course that was going to colour everything. She shook herself. None of it mattered. What mattered was getting Dino settled, and getting him the clothes that he'd need. He could have some of Jessie's things for now, and the rest could wait until tomorrow.

Sam, she thought to herself. Where are you – what's happening for you – how deep are you in and how can I get you back up?

Freya went inside with the bag, and found Louisa waiting in the hallway. 'Can I help?' Louisa asked.

'No, don't worry. There isn't much.'

'OK.' Louisa shrugged.

'You all right, love?'

'Sure,' she said, nodding. 'It's just . . . It's just a bit weird, I guess.'

'I know. I know. It's a big change. Thank you, for being great.'

'It's all right. I'm not really doing anything.'

'You are, though. Believe me.' Just by accepting Dino into their house willingly, Louisa was helping.

'Mum – now that my exams are over – can I speak to Matt again?'

Freya hesitated. Louisa had been generous, and now it was her turn. She forced herself to let go. 'Sure. Yes, you can.'

'Great!' Louisa said, her face lighting up.

'But Lou – take it slow, won't you?'

'Yes, Mum.'

That night, Freya was restless. She was relieved to have Dino there, under their roof, but a thousand questions still buzzed in her head. She wanted him to feel happy and safe with them, but she knew that to him she and the girls – his cousins – were strangers. Hopefully tomorrow their home would feel slightly more familiar to him. She wanted it to. Perhaps it would be the girls, rather than her, who would make that first connection with him. Help him feel confident enough to speak. It didn't matter who it was as long as someone did.

There were times when she still, instinctively, looked over at where Joe used to lie sleeping beside her. She would once have touched his shoulder gently, and rested her hand there a moment, on the warmth of his skin. Chatted to him, softly, about the things that had happened that day. They were still a team, in many ways, but not like that. And in this – creating a home for Dino – she was on her own.

She strengthened her resolve. She could do it, and she would – she'd find a way to help Dino feel comfortable and happy here.

In time, Sam would come, and be part of their family again too. She'd been offered a strand of hope that led back to the sister she loved, and she wouldn't let it go.

Cassie texts me to say she's on her way back after dropping Dino off.

I've been sitting here chewing my nails so badly one of them is bleeding. When they get bad like this, which they do sometimes, I just paint them and you can't tell. I'll do that tomorrow. But right now I'm just biting and biting.

I text her. How was he?

She texts back. He was quiet.

Of course he'd go quiet, in a situation like this. It's normal. Or even if it's not normal, it's just how Dino is. How he's always been.

Cassie's said I can stay the night. Actually, she's said I can stay as long as I want to. But I'm just going to do the night. As much as I love her, this friend who's been through a lot with me, I can't do this with her. Because she's part of it. I have to cut my ties with her. Tomorrow this is all starting, properly. I'm going back to the flat. It doesn't matter that it's damaged by the fire. I'm going to stay there, lock the door, until this is over and I'm clean. Then, I'll get him back, and this will all be in the past, and it will all be better.

*

This bed is a soft bed. I sink into it. Jessie gave me some of her toys to put in it. I have the Tigger one, that bounces when you press it hard into the carpet. It's like a baby toy really. But I hug it anyway. Jessie is next door in her room and I can't hear her but I know she's there.

There are posters of animals on the walls. They aren't scary ones, just pandas, koalas, that kind of thing. But it feels really dark in here. And even when I pull the duvet right up I feel cold.

I think of Mum. I wish she was here. I wish she was here so much it makes me hurt inside, in my tummy.

I'm going to keep the promise I made to her. Even if it means not talking at all. I won't let her down.

71

Chapter 8

Dino woke early, before either of the girls. Freya had heard him stir, and wanted to be there to get him his first breakfast. She wasn't a morning person by nature, but these weren't usual circumstances. Now, with a packet of Weetabix between them, she was struggling to think of how to fill the silence. This boy was her nephew, her own sister's son. But he felt like a stranger.

The fairest thing was to avoid talking about Sam. She would keep any conversation anchored in his life, and in the here and now.

'I thought maybe me, you and Jessie could go out to the beach later,' she said, pouring milk on her own muesli.

He was pressing a spoon into one of the wheaty islands, cracking the dry part so that it crumbled down into the milk. 'Sure,' he said, without lifting his gaze.

'Some days I'll have to work,' she said, 'and you and Jess will go to your grandma Jilly's. But I have a few days off. I wanted to show you around, help you feel at home here.'

He carried on looking down at the pool of milk. 'OK.'

This was going to take time, she saw that now. But this boy

in front of her was her nephew, and she would be there, however long it took.

'What do you normally have for breakfast at home?' she said. 'I didn't know what to get, but I could get Coco Pops if you like. Or Rice Krispies . . . '

He shook his head. 'This is fine.'

'Does your mum—' Her heart clenched as she pictured Sam. 'Does your mum usually get—'

'This is fine,' he said again.

A blast of music came from upstairs. Dino jolted, his eyes wide. He looked instinctively to Freya. His hands were shaking.

It was 'Walking on Sunshine', the song Louisa woke up to each morning.

'Oh, love,' Freya said, startled by his reaction. She touched his hand. 'It's just Louisa's alarm clock. She has it loud enough to wake the dead. Anything less and she'll sleep right through it.'

She smiled at him, and he seemed to settle a little. But she'd seen it flash in his eyes – uncertainty. Fear.

I'm back at the flat now. It doesn't look good – the living room walls are blackened, near where the curtains caught light. I open the windows up to get some fresh air in. I told Cassie not to smoke in here, but she's never listened to me – never listened much to anyone. It's one of the things I like about her and that drives me crazy about her, all at once. Anyway, remembering how her actions messed this place up reminds me why I want to do this alone.

I'm still carrying her roll-mat. It's one from India. She still talks about it, how spiritual it all was, how she met a man there and they rode on mopeds for months and months, seeing new places. I roll it out, running a finger over the golden embroidery. Elephants. I'd like to go there one day. Maybe even take Dino. Show him the real elephants.

But I know the order of things, the way it has to go. I've learned enough to know that there are no short cuts. I sit down on the mat, and put a bottle of water next to me. I check the TV – it's still working. The electric hasn't been disconnected, so that's good, and Cassie put some money on my card to see me through.

I pull a blanket around me, because I'm starting to feel shivery. I don't know if it's the windows being open, or not.

I focus on the TV. I can do this. I am going to do this.

Later that morning, Jessie showed Dino around the house and garden and he seemed to warm and respond to her. For the most part, he was quiet. Freya's questions went unanswered and her attempts to engage him fell flat, and he continued to startle at loud noises. He didn't seem unhappy – but he didn't seem happy either. Freya reminded herself how he must be missing his mum, and home, and told herself not to expect too much from him. She had no idea what his life at home with Sam was like, and what he was used to. In time, he would start to open up, and they'd make changes accordingly. They would all have to adapt. They would do it willingly – what mattered most was making Dino comfortable, and doing all they could to make their house feel like home to him.

Freya walked Dino and Jessie into town, and Jessie narrated their trip brightly, pointing out her school, the tea rooms, the children's bookshop. They went home the long way, along the coast. 'Any interest in ice creams?' Freya asked. Jessie gave a whoop of delight, Dino gave a nod, and smiled. Next to the beach was a kiosk that stayed open year-round. Johnny, the owner, knew everyone in the small town by name, and he greeted Freya and the kids. His eyes for a moment rested on Dino, as he handed over two Fab lollies.

She saw it flicker across his face: the question. The same one everyone in the community would have. Who was this boy, and where had he come from?'

She paid him the money, smiled, and shepherded the kids away before he could ask.

They walked along the beach, and Jessie took Dino off to look for pebbles. Freya wished it were easier to explain. People in the town deserved to know that Sam was alive after supporting the search for her all those years ago. But the truth wasn't only hers to tell.

Jessie's gentle chatter carried on the wind; she was talking Dino through the different shapes and colours of stones and shells. He watched her intently.

As Freya watched the kids play on the beach, she felt the presence of someone beside her.

She turned and saw it was Eliot. She hadn't seen him in years. His presence was familiar and unsettling all at once.

'Hey,' he said. He passed her a coffee. 'I saw you over here, I thought you might want one.'

'Thanks,' she said, politely taking it. She didn't smile. 'How come you're in town?'

'Visiting a customer,' he said, pointing to a workshop by the seafront. 'There's a new café opening, and they want to buy in some of the furniture I make in bulk. And you? You still location scouting?'

'Yes,' she said. Part of her wanted to tell him more, but she held back. We're talking like we're friends, Freya thought. But we're not friends. We never have been. We never will be.

'And you're OK?' he asked.

She could feel his eyes on her, waiting for a response.

She should keep it simple. Light. *I'm fine.*

'Freya?' he prompted her.

Her chest felt tight.

Jessie and Dino were playing in the surf, daring each other to go closer to the sea. Jessie kicked up the water and Dino let out a squeal.

'You see the boy playing with Jessie?' she said, motioning over to him.

'Yep,' Eliot said. 'Who is he?'

Emotion rose in her. It would mean something to him, as it did to her. It would bring everything back, from that time. It wasn't too late to stop from saying it.

She looked at him, and for a moment it all flooded back. The pain of what they'd both lost.

'He's called Dino,' Freya said. 'He's Sam's son.'

After Eliot left, Freya called the kids back, telling them it was time to head back home.

Sam and her friends had met Eliot when he was playing in a band at an open mic night. She remembered when Sam had been getting ready to go out to see his band play with the rest of her friends – Echo and Anya, the girls she'd been hanging out with that summer.

That night, Freya had been watching her sister get dressed. 'I want to wear that blouse, the one with the blue and grey flowers on it,' Sam had said, flicking through her wardrobe.

'Top drawer, on the left.'

Freya had an encyclopaedic knowledge of her sister's wardrobe. She knew every item of clothing she'd bought, when and where, and which significant events she'd worn them out to. She wasn't allowed to borrow Sam's things. She was only, on rare occasions, allowed to touch them. But she was allowed to remember where the things were, and which were in the washing machine.

Freya found the top, and Sam took it, without thanking her. She got dressed, and drew her pink hair up into a topknot, strands falling loose around her face. She brushed on eyeshadow, silver dust colouring her eyelids, flecks scattering on her cheeks.

She liked him, Freya could see that. Whoever this man was, who'd come seemingly from nowhere.

'What is it about Eliot?' Freya said.

Sam raised an eyebrow, surprised. She laughed.

'Oh, Eliot? Well, he's gorgeous ... Dark hair, stubble. Good bum in jeans. You know.'

Freya raised an eyebrow. 'Anything else?'

'Who needs anything else?'

Dino and Jessie were in bed, asleep. Freya sat on the landing stairs and typed out a message to her sister.

Hey, Sam. I wanted to let you know that Dino's settling in here OK. I hope things are going well for you.

Freya thought again of the near-empty sports bag Dino had arrived with. How could things be so bad that Sam couldn't have got together some clothes for him? She'd cobbled together a few bits of Jessie's, and of course she'd go shopping – but she was still struggling to get her head around it.

He's quiet with us so far, but I'm sure that with time he'll start to open up.

Where were you? Freya thought, a bitterness chewing at her insides. Why weren't you there? The disappointment at not seeing her sister had left a wound deep inside her that was raw.

When you're ready, I hope you'll come and see us here. I'm not saying collect him, just see how he is.

I miss you, Sam. I miss you so badly it hurts, but I feel like if I let you know that, you'll run again.

She sent the message.

As she was lying down to sleep later that night, a reply came.

Freya. Thanks for taking care of my boy.

I'm sorry I wasn't there to meet you. That wasn't OK.

I'm not in a good place at the moment.

I will be. Just look after Dino for me, and I will be.

Chapter 9

Freya took Dino and Jessie over to her mum's house. It was only a few minutes' walk away, and the route was as natural to her as breathing now: the familiar path, the same steps.

They passed the ramshackle bungalow with a tangle of weeds out the front, one Freya must have passed a hundred times. Today Adriana was out on the veranda, her grey hair loose, watching them go by.

Her house wasn't like the others, and Adriana wasn't like their other neighbours. She kept herself to herself, but she was always watching. There'd been a man living there with her once, when Freya and Sam were small, but she hadn't seen him for years.

When Louisa was a newborn, Freya had paced these same streets with the pram, doing what she could to quieten her daughter's wails. In those days of being a new mother she'd walked, fuzzy-headed, until Louisa was quiet again and her eyes began to glaze over. Then, in that precious time, she would sit on a park bench and wonder when – if – she'd ever feel like herself again. But the route, that was one of her constants, when everything else was uncertain – Louisa's nap times, and teething, how she'd sleep at night; what, if anything, she'd eat of the purees Freya had painstakingly prepared. But she always knew she would walk past that house on the corner, and, while it sent a shiver over her skin sometimes, it would also remind her that she was lucky. That she wasn't, and hopefully never would be, as sad and empty as Adriana, the woman who lived there. It was a cruel thing to think, and Freya knew that, even as she thought it. But she had been at a low ebb, with Sam gone, and she was prone to thoughts that were less than kind. She kept those thoughts to herself and hoped people couldn't see them when they looked her in the eye.

She'd seen the old lady out on her veranda; she'd seen her at the window. She'd seen her watching. That uncanny feeling when you walk without looking back but you know eyes are burning into your back.

Freya had seen something dark in the woman on the corner – in her house – in the way she looked and watched. She still saw it now, though her children were older and she had not the vaguest of excuses for thinking unkind thoughts of people any longer. People – shopkeepers, other mothers – remarked that they felt sorry for Adriana that her husband had left her. But Freya had never bought it. There was more going on than abandonment, she was sure of it.

Back when Sam was still with her, she'd had her theories, and voiced them to Freya. She said she'd been yelled at so many times for playing out in the street in front of the house, for bouncing balls up on to that veranda, that she was sure Adriana had driven whatever love she'd once had out of her life, because there was no space for love in that house.

Freya hadn't believed her – Sam was exaggerating, she told herself – until today.

She saw the way Adriana looked at Dino. She looked at him

as if he didn't belong. She looked at him with a hostility that was charred black.

Adriana's seen Freya pass by the house various times over the years. Freya is the older, plainer one of the sisters. It was always that way, even when they were young. Freya's own two girls are more beautiful than you'd expect; presumably the genes are from their father. Freya's got that unflattering haircut now – short, too blunt for her face, really. Their hair is long and tidy, up in ponytails or plaits. Sweet little faces they have, chins a bit pointed, brows quite dark – the little one, now she's a child you'd notice. Striking, she supposes you'd call them.

Freya should take good care of them. Adriana's overheard things in the corner shop. She never gets much further than the corner shop. There's no need, is there – now that you can get your shopping delivered to your door? But on the occasions she has gone out, she's heard about that strange set-up with their father. And now this. Another child, coming into their family.

Adriana saw the boy play up with Freya today, stop dead and refuse to come with her. Adriana had watched from the porch, and saw how he wouldn't budge. She could see Freya being soft and patient with him – too soft. Adriana can't help thinking that what he really needs is a good firm talking to. You can see he's stubborn. Difficult. There's something in him, you can see it, even from afar. There's something in him that's not right.

That young woman, Freya. She's sure she has good intentions. She was always the sensible one, of the two of them. But if she thinks that makes her a miracle-worker, she's mistaken.

The boy has come from nowhere. And you don't know what's happened to them there.

Some children – they've been broken. You've got to protect your own.

That evening was not going well. Freya was sitting in the hallway with her back against the wall, hoping that Dino would calm down. His bedroom door was pulled tight shut. She could hear him throwing things against the wall, roughly, hard, and worried that he would hurt himself soon.

Freya couldn't make sense of his behaviour – she'd never seen anger like it. She'd asked him to sit with her for a while, suggested they look through some photo albums of her and Sam when were kids. When she saw the shadow fall over his face, though, she'd instantly regretted it. He'd gone quiet, then run up to his room and slammed his door shut. Freya had got inside and that was when he'd really started to lash out, flailing his arms and hitting the walls. When she'd tried to hold him tight, he'd pulled away. He'd told her to get out, and in the end she had. She would be here for him, but give him the space he needed. He clearly missed his mum more than she'd even realised.

Freya could see Jessie in her bedroom, sitting in her wigwam den, leafing through a book. Or pretending to leaf through a book, more likely. It would be hard for anyone to ignore the noise from Dino's room. This must be affecting her, Freya thought. All this rage.

I miss Mum. I miss the way she used to hug me, and how her voice was when she spoke all quietly. She did that sometimes. I think of her especially at night, when it's dark. Even with the night light in here, with planets made of light that go across the ceiling, it's still too dark. Once when we were back home they stopped the electricity and Mum and I lay under her duvet and ate marshmallows until we fell asleep. Sometimes I miss her so much it makes my eyes hurt, but I never cry. I'm never going to cry. Not about her, not about anything. I push that feeling down, down, down and I squash it, and I don't know, it doesn't really go away but it doesn't come out as tears so I guess it turns into something else.

*

I told Cassie to leave me for three days, then come around when I'm clean. I bought enough food to tide me over until then.

It's been two nights, and already I feel hollowed out and crappy. I should've known there was no point buying food. I haven't eaten it, and I don't know why I even started doing this. I'm a shell. This is harder than I thought it was going to be. I feel like the walls here are closing in. This small place getting smaller. I can't stay here another night, another day.

All I feel in this place in emptiness. What I gave up, what I've lost. I need Dino, I need his help to get me straight. I need to get him back. I don't know how, but I have to.

I pull on my hoodie and I'm out the front door, and I keep walking until I get to the beach. It's cold out here. Dark night. I look at the sea. He's near the sea, too – a different one. I'm going to get Dino back, and I'm going to get things right again.

I feel around in my pocket for my phone, and get it out to call Freya. I don't have any money for a train fare, but she'll bring him back, I know it. And, when she does, I'll make it all right. Make up for everything that happened before.

A voice calls out, interrupting my thoughts. 'Hey! Is that you?'

I turn, and see Cassie walking along the seafront with Al. He's a guy we hang out with from time to time, and who we get our drugs from, mainly.

'I thought you'd still be at home,' Cassie calls out. She's got this big smile that makes you feel like everything's going to be all right. 'Come for a drink?' she says.

It turns out her smile is what I need to see tonight. 'Sure,' I say. I walk over.

I take Cassie's hand.

*

When Dino's room finally fell quiet, Freya stepped inside, cautiously, and found him in an exhausted heap on the beanbag. He looked so peaceful, and vulnerable, curled up like that. She brushed her hand across the soft skin of his cheek. Then she lifted him into bed, straining under the weight, and tucked him in. She would have to go slowly with him, tread more carefully from now on. She checked on Jessie, and then went downstairs.

She poured herself a glass of wine, and then sat down to call Joe. She needed to talk to him about a couple of things to do with the girls, but she also just wanted to hear his voice, the comfort of it, the familiarity. She longed for that tonight.

'Hey, you,' he said, picking up. With those two words she felt whole again. 'How's it going?'

'I've had better days,' she said.

'What's up?'

The noise and anger from Dino was still with her. She could still feel in her arms how he had fought to wrestle himself free. She felt as though she didn't have the skills yet, to help him manage his own feelings. She'd dealt with tantrums from the girls over the years, but never anything like this.

'It's Dino,' she said.

'Teething problems?'

She thought of the long silences, the unexpected flashes of rage. She didn't want to admit to Joe how difficult she was finding it – how far from natural it felt to make him part of their family. 'Something like that,' she said. 'I think he's really missing his mum.'

'It can't be easy for him,' Joe said, his voice soft.

'No. I don't think it is.' It's not easy for me either, Freya thought. She stopped herself from saying it. She was the adult here, and she had to remember that.

'Do the girls get on OK with him?'

'Yes. I think so, yes. Jess seems to really like him.'

'That's good,' Joe said. 'She was always on at you about wanting a brother.'

Freya felt a pang of nostalgia. Jessie used to say it when they all still lived together. When having another baby had been something closer to a possibility.

'Listen, it's actually Jess I'm calling about,' Freya said, forcing herself to get back to the practical. 'It's her gymnastics competition tomorrow. This one is a biggie, her teacher said. Are you able to make it? She's been practising really hard. Sorry, I meant to tell you earlier, but with everything that's been going on, I forgot.'

'Ah, Freya. I'm sorry. I can't – I've got plans this weekend.'

'OK, no worries,' Freya said. Plans? Joe never had plans.

'Next time,' Joe said.

'Sure. I'll explain.'

'Thanks, Frey. Give her a good-luck kiss from me. And take a video? I really hate to miss it.'

'I will do . . . Listen, you don't fancy coming around for a glass of wine tonight, do you?' she asked him. 'Talk about how fast our girls are growing up, Louisa's got her prom just around the corner . . .'

'Oh, you know I'd love to, but I've got to get up early tomorrow morning.'

'OK. Sure. Totally understand.'

'Cool,' he said.

They were silent for a moment.

'Freya,' he said at last. 'I'm here for you, whatever happens. I hope you know that.'

'Yep,' she said. 'I know that.'

She hung up, and suddenly felt very alone.

It wasn't meant to be this way. Christ. I've really fucked up this time, haven't I? I'm on Cassie's carpet again, waking up with that rough texture against my face. I open my eyes, it takes me a minute, and at first I can't work out who is in the room with me. Then I see that Cassie and Al are crashed out in her bedroom, a bundle of limbs. We're fully dressed, all of us – so I guess things got messy but not that messy.

This would've been no big deal, a few years back. Seven years back. And I guess in some ways it's better right now because I know Dino's safe, I don't have to worry about getting back to him – I don't need to worry about having left him on his own.

But what's shit about this is that all my hope has just popped like a balloon. Maybe I shouldn't have believed my own crap in the first place – but I did. I really did this time. Because my love is so big, and I thought that at this point in my life – knowing everything that I do – I really thought it might be enough.

Now I've remembered how hard this stuff is, how you have to be so focused. How getting well has to be everything, you have to be so strong, all the time, every minute, and you have to want to get well so much you give up the escape routes, the highs. You have to want to be well more than anything else.

The next morning, Freya brushed Jessie's hair and wove it into a French plait. They were sitting together in the bathroom, facing the big dressing table mirror. Freya smiled at the vision of her younger daughter in her silver leotard and leggings. Her dumpy, cuddly toddler had transformed seemingly overnight into this long-limbed gymnast, ready to compete in her first trial.

She put her face beside Jessie's, feeling intensely proud of how much her daughter had grown and what she had already achieved.

'Are you looking forward to today?' she asked.

'A lot,' Jessie replied. 'Mum – when I'm up there. I feel like myself. I feel free.'

'We'll all be right there, watching you,' Freya said. 'And your dad and granny will be thinking of you too.'

'Thanks, Mum. I'm going to make you proud. I want to make you proud.'

Freya kissed Jessie's cheek and squeezed her hard. Her heart swelled with love for her daughter, her girl.

'You doughnut,' she said. 'You're already my everything. You don't need to win anything to make me proud of you.'

Ten a.m. Freya looked at the kitchen clock and mentally calculated what they still needed to do. Jessie's gymnastics competition started in exactly half an hour, and it would take them fifteen minutes to drive, if she put her foot down. Jessie was dressed in her leotard and tights, trainers and jacket on, sitting on the bottom step, waiting to go, just as she had been since Louisa had left to go shopping. The bag was packed with water and snacks, and a change of clothes for afterwards. But they weren't ready to go – not by a long way.

The inside of Freya's head throbbed. Dino was crouched down in the kitchen, and he wouldn't shift.

Freya crouched beside him, and put a hand on his arm. He stiffened beneath her touch.

'Dino, I can't leave you here.'

'I can't go,' he said. His voice was rough with emotion. 'I don't want to go.'

Freya told herself to ignore the clock's tick, to focus on him and how he was feeling.

'Mum?' Jessie called out. 'Mum . . . Are we going to be late?'

No, they would not be late. Jessie deserved to be there on time, arriving calm and focused, so that she could perform to the best of her abilities. They would do that. She would make that happen.

'Dino,' Freya said softly. 'What is it? What can I do?'

He shook his head, then buried it back into his raised knees, his arms wrapped around them. He said something, but it was muffled.

'What is it?' she asked again. 'We really need to go now.'

'No,' he said, softly.

'But—' Her heart raced. 10.20. They'd wasted too much time already. They would be late. Jessie would be late getting on stage.

'No,' he said again, shaking his lowered head.

'It's time for us—'

'NO!' he shouted, raising his head. His eyes pierced into Freya's. He turned and began to bang his head against the wall. 'No, no, no, no, NO.' It got louder and louder, and anxiety prickled in every part of Freya's body. She'd never encountered anger like this before, and she was terrified. She had to stop it – stop this – stop him from hurting himself.

The banging got harder and Freya reached in, made her arms a physical barrier between his head and the wall, wrapped her arms around him. She held him so tight that he couldn't move, and although he pushed back against her, his arms pushing her away, he couldn't hurt himself any longer. She held him until his resistance lessened. She held him until she had calmed him. She held him until Jessie came, sat beside her. The three of them sat there on the kitchen floor, silently. As Dino finally stopped pushing back, Freya reduced her grip on him, and took one of her arms away. With that hand, she took her little girl's hand in hers and squeezed it gently. Hoping she could convey, in that touch, that it was all going to be OK – and just how sorry she was.

They didn't make it to Jessie's gymnastics competition. They spent the afternoon watching *101 Dalmatians* – by the time Dino had calmed down, Freya hadn't had the energy to do much else. Her nephew's emotions had been a lot for her to contain, and it was starting to sink in that having him in their home was going to impact on all of them. Freya felt crushed that Jessie had had to miss out on something that was so important to her. Jessie had been great about it, considering. Freya knew how much it mattered to her, it must have been heartbreaking for her to have to miss it, but she'd said it was important Dino felt OK, because maybe he needed time to feel settled. She had sounded so grown-up when she said it, and it had made Freya feel desperately proud. While she was struggling to understand and forgive, Jessie was already there.

That evening was Louisa's prom. Freya tidied the kitchen and could hear Louisa and her friend Ava laughing as they got ready upstairs. She was glad to be distracted by their teenage puppy energy. Distracted from the fact that she was struggling to cope. That having her nephew with them was harder than she could ever have imagined.

Her elder daughter had come so far – she'd studied hard and got through her exams, and she'd built really strong friendships at the school. She'd been looking forward to the party tonight, and Freya had promised Joe she'd take photos so that he didn't miss out. Freya knew that Louisa and Matt had been back in touch since her exams ended, and Louisa had mentioned he'd be driving the girls to the party that night. Freya had asked if she could meet him – if this man was going to be in her daughter's life in some way, she wanted at least to get the measure of him.

Louisa and Ava walked into the kitchen, chatting and laughing. Ava was in a turquoise dress, and Louisa was dressed in a silver one, her hair twisted up into a topknot and sprayed with glitter. Freya's breath caught.

'Wow, girls. You scrub up pretty well.'

Ava smiled and touched her red hair self-consciously. Louisa just beamed. She seemed so much more confident and self-assured than Freya remembered being at the same age.

'You both look beautiful.'

She gave Louisa a squeeze and told herself not to get senti-mental. It was only a dance, only one night. Louisa was growing up, and that tugged at her heart, but it was the way things were meant to be.

'Now – photos,' Freya said, getting out her camera. 'Your dad made me promise.'

The girls posed, and Freya took photos until they were interrupted by a car tooting its horn outside.

'That'll be Matt,' Louisa said. She picked up her handbag, and gave her mum a hug goodbye. The girls put on their coats.

'Get him to come in and say hi, won't you?' Freya said.

'Do I have to? It's embarrassing.' Louisa said, wrinkling her nose.

'Yes, you have to.'

Freya watched out of the window as they went outside. She could see where Matt had parked his car to the side of their drive. Ava got into the back seat, and Louisa leaned in towards the driver's window to talk with him. He got out of the car, and walked with Louisa up to the house. He was tall, with short dark hair and glasses, and his shoulders were a little hunched over.

'Hi,' he said.

Freya tried to work out if he recognised him, as she did most of the younger people in Fern Bay, but his face wasn't familiar.

'Hello, Matt,' she said. She took in the rest of his appearance – indigo skinny jeans, a long-sleeved band T-shirt. 'Are you going to the prom too?'

He shook his head, then looked up to briefly meet her eye. 'I'm just dropping them there, and I'll pick Louisa up later. School dances aren't really my thing.'

'OK,' Freya said. She'd had a dozen questions in mind to ask him, but now couldn't think of a single one. Something about this young man unsettled her. She didn't want to let Louisa leave with him.

'We've got to go now, Mum,' Louisa said. 'It's about to start.'

'OK, sure,' Freya said. The prom mattered to Louisa, and Freya would have to put her own reservations aside, at least for tonight. 'Right, then. Off you go. Back by midnight.'

'Yes, yes, yes,' Louisa said, skipping off down the drive. 'I will be.'

They left, driving off in the direction of the school. Freya felt the invisible thread that had connected her to her elder daughter for so many years pull tight, and snap.

Chapter 10

To: Freya
    From: blackbirdsinging
    You and Dino are doing OK, aren't you? Things are going all right here. But it takes time. I've been trying really hard. But I had a few . . . I don't know. I took some backward steps, Freya. I'm not going to lie. You know me. I go in and I go hard and that trips me up sometimes. I'm not perfect and I'm sorry. Because Dino deserves more perfect than this.
    It's good knowing he's OK – that he's got you.
    He's still got you, hasn't he, Frey?

The next morning, as she was making coffee, Freya looked out of the kitchen window. She'd replied to Sam, and told her not to worry. That she understood. That she should take all the time she needed.

Dino was out in the garden, sitting by the apple tree, holding something in his hands and staring intently at it. She put the kettle on, just watching him through the window. He looked up and noticed her. He kept looking, held her gaze. He didn't smile.

But he wasn't looking away. She reasoned it was as much of an invitation as she was likely to get.

She went out and sat beside him. He was making something out of twigs.

'Do you need anything, for what you're making?'

He nodded, vigorously. 'String. Something like string. I could really use it.'

'OK, sure,' Freya said, going back inside and returning with a ball of it.

He worked the twigs into a rough circle shape and started to bind them.

'You're working hard at that,' Freya said gently.

'I like it,' he said, picking up a feather and gently weaving it in.

'Can I ask what you're making?'

'Just a thing,' he said. He wound the string tighter, and then criss-crossed it over the circle.

Freya spotted a feather with shimmering blue on it, lying on the lawn. Behind it was the area of the garden that she'd let grow wild, with poppies and lavender and colour that brought the bees.

'Here you are,' she said.

He smiled. A real smile, that went to his eyes.

She crossed the grass over to the bird-feeder, and found him another two smaller feathers.

'You know.'

She nodded.

He knotted the string, attaching the feathers so that they swung beneath the circle of webbed string.

'I used to have bad dreams too,' she said.

I'm up in my room. It's bedtime, but my room is still a bit light from the crack that the door is open. I hang the dreamcatcher I've made up at the window. It will always be there now, to catch the bad dreams. Mum got me one of these when I was five, when my nightmares started to get really bad, and she hung it up over my bedroom door, in the old place. But then there was the fire, and it was one of the things we couldn't save.

I'm hoping tonight that it'll catch all of the bad dreams, especially the ones that wake me up and I'm all sweaty and there's that racy-head feeling. I hate that racy-head feeling. Like I can't keep up with my brain, and I can't find any way to slow it down. Sometimes my heart is beating so fast it takes me ages to get back to sleep again.

Back at home, in Margate, I'd climb into bed with Mum, curl up close to her, feel the heat of her legs and tummy against me and how soft she is and then I'd get back to sleep again. But here – I just have to lie in bed and wait. And sometimes it takes ages.

Last night Mum was there, and for a while it was a happy dream, but then Neil got in it and it all went bad. And I don't know why he was in it. Then I felt in my mouth and my tooth fell out. Then another, crumbling. And I've had teeth fall out in real life, loads of them. But this was different, this was like all of them all at once so I was going to end up with nothing in my mouth to eat with at all. The dreams don't really make sense anyway, but then I wake up and well, it's stupid really. But it's a scary thing and tonight I don't want it to come back.

I'll see Jessie in the morning, at breakfast. She'll have Rice Krispies or Weetabix, only one cereal. I'll have a mix of all of them, Frosties on Freya's Special K on Coco Pops on Rice Krispies. Freya said it's OK. I like those cereals. We don't have them much at home, only sometimes and then never all at once like that. When I mix them they pop and rustle around like they're trying to jump right out.

Here at Freya's house each day is pretty much like the next day, and you know what's coming and sometimes I even know what we're going to be eating for dinner. It didn't matter to me with Mum that each day was different. Only when things went wrong sometimes. But when things are the same, it's definitely easier. I think for Jessie and her sister things have always been like that. I don't tell them what my home was like, even

93

though they keep asking questions. Lots of people ask me questions. But I don't say anything.

I promised Mum I would do what she asked me to, and I know it's not right to lie, but I won't ever break that promise.

Jessie and Dino were watching TV, sitting next to each other on the faded sofa in the living room. The sofa had seen them through years of breastfeeding and snacks and pillow fights, and was still somehow in one piece. And now Dino was in the middle of it. Little by little, he was starting to belong there. That morning, Freya and Joe had waved Louisa off with her friend's parents, to France. Her first holiday without either of them. Freya felt a pang at letting her go, watching her grow up and become more independent. But at the same time she knew it was exactly how things should be.

'Mum,' Jessie said. 'Do you want to come and sit with us?'

'I'm fine, thanks, love, I have a couple of things to do in the kitchen.'

Dino had the remote control and was flicking through channels on the TV.

'When's Louisa back?' Jessie asked.

'In a week,' Freya said. 'Why, are you missing her?'

'I guess so. A little bit,' Jessie said.

Freya went to sit beside them on the sofa, and ruffled Jessie's hair. 'You guys spend all that time squabbling, but you actually like each other, am I right?'

Jessie nodded. 'She's never been away for so long before.'

'Do you want me to see if some of your friends are around, have someone over for a sleepover?'

'Nope,' Jessie said. 'I'm OK.' She pointed at one programme. '*Operation Ouch*, Dino. That's brilliant. Leave it on that.'

'You sure you don't want a sleepover, Jess? I could call Hannah's mum.'

'Yep,' Jessie said. 'I'm not lonely. I've got Dino.'

Freya glanced at him, and there it was again – that small sort-of-smile that she was seeing more of these past few days. He put the remote control down and left the programme to run.

Was that progress? She hoped with everything in her heart that it was. That the smile could come and be followed by more.

Chapter 11

Jessie and Dino were casting pebbles out into the sea in Fern Bay. Dino threw his flat stones with vigour, his little arm swinging right back before flinging the stones into the water. Jessie had a turquoise bucket in her hand, full of seaweed and shells that the two of them had collected. Freya thought of work – after these days at home she was looking forward to really getting started on the new project. She and Sian had been talking regularly, and Freya had done as much as she could remotely. Louisa was away in France still, with her friend's family, and Freya was contenting herself with photo messages and texts. It looked as though Louisa was having a good time, and with any luck she'd start to forget about Matt.

When she and Sam were kids they would come down to the beach with their dad most weekends. Searching for the perfect pebbles just as Jessie was doing now. Sometimes they'd played together, until the sky grew dark. Other times they'd bickered and squabbled and their dad had sighed, then laughed, and told them it was time to get home and have dinner.

They'd always had their difficult moments. But it wasn't until the summer that Sam left that the tensions between them had really started to grow.

July 2001
Beech Close, Fern Bay. Five weeks before Sam's disappearance.

Sam's friends came over to the house that evening, the newer ones that their parents disapproved of, the ones they'd never have let in that night, if they'd known about it. Jilly and Harry had driven up the coast and rented a remote cottage for a month, so that their dad could finish a book he was writing. They had left Freya, back for the holidays, and Sam, on their own in the house.

Sam walked in with a girl that Freya recognised from school. Echo, that was her name. She'd once been called Nicola, everyone knew that, but she'd renamed herself, and started to dress like Courtney Love. There was another girl called Anya, and a couple of other people Freya didn't know.

One of them was Eliot – tall and dark, as Sam had described him, in jeans and a faded blue band T-shirt. They filled out the kitchen with their noise and laughter, and Freya felt strangely protective of her parents' house, of the tea sets and antiques her mum had collected and treasured. They emptied the fridge of food, these near-strangers, and put it out on the kitchen table to devour. Freya watched from the doorway. The way these people were trekking through the house – it irritated her. They'd swarmed in, dropping a trail of jackets and mud-covered Converse.

Eliot wasn't with her sister, or the rest of them, but smoking a cigarette out of the half-open back door. He looked over at Freya, and their eyes met for a brief moment. Sam was propped on the edge of the table, her toes, clad in fishnet tights, pressing into a chair-back and tipping the chair up. She looked like a different person when she was with these people. Her hair, previously light

97

brown, was now candyfloss pink, and her vocabulary and mannerisms had changed almost as much. It might not be as visible to everyone, but Freya could see it.

'Want to come and join us?' Echo said. 'Frankie – that's your name, right?'

Freya bristled. She was doing it on purpose. 'It's Freya, actually.'

'Freya, then. Whatever.'

Standing there in her flowered dress and pumps, Freya felt as if she was from a different generation. They'd gone to the same school once, but those years had gaped between them, and even now they weren't much closer to closing up.

'Do you smoke?'

Freya shook her head. She inched towards the group, and perched against the radiator.

'So Sam tells us you've met the love of your life.'

Freya felt her cheeks flush. Her body had a habit of betraying her, and she resented it.

'C'mon, I didn't put it like that,' Sam said, her eyes meeting her sister's. 'I just told her about Joe.' She took a swig from a bottle of San Miguel.

Freya shrugged. 'Joe's just a friend. Now, anyway.'

Echo smiled, in an indulgent way. Again, Freya felt as if she were the kid there, rather than the oldest person in the room. 'Well, good luck getting him, then.'

'He's not a prize,' Freya said. 'He's a person.'

Echo looked at Sam, her eyes dancing with mischief. 'Oh, she's got sass,' she said. 'I guess there's more to your sister than we thought.'

'And she's right,' Sam said. 'He's definitely not a prize.'

Freya bristled. She didn't like these people, but, more importantly, she didn't like who her sister turned into when she was with them. 'Listen, Sam. I'm going to go upstairs. Clear this place up when you're done, OK?'

Sam gave a salute.

Freya sighed. Bit her tongue. It wasn't worth it. Really, it wasn't.

The doorbell rang again, and more of Sam's friends came in. Freya could hear the clink of glass and the rustle of plastic as beer bottles and cans came out of bags. She could hear people going into the kitchen. Freya sat in her bedroom and pulled her knees up towards her chin. She made herself take a breath. Why was she letting it all bother her so much? It unsettled her, these almost-strangers in her house, touching their family's things. It mattered to her parents to have their home in order, and so it also mattered to her.

But it was more than that. The way that Sam had spoken to her in front of everyone – it stung.

She thought back on all of the times she'd picked her younger sister up, from a fall off her bike or a school bully's harsh words. She and her mum had been a team – picking up the pieces of Sam again and again. Each time she left, usually after an argument with her dad, Freya would start the search, and each time Sam returned, unrepentant, and full of fury.

There was a knock at her bedroom door. It would be Sam. Freya didn't know if she wanted to see her sister right then. But when she opened the door it was Eliot standing there. He asked if he could come in. She'd never imagined he'd be polite, but then she'd never imagined he would come up to see her, either. He'd barely looked her way before. She nodded, and he opened the door, closing it behind him. He sat on the end of her bed. This man, whom her sister seemed so caught up in, had for some reason come up to see her.

He opened a beer with a bottle opener, and held up another

one. 'I brought you this. Couldn't have you being left out of the party.'

'I don't want it,' Freya said, stiffly.

'Right,' he said. 'Sure.' He opened it regardless and put it on the desk beside her.

She glanced down, feeling awkward. To soften the feeling, she took a sip from the beer. They sat together in silence.

'You OK?' he asked. His voice was softer than she'd heard it sound before. There was the trace of a northern accent, something you didn't hear often in their town.

Freya shrugged. 'Yes and no.'

'You're not mad keen on having us all round, am I right?'

'Not really,' Freya said. 'I don't know. I guess I'm not good with big groups of people. I never have been.'

'I get that.'

'Is that why you're up here?' Freya said.

'Kind of,' he said. 'Also, I was curious.'

'About what?'

He looked at her. Right at her. Green eyes, flecked with brown. She'd been looked at like that before – on holiday, by warm Mediterranean seas, where men didn't consider it impolite to look, and look, their eyes boring a hole in you. But here, in England, where that intensity was awkward, was equated with rudeness, it didn't happen often. She'd spend whole evenings with Joe while his eyes flitted around the room, where he fiddled with his phone, his wallet, his cuffs. Where he didn't look at her the way that Eliot was doing right now. Eliot's stare – the confident look that didn't need anyone's permission – held her captive.

'About you,' he said.

She wouldn't let him know about the shiver that danced on the skin of her forearms. She wouldn't let him see the goosebumps that had appeared there. She wouldn't – she couldn't – let him

100

see how his simple presence made her feel as if she, for the first time, was truly there. That she existed.

'So?' he said, smiling, because she still hadn't replied or responded.

'What about me?' she said.

'You hang around in the shadows, and I don't know why.'

'What a thing to say,' she said. It was stupid. It wasn't who she was at all. She just preferred for things to be quiet. 'Those girls are not my scene, that's all. Not all of us need attention.'

He looked around her room, glancing at the photos she'd taken, the ones that were pinned to her walls. She could hear Sam and her friends laughing downstairs, but Eliot didn't seem to register it.

'You sure you wouldn't rather be down there?' she said.

'I could be,' he said. He looked from the walls, back to her. 'But I'm not.'

'Why not?'

'Maybe they're not really my scene, either.'

Eliot was Sam's – either that was already true, or the plan was that soon he was going to be. Sam had made that clear before the summer started. She was his friend, and she wanted him to be more than that. Sam had never given Freya an update, so she didn't know what, if anything, had happened between them – but Sam had staked her claim. She seemed to be playing it cool, though; Freya had barely seen her sister talking to him. She and Echo were together most of the time, making food, whispering, laughing.

The thing was, when Eliot looked at Freya, it didn't feel as if he was Sam's. When he looked at her, it didn't seem like that at all. It felt as if he was looking right into her soul, and it unsettled her. He made her feel something she wasn't comfortable feeling.

And she knew she had no place – no right – feeling it for someone Sam liked.

Freya was used to the background. Maybe what he'd said wasn't so far from the truth after all. She was used to being there, unseen, and that suited her. She could watch, she could see, but she didn't have to be at the centre of things. When Eliot was close to her, though, she felt pulled right on stage. As if this was the show of her life, rather than something she was performing a reluctant, half-hearted cameo in. He made her think that maybe she could do this. That maybe she could make a life of her own, rather than fitting into the shape that Sam had left her. That maybe she could be braver that she'd previously thought.

She loved Sam. Sam was the one who knew her better than anyone else. But maybe that wasn't what she needed around her. Because Sam knew all of it – and that didn't leave much space for what could grow and what could be new. Perhaps she was defining Sam as much as she was being defined by her. Maybe this wasn't good for either of them at this point in their lives.

The way Sam had spoken to her earlier had made her realise how little her sister cared. It felt as if things between them had changed. And now here was Eliot, looking at her, seeing her. Seeing all the way through her. He touched her cheek and a rush went through her. This was happening. It was real. She hadn't imagined the way he looked at her, and what was in that. In that touch – in the way he reached out across the space between them, and in that one movement made it disappear completely – he told her in that touch that he wasn't Sam's, not at all.

Sometimes the unexpected can feel so natural, so familiar, that, while you might tell yourself you'd never ever do it – you find out that it is the very thing you were always going to do.

Chapter 12

It's not hard for me, keeping quiet. I've done it lots of times. When Mum was out it was what we agreed. I'd keep quiet, and she'd come back. She didn't want neighbours asking questions, she didn't want the police knocking on the door. She told me that if that happened they'd come and take me away, and I didn't want that. It wasn't easy being on my own for that time, but she'd always come back, and she'd bring something with her, usually.

I would just go upstairs, play with the tablet she left, an old one with a cracked screen but it works OK still. Anyway, I'd play on that for a while and then the battery would run out and she would forget to put out the charger. Then I'd watch TV or play with some Lego. The days felt long. I'd watch it get light and then dark again and nothing would really have changed. I could hear the kids playing out in the street, but knew that I couldn't go. I wasn't allowed to go out there, not until she was back. I didn't count the number of times she'd gone away.

Then, when the sun had been up and down a couple of times, I'd hear the key in the lock downstairs, or sometimes I'd see her outside the window, walking down the street. Sometimes she'd be on her own. Sometimes she'd be with other people. I liked it better when she was on her own. When she was back, I'd sleep again. While she was away I wouldn't sleep very much. I'd just lie there looking at the lights from Dreamland. The red, green, blue of them. I wanted to go there, more than anything.

*

I've left Cassie and Al, and I'm back at the flat. Everyone's entitled to a blip, and that was mine.

But this time, I'm truly ready. This time, I'm focused. I'm doing this. I'm getting clean.

I found a photo of me when I was young, not long after I came here. Even after what had happened, there was some hope in my eyes. I've stuck it up on the fridge to remind me not to throw it all away again. To keep me focused on what I could be.

When I first got here, that summer, lying on the sand. Lying low. It was good. Better than Fern Bay. That first winter was hard, without any money for the heating. But that summer, pregnant – that was good.

There's no money for the meter, so the TV doesn't work. The gas is still on, though, so I make myself a cup of tea in a pan on the stove, and put a load of sugar in it to make up for there being no milk. I'm trying to shrug off this hangover, and I'm nearly there.

I sit down, on the orange school chair. I look at the front door, closed. I look at the curtainless windows, and grey skies.

I am going to do this.

And then a lump comes to my throat.

Because I feel trapped.

Really trapped.

Even though I can leave any time I want.

And then I remember how Dino was sitting here once, and how he couldn't.

Freya got in from work and poured herself a glass of water. It was a hot day, and the set had been busy, but they'd made good progress, resolving issues as they came up. They'd lost a couple of days to bad weather earlier in the month, and now the filming schedule was tight and everyone was feeling the pressure, but Freya had kept her cool.

The doorbell rang. It was Jilly, dropping Jessie and Dino back. Freya felt a wave of gratitude that her mum was around to help. She opened the front door, and the kids ran through into the kitchen, pouring drinks for themselves from the fridge. Her mother's face was pale and strained, and she saw right away that something wasn't right.

'You OK, Mum?' she asked. 'You look tired. Come and sit down.' She took her through to the living room. 'What's up? How was today?'

'I haven't been feeling well, Freya. I'm having migraines again.'

'Oh, Mum,' Freya said. Migraines. Like the ones she'd had for months after Sam disappeared. The place her mum's pain ended up, when there was nowhere else to put it.

'I've made an appointment at the doctor's for tomorrow,' Jilly said. 'I'm sure I'll be feeling better soon.'

'Good,' Freya said. Doctors couldn't medicate for this, though, could they? For the pain of thinking you were going to see your younger daughter again after so long, only to have that wrenched from you.

'I don't want to let you down,' Jilly said. 'But looking after the two of them – I'm finding it too much at the moment.'

Freya's heart went out to her mother. Freya had been so caught up in organising things so she could work, she hadn't thought properly about the impact on her.

'Don't worry, Mum,' Freya said, giving her a hug. 'The most important thing is that you have time to get your strength back and feel better. Everything else will be OK.'

'Yes, yes, it will be.'

She sensed there was something still unsaid between them. 'What is it, Mum?'

Jilly spoke softly. 'I feel awful saying this, Freya. Dino's my grandson.'

'What is it, Mum?'

'Jessie's very fond of him, I can see that. But he's barely said a word to me since he arrived. It's just this silence. All this silence. I've never met a child like him, Freya. There's something in him that I don't understand – it's almost like I don't know how to reach him. He's part of our family. But it doesn't feel like that.'

Freya nodded. 'I know what you mean. But I do think he's getting used to us, slowly.'

It was early days, and they had to help him see that he could trust them.

'You can't look after him yourself, though, can you, not with your work?' Jilly said.

Freya thought of her schedule for the coming week, and had to accept that her mother was right. It was crammed full of meetings with Sian and the team, budget planning and liaison with local residents. There was no way she could do it all while taking care of the kids. And she wasn't about to put Dino in a holiday club full of strangers.

'No. Louisa's back tomorrow, but only at midday – and she's got activities planned all next week. She might be able to help out here and there, but I can't ask her to look after Dino the whole time. And Joe's got his hands full with his studies.' She racked her brain for a solution, but there didn't seem a straightforward way round this. 'I'm going to have to talk to Sam.'

That evening Freya emailed her sister, and told her they would need to talk. She thought of the week ahead, the filming schedule, the things she'd set up – she had her assistant Annabel, and she was great, but she was inexperienced still; these weren't things she could just hand over and then pick up again in a couple of weeks.

106

More than that – Freya wanted this. She'd wanted to work on a drama like this since she first started scouting. She knew that Dino needed her – and she wanted to be there for him – but she also wanted and needed to work.

Sunday morning came, and there was no reply. She thought of calling the emergency number she had insisted on getting, but Sam had made it clear that she wanted to be in touch only by text or email – that she couldn't handle phone calls, even from Dino. Whatever was going on for her, she needed to distance herself from her son for a while. As Freya got lunch ready, though, she grew restless and frustrated. Monday morning was getting closer and it was seeming more likely that Sam wasn't going to help her fix this. If that was the case, she'd need to call Annabel and sort something out with her work.

Joe came around and they got Sunday lunch ready together while an excited Louisa, just back from her holiday, showed Jessie her photos in the living room. Freya filled him in on what had been happening.

'You've heard nothing at all from her?' Joe said.

Freya shook her head. 'Not a word. And it's a big week at work. I need to sort this out.'

'Can't you just call her?'

'She asked me not to.'

Joe raised an eyebrow.

'She doesn't even want Dino calling. Which is hard on him. But I guess whatever's happening for her at the moment, she needs to focus on it . . . ' She noted that Joe's expression was sceptical still. 'What?'

'She's not really back at all, is she?' Joe said. 'Not in any way that means she's there for you.'

Freya felt emotion rise up in her. 'I know she's *alive*, Joe. I know she's out there, and she has a family. Maybe she can't be there for us right now, but that's not nothing. That's pretty much everything.'

She sat down at the kitchen table and cradled her head in her hands. It all felt like too much.

'I'm sorry, Frey,' Joe said.

'I have to do something,' Freya said. 'I can't let everyone down at work. But I can't let Dino down either.'

'Sam shouldn't have put you in this position,' Joe said, firmly. 'It's not fair of her. I know you don't want to, but I think you need to call her.'

Freya chewed on her lip.

'And look, I think there's another reason you need to speak to her.'

Freya looked up at him. 'What?'

'I don't want to be the one to say this, believe me.'

She knew what he was going to say. She knew, because it chimed with the nagging doubt that she hadn't let herself listen to.

Joe sat with her, and looked her right in the eye. 'You get an email, out of the blue – don't you think you should question that? Anyone can send an email.'

'No,' Freya said. 'I could tell it was her.'

But the doubt was there now, like grit in an oyster.

She looked at Joe. She knew he wouldn't have raised the doubt unless he'd felt it was necessary.

'They're my daughters, too, Freya,' he said. 'I need to be sure.'

Freya got out her phone. She found the phone number Sam had given her, and called it. No one picked up. She tried again, Joe's words were still in her head.

'Hello?'

'Sam?' Freya said, her voice filling with emotion. This was her. This was her.

'Hi, sis.'

'Are you OK?' Freya asked. 'I know you said not to call, but I need to talk—'

'I'm sorry. I'm so sorry.' Her voice was faint.

'I can hardly hear you.'

'I'm just – it's too much.'

Freya wasn't sure if she was crying or not, but her voice wasn't clear. 'Do you need help?'

The line started to break up. 'I can't talk—' she said. 'There's no reception. I'm sorry.'

The call was cut off.

Freya felt as if she couldn't breathe. They'd been there, together, for a second. She'd had Sam there, and then she'd slipped away.

She called back. No answer. Again. Silence.

I put the phone on the side, and push it away from me.

I didn't mean to hang up – I didn't plan to, I just panicked. Hearing Freya's voice, and how glad she sounded to hear from me. It was like I couldn't breathe. I don't want to remember. I don't want to be back there.

It all feels so heavy. I've opened the door now to Freya, to the past, and there's no shutting it again.

That evening Freya called Sian. It was clear that there was no other option for the next day but for her to take time off work – so she briefed Annabel on the day ahead, reassuring her that she'd be on the end of the phone if anything came up. Freya pushed down a quiet fury, stifling it. She didn't *do* this – she didn't not show up to work, she didn't let people down. She was a professional, and against her will that was being dented. It all felt so frustrating – this wasn't something she'd ever done, even when the girls had been young. She'd always known she would have to

109

make adjustments for Dino, but she hadn't expected it to feel like this – as if her life was slipping out of her control.

As she got into bed, her phone buzzed with a message.

Freya.

I know I'm asking a lot, and you're getting nothing back right now.

I'm going to make it up to you, I promise. I'll be there for you, for Mum — and for Dino. I'll be the sister and daughter and mum that I want to be.

I may not always have shown it, but you're the only sister I ever wanted.

I would give you my last Haribo cola bottle, always.

Sam x

Chapter 13

Before the night that Eliot came up to her room, Freya had thought she could control most things. She'd thought she knew the steps, the rules, the things you did that made one thing follow another. The words you could say, the moves you could make, to make a perfect chicken roast, to pass an exam, to make things right with a friend you'd unwittingly upset, to plan a route to a new place that was smooth and hassle-free, to pack a suitcase that had a complete outfit, with accessories, that was right for each day of the holiday. It wasn't that she didn't feel things – she did, like anyone – but, as with everything else, she knew when to take herself out of a situation and take a deep breath and do what she needed to do.

But what Freya hadn't counted on was desire. Messy, powerful desire, that blurred all the boundaries. A yearning that continued through that week, when Eliot came into her room again, and talked to her. One that built up with every caught glance across the living room, until it threatened to consume her. Being around him made her feel she could escape herself. Or escape, at any rate, that mould she'd been in for years. Being the practical one, the thoughtful one – the good one – there had been a time she'd embraced that, but now she was seeing that those words had become a cage. She longed to get out and be someone new. But she wouldn't. She couldn't. Because he was Sam's.

One morning, a week after the day he'd first come up, she was with Sam at the breakfast table. It wasn't a big thing. But it sat on top of all the other things that had happened between them lately. Freya snapped at her for eating the last of the cereal. Their argument escalated until Sam was shouting. It wasn't how things ran – it wasn't how things were meant to be between them.

'You're so selfish,' Freya shouted. The volume of her own words startled her. But it was more than that. She felt – she heard – her own power. She felt the release of letting go of the control she'd held tight to all her life. She said the words and she felt the boom of her voice opening her right up. This – this was what she was capable of – and she'd never known it.

'I'm selfish?' Sam said. '*I'm* selfish?'

Sam didn't say anything else. She didn't elaborate. But the words, hanging there, were enough. Because Freya heard them back. It was as if she knew – maybe she did. Because it was Freya who was selfish now, wasn't it? It was Freya who was thinking about Eliot every waking moment, and most of the non-waking ones too. It was Freya who wanted him so much she could hardly breathe when she saw him.

'Maybe we both are,' Freya said.

That summer she and Sam found a way to live alongside each other, but the tension was palpable and, as July spilled its heat into August, it increased. They would bicker over what TV to watch, they would snap at each other about not having bought the milk. Freya sought out conflict, without really knowing why.

She wanted something to make her feel better, more justified, about the way she was feeling. She'd study up in her room, or out in the garden on the warmer days, and put on her favourite dresses to do it. Thinking, wondering if maybe Eliot would come.

Joe would text, saying that it was quiet without her. He'd tell her these funny little stories about things that had happened in the pub, and it would make her smile. He'd say he couldn't wait for her to get back to Bristol, and she'd say she felt the same, but she felt empty saying it, because it wasn't true. All she wanted was Eliot. The rush she felt when she saw him, even if it was just for a moment. She relished the sweet humidity of the days, knowing that in the evening Eliot would come back.

Perhaps saying she was fated to do it was the easy way out – because, looking back from her late thirties now, it had always been a choice. It had been a choice to meet Eliot's gaze across the room. It had been a choice to leave the room just after him, so that when he came back from the bathroom they'd pass in the hall, and she'd feel for one fleeting moment the touch of his arm against hers, as they passed wordlessly.

Freya had felt that summer that her body, the skin she'd lived in for nineteen years, was coming alive for the first time. She'd felt conscious of parts of her body that usually just served her. Each part of her felt vulnerable to the excitement, to the electric charge that came when he looked at her. She'd never understood what her friends were talking about – when they went off with the boys in cars, when they skipped school to sleep with crushes who left them crying, when they emerged from bedrooms at parties after fumbles on the coat piles. She'd never understood it – and she had found it strange to imagine crossing that line with Joe. Joe was a good friend, and she knew what everyone thought – her sister, her friends at uni. That it was just a matter of time. But what if she didn't want that?

This – what she felt for Eliot, the feelings that made her skin prickle and disrupted her focus – this was something new, and so unfamiliar. And it was *addictive*. There was nothing she wouldn't give, nothing she wouldn't trample on, in order to see him and talk to him again. To have him look at her in that way that said I know you, I get you, I hear you, and, buried deep in all of that – I want you. I want you for all of that. I want you for that and all the things I don't know about you yet, too. I don't want to meet you in the illusion of your perfection, I want to meet you deep in your flaws, I want to get to the heart of you, and make it bigger, make it newer, make it feel everything it can feel.

That was what his look felt like to Freya, and those thoughts were the ones that she had about him. In her own mind, it went deeper still. She'd find herself thinking: I want to make you feel every good, deep thing that exists. I want to shut the door on everything else, and let this bubble be all that exists for a while. I want us to exist beyond what's right, what's wrong. I want there to be enough space that I can know you, and maybe make a little dent in you that's the shape of me. Then, when we're done, when we're really, truly done, I want to go outside with you and look up at the night sky and say: What do those stars and those wispy wandering clouds look like to you? And the answer doesn't matter. I don't care if you see it the same way, or differently, but what pulses in me, with an urgency that just won't quit, is that I need to know. I need to see what shape the world is to you.

At night she could barely sleep for reliving every time her eyes had met Eliot's, each word he'd ever said to her, the fleeting seconds of their chance meetings that had never happened by chance. The wishing and hoping that this thing – this uncapturable thing – might turn into something real. Something so real she could touch it and taste it – touch and taste him – rather than just make it a little less under the sheets by herself each night. She could keep the feeling in abeyance, keep a modicum of control that way, but it never went away. Then there were the nights when it caused a surge in her that was the opposite of what she wanted, that augmented the feeling which already threatened to consume her. She knew then that it had the power to take her over.

And one night it did.

One night it did, and she let it. One night, when everyone was downstairs, Eliot came to her in her room, and instead of doing what she should have, telling him to go downstairs again and rejoin his friends, go back to Sam – instead of doing any of those things, those Freya-type things, she got up and pulled the lock on her door across, and tried not to think about why she was doing it and what it meant.

When she turned around to face him, he was so close that he was almost pressed up against her. His thumb ran over her bottom lip and there it was: the die was cast. She felt what she'd longed to – the weight of his body against hers, and the musky smell of him. She could feel him breathing, see the rise and fall of his chest – and she wanted that breath to be something they shared; she wanted it to be a part of her. Her own edges started to soften and merge with the parts of him. And it was the most irresistible thing she'd ever experienced.

This wasn't about her sister. This wasn't about anyone else but the two of them – the two of them that here – damn, she felt her heart beating so hard – had a world all of their own. Her heart was beating as if it wasn't inside her chest any more but somewhere between them. This heat that she'd played a part in creating immersed her. This new self she was becoming. This hot, powerful force that had built up in her from the energy between the two of them, in this moment, suspended in time.

Right and wrong had ceased to be clear – or even to matter. They weren't the measure of this. What swept through Freya was a rush, not just of desire, but of becoming herself. As Eliot's mouth found hers, and his hands held her hips, bringing her in closer towards him, she felt the intoxicating freedom of stepping outside everything she'd thought she was, and becoming someone new.

That summer she held the truth of her time with Eliot close to her, and shared it with no one.

Because in spite of everything else, Sam was her sister, and moving in on the man she wanted was not what she should've been doing, she knew that much. Freya knew deep down that whatever Sam had done to cause friction between the two of them was minor compared to the fire she had lit under their relationship.

Freya had never felt the heat of it before, never understood how it could be to turn your back on your own self and the morals you thought you held dear. At nineteen, she should know better, right? She told herself stories – that Sam had never really known Eliot, had never really seen him or understood him in the way she did. That he'd never truly belonged to Sam the way he had, for that night, belonged to her. The way he'd laughed, the way they had sparked off one another when she'd let him become part of her . . . sometimes she wondered if she'd somehow made it happen. If she'd conjured Eliot into being that night. If – because it had crossed her mind – she was somehow responsible for him coming up to her room: perhaps her willing their encounter to happen had been enough to make it possible.

But why shouldn't she be the one to live in the moment, and see colour flood in, just for once?

She tried to tell herself that Sam hadn't had any right to Eliot, he was a free agent, but, as much as she wanted it to, it didn't ring completely true. Usually, if she told herself something often enough, it started to feel real, but she knew deep down that Sam had found Eliot, and that she'd staked her claim early. The things that usually helped Freya make her world slot together no longer did. She couldn't make right the wrong thing that she'd done. She'd couldn't even tone it down.

In the childhood days that she and Sam had shared, she never could have foreseen that one day they'd be here, slotting together awkwardly, almost like strangers. They hadn't argued when they were younger – but when Freya looked at it now she saw that it was because, elder sister or not, she'd always been the one who conceded. The one who gave in to keep the peace.

That summer, everything had shifted. Their dance as sisters had become a different kind of dance, and each of them felt out of step.

The next time Eliot came up to her room, the same thing happened. The third time, he'd messaged her and asked her to meet him in his car, at the end of their road. She'd gone out to meet him, and he'd driven her over to the woods. When they got there he'd kissed her, hard, and pushed her up against a tree. His body against hers sent a rush through every part of her, and, when he touched her, she cried out, and pressed her mouth into his chest to stop the sound. The good sister she had been was gone for ever.

Sam would still talk about Eliot. Freya would hear her on the phone, to Echo, or some other friend, mentioning him. Freya would listen, trying to hear exactly what she was saying, knowing that later that night she would meet with Eliot and make the same mistake, if that was what it was, again and again, and it would feel like heaven and earth and everything in between.

Freya couldn't understand, even now, why he'd chosen her, in her mousiness, in her straight-up-and-down-ness, when Sam had the sort of figure girls envied and men couldn't resist. She couldn't understand it, but, in the moment of being chosen, the buzz had been intoxicating.

Chapter 14

Freya was starting to accept that her life was going to have to change. This job was everything she'd been wanting, but her family – and Dino was part of that – had to come first. She would be there for her nephew, whatever it took, and even if that meant making sacrifices. On Monday afternoon she called Sian with a heavy heart. She told her that she had unavoidable family commitments and would have to pull out of the project. Sian – the director Freya had wanted to work with for years – tried to be understanding, but Freya could hear the stress in her voice. Freya knew better than anyone how inconvenient this would be for everyone involved – she was letting all of them down. Freya was technically breaking her contract, and it nagged at her that it could damage her professional reputation when word spread in the industry, as it invariably did. She thought of all her plans for the series, and the hopes she'd had that this project might lead her to a new stage in her career. It felt like a lot to let go of, and it stung. She'd wanted this. She'd worked hard for it, and she'd really wanted it.

When she put down the phone she felt a huge sense of loss. She might never again have a professional opportunity as big as this. But then she might never have the chance to do this for her sister again, either. This was her family, and this was the commitment she had made – and she would stand by that promise, no matter what.

Freya was playing with Dino in the living room. Upstairs she could hear the girls playing in their room, or rather the opening and closing of doors as Jessie tried to convince her sister to join her in the game. Louisa was more concerned with being on her phone to catch up with friends, much to Jessie's disappointment. Guess Who. Freya was the blue board, Dino the red. He lifted the little flaps and then closed them again. He picked them at random, different people, different rows. His green eyes were cast down and there was a frown line between his brows. Freya asked him if he wanted to pick a card, so that they could start playing properly, but he didn't reply.

Another silence. Freya was growing used to them. They weren't comfortable, but they were becoming familiar. She just had to draw from that well of patience deep within her.

'Dino?' Freya prompted him gently. She passed him the small pack of cards to choose from. Bill, with his red beard, Paul with his white hair and little glasses. It was an old version of the game, one she and Sam had played when they were kids.

'Have you spoken to my mum?' he asked.

'Yes – I got a message from her. She misses you.'

'Can I call her?'

The messages had asked for her to be left in peace, said that she needed space from Dino for a while. Freya had to respect that.

'I'm sorry, love. Whatever it is she needs to do, she needs to do it on her own right now. It won't be for long.'

Dino went back to the opening and closing of the flaps, then started to take out the card inserts, bending them, ripping one.

119

Freya flinched a little. The old game had some sentimental value for her. She didn't want to see it get damaged like this.

'Dino,' Freya said, more firmly. 'Don't do that!'

It came out louder than she'd meant it to.

Dino shrank back a fraction, his eyes wide. Freya felt awful. She'd scared him. She wanted to wind back that minute, but as she opened her mouth to speak she saw it was already too late. He turned away from Freya and buried his head in his own shoulder, hiding his face. She reached out to touch him, her hand grazing his upper arm.

His arm swung out, defensively, and hit her hard on the cheek. She felt a sharp sting across her cheekbone, and her hand instinctively went to it.

'What was that?' she whispered, reeling.

Dino was looking up now – still scared. But a different frightened now, as if he wasn't sure of his own power, his own strength. 'An accident,' he said, quietly.

She didn't know whether she believed him.

When they were young her daughters would knock and bruise her, she'd laugh about being a toddler climbing frame, they'd run too fast in their games and use her as a brake. She had never expected to be treated like precious china. But this was different. This had hurt. He'd said it was an accident – but she hadn't seen his face. Had it been? Or had he intended to hurt her?

Jessie burst into the room, beaded necklaces strung around her neck and a smear of lipstick on her mouth. 'Mum!' she called out. 'Look at me.'

Her hazel eyes were bright. Freya couldn't let her know that anything was wrong.

'Wow,' Freya said, pulling herself up straighter and forcing a smile. 'That's quite a look.'

Dino was still slumped, not saying a word.

Louisa appeared beside Freya. 'Mum, she took my make-up without asking, and she's smashed my bronzer, look ...' She held out a Clinique box, with crumbled fragments of make-up still in it. Then she paused. 'Christ, Mum. What happened to your face? Your cheek's really red.'

Freya put a hand up to cover it. She glanced over at Dino. She felt confused, but also sure that what mattered most was reassuring him. We are on the same team, she tried to tell him silently. We can work this out.

'It's nothing,' she said.

'It doesn't look like nothing,' Louisa said.

Freya scrambled around for something to say, but she couldn't think of anything.

Dino's eyes were fixed on the floor. He was trembling.

'Just an accident,' Freya said. 'Listen – I'm pretty sure it's time for dinner.' She brightened, on physical autopilot, because she didn't know what else to do. Her smile extended to Dino, who was now looking at her, blank and cold. 'Who wants to come and help me get it ready?'

I'm looking at my hands. I ball them up, like I did earlier, when I was angry.

It hurts, this feeling. Like I'm not enough. I can't make her love me. I don't feel like that about my dad, because he left before I was born. He never knew me. But she stayed to get to know me, and in the end, this was what she decided. That life without me was better, was easier. That I got in the way.

It's not Freya. It's not meant to be Freya. But when it all builds up in me it sometimes just comes out all in a rush, and I don't have time to think – it's just out.

When she looks at me all sad and hurt I feel bad and then sometimes I just feel angrier about the fact she's making me feel bad.

You can talk to us.
They all keep saying that. Freya, and Joe, and Jessie. Even Louisa.
What if I told them?
What if I told them I can't?
That I promised, and I can't.
I won't.

Freya put Dino and Jessie to bed. She read them their stories together, then said goodnight to Dino. For a moment she could fool herself that nothing had changed – but it had. Something inside her had been pulled tight – she was unsettled. She hadn't hugged Dino goodnight, this time. It hadn't been a conscious decision; she just felt herself instinctively holding back.

She'd find a way to be there for him, in the way that he needed. But she couldn't right now – because she needed to work that out, put her own boundaries in place, and be sure that the girls weren't at risk from his outbursts. She led Jessie out of the room and into her bed. She kissed her gently on the cheek as she lay down to sleep. Her daughter seemed somehow more fragile, and she found she was holding on to her hand a moment longer than she needed to.

She had to get things in perspective. She was mother to three for the time being, and there was no changing that – that was the deal she had made, and it was a promise she would keep. The only option, the only thing she could do, was to dig deep and search within herself for a little more strength to help her be there for the child who needed her most.

That evening, Freya didn't want to look at her reflection for long. The area around her cheekbone throbbed, and, though the bruise hadn't come up yet, she knew it was likely to, soon. She found some arnica cream on the bathroom shelf – something she'd used on Jessie's bruised knees and elbows in the past, but never on herself. It had always seemed to stop the swelling where her little girls had fallen down.

The next day at breakfast, Freya looked at Dino across the kitchen table. His eyes were cast down. She longed for him to look at her – even in anger. She'd take that. Something, anything, other than this silence. The silence that told her nothing. The atmosphere was heavy, and Freya felt the ache of it – if he were glaring at her she could at least feel hateful towards him, however unfair that might be. This child in her house who seemed so full of resentment towards her.

'Dino – can we talk?' she said, gently.

He looked up now, and instead of anger his eyes were pools of sadness, emptiness – something she was worried she wouldn't be able to fix.

She'd thought the shared blood in their veins would make it all easier, help her to understand him. But it didn't seem to be working out that way. He had hit out at her. He'd hurt her. She now had a dark bruise on her cheek to prove that it had really happened. She imagined how the other parents would look at her in the playground – knew the foundation she'd put on could only hide so much. It felt like a strange, guilty secret to have been hurt by a child. As if it was something she had somehow provoked, or something she should have been able to avoid.

She needed to be patient. But the virtue she'd once been certain she possessed had been tested to its very limit, and she didn't trust that she even had it in her any more.

As she looked at him now, she wished she felt something else – something more straightforward, something that would enable her to turn her back, to say enough was enough, and hand him back. But what she had started to feel for Dino, in spite of everything, was love. Love that bonded her to him, and love

123

that meant whatever he did, however he acted, she had to try to understand.

It's been days. It feels like weeks, but when I make my brain do the numbers it's been twenty-six hours. The cramps are kicking in. I've been so tired – tired so I can't keep my eyelids open – but sleep won't ever come. The first time I got this stuff, it was from my doctor – it was meant to make my back better. It did, for a while. Just so long as you don't stop.

Hearing Freya's voice on the phone was hard. It brought me right back to Fern Bay. To the person I was back then, before I got free of it. It wasn't all bad – that summer we were all together, met Eliot, and the group of us would go to gigs and have barbecues on the beach and he and Anya would play guitar. I felt good then, sometimes. But there was always the memory of what happened to me there, in my own home. Those streets, that beach – I was never free of it. Hearing her voice took me back there.

I can't do this any more. I don't care if it's failure, I don't care about anything at the moment other than feeling better than this. I pick up the phone and call Cassie. Is Al there still? I ask. Because I'm coming over.

Freya went into Dino's room at bedtime and listened to him read a bedtime story to her. He was a little slow, somewhere around Jessie's level in spite of his extra year, but still able to get there with most words. She focused on the story, a chapter of *The Magic Faraway Tree*, and tried not to think about the day before. They needed a chance to start over.

When he'd finished, she touched his cheek gently. She would bring tenderness to the rawness that remained. She wished him goodnight and he leaned in towards her touch.

'What's going on for you, Dino?' she asked.

'I don't know,' he said. 'I feel all mixed up, I guess.'

She put her hand on top of his, did what she could to calm him.

'Everyone feels like that sometimes. Do you think you're scared of something? Or sad?'

He shrugged, but his eyes grew shiny, giving his hurt away. 'I don't know.'

'So it's a feeling, but you're not sure where it's come from?'

'I guess so. Or maybe I do know.' He looked down at the duvet, tracing a path on the robot picture printed there with his finger.

'What is it? You can trust me, Dino.'

'I'm worried that I'll be on my own.'

Freya squeezed his hand. 'You're not on your own, love. You've got us.'

'But that's only for now. What about later? What if she doesn't come back for me?'

'Your mum?' Freya said.

'She's done this before.' He seemed more numb than anything else. 'She goes, and she doesn't say when she's coming back.'

'You mean back home – she leaves you?'

Dino nodded again. There was a flash of pain in his eyes.

Freya's pulse picked up. 'Let me get this straight – she leaves you, what, with her friends?'

'Sometimes it's Cassie. Sometimes it's just me.'

He went quiet then, as if he'd already said too much.

'She leaves you at home on your own?' Disbelief merged with a quiet fury. This boy was seven, for Christ's sake. Far too young to be left alone. 'And she goes out for, what, a few hours?'

He shrugged. 'Days, sometimes.'

Freya felt a protective rush towards Dino. She could tell he wasn't exaggerating – he looked ashamed, as if he was somehow the one at fault. So this was what had been happening for him – no wonder he was finding it hard to sleep.

Sam hadn't changed. She was still, ultimately, as selfish as she'd been as a teenager. But now, instead of Freya and her parents being the ones left behind, it was far worse – now it was a child.

She took a deep breath and tried to stay calm. Letting her feelings show wasn't going to help the situation.

'Your mum will come back,' she said, soothingly. 'She promised me she would, and I believe her.'

All along Freya had told herself not to judge. What did she know about Sam's life these days? Nothing. Nothing at all. But this was different. This – she could see too clearly to ignore – was neglect.

'I'm OK at home,' Dino said. 'She always leaves a lot of food for me. But sometimes she forgets to leave out the iPad charger, or the remote control gets lost, and then it's really quiet. I don't like it all quiet like that. The bit that I don't like is not knowing. I watch the hands on the clock and the sun come up but it doesn't really make a difference, because she hasn't given me a time. She just says *I'll be back soon.*'

'And this time? What did she tell you?'

'*Not long*, she said. But it's not true?' His eyes flashed with hurt. 'Freya, it's not true, is it? It's been a really long time, hasn't it?'

'It has,' she said, softly. What else could she give him? She couldn't make any promises. There was nothing more she could say. 'You've been waiting a long time.'

He nodded, and looked disappointed, a little broken. Like no seven-year-old should look.

'You deserve more than this,' Freya said, a new determination coming in. 'So let me promise you this much, Dino: whatever happens with your mum – I will keep you safe.'

Chapter 15

What had started out feeling difficult to Freya was starting to get easier. It was starting to be her life – a different kind of life, with Dino right at the centre of it.

The next day, a Wednesday, Dino was putting things away in the kitchen after breakfast. He placed the cutlery back in the drawer, slowly and deliberately. Freya had only had to ask once; it wasn't like with her daughters when she sometimes felt that they didn't hear her voice at all, only a noise that they often to ignore. Dino had taken to the task, doing it diligently, without any fuss at all.

The sun was out, and the back door was open, leading out to the garden. Discarded footballs and outdoor toys lay on the lawn. But he didn't waver from what he was doing. He picked up each spoon, fork and knife carefully, and put them away. He seemed to enjoy these small, focused tasks.

She went up to Dino, and bent slightly to his level. 'Thanks for that,' she said.

He looked at her, and she saw something close to a smile. She reached out to touch his hand, and he let her take it. It warmed her inside to see him start to trust her. The aggression had started to fade, or at least she hadn't seen it lately. Perhaps they could get there. Perhaps, slowly, together, they would get there.

I've been crashing on Cassie's floor for – how long? – it feels like weeks now. Al comes, and Al goes. Al brings what he has, whatever I need to chill out, or to lift me back up. Al chats with us as we rise and fall. This isn't the family I was born into, and it's not the family I gave birth to – but these guys, they are my family – in that they accept me. They see me get messy, and they're there when I talk wild, they laugh with me, and they hold me, if I need it. They are there for me, truly.

So I'll stay here, wake with my face on that scratchy carpet in a room that smells of smoke. I'll drink my tea without milk because the milk's all gone bad, because this is family. And I can look after them, just like they look after me. I can do this, because their needs – it's not the same. It's not like being a mother where you lose sight of it all. Where you can lose sight of yourself. Losing myself with these guys – it's more like finding myself, really. Remembering how it all was, when I first arrived here in Margate, and everything was fresh and everything was new, and I thought I could be the kind of person anyone would want a piece of. Before Neil reminded me that all I ever was was no one.

Dino's eyes were fixed on the cages in the pet shop. Freya had got him here by saying it was the nearest thing they had in Fern Bay to a zoo; she'd hoped it might help them to reconnect. There were the regular pets – rabbits, guinea pigs – and he'd crouched to look at them for a moment, the tiniest of smiles on his face. But it was when they got to the reptile area that his face had really brightened. The owner must have caught a glimpse of it, because she appeared by their side and bent to open the cage. 'Would you like to hold the chameleon?' she asked. He nodded, a gentle smile breaking out on his face. It changed the whole way he looked – his cheeks rising up, his eyes sparkling. He looked so different when that happened, almost like another child altogether.

He held the reptile on his right arm, tentative and nervous, but still smiling. 'It feels weird,' he said, to the shopkeeper. 'Its claws are digging in a bit.' The animal moved, and Dino giggled. Freya felt as if her heart was filling up. This boy was not a lost boy – he was just a boy who had been waiting to be discovered. And seeing what lay underneath – it was a gift.

'Do you want to hold it, Freya?' he asked, reaching his arm out towards her.

She opened her mouth to say no – of course she wouldn't hold it. She wasn't a kid. She wasn't a little boy, she wasn't—

'OK,' she said. The chameleon moved from Dino's little arm to hers, and as they peered close to it together, watching his eyes swivel around, she wondered what had taken her so long. She felt brave, for the first time in a long time.

Freya has short hair. It comes to her chin, and it's straight and swingy. She likes things with lines on them, stripy tops, long earrings that are like lines of silver. It's like everything with her is neat and in order. I can see those bones by her neck, a horizontal line above her top sometimes. It's like she's made up of all these straight edges, but now, here in the pet shop, they've disappeared, and she's become curved, and soft. I like her better this way.

Freya felt buoyed up by the way Dino was starting to trust her, but her concerns about his behaviour hadn't gone away. A couple of days ago she had confided in her mother about Dino's angry outbursts, and admitted that, as much as she wanted to support him herself, she felt out of her depth. Jilly shared her concern, and had said she'd heard about a local group that might be suitable for him, run by a woman called Joanna. She'd passed Freya the flyer. It was advertised as teaching mindfulness, with play therapy. Freya called up and booked Dino a place – and two days later they were here, at the Community Centre. Dino had been really reluctant to go in, and Freya hadn't wanted him to be uncomfortable, but she had gently encouraged him until he finally let go of her hand. Now, she was on her own in the foyer, waiting, and hoping, that something in there would help.

Freya's brought me here, to this woman's office. Joanna. She told me her name. I told her mine. She said it back, 'Dy-no.' I don't know why she said it that way. Like she didn't hear me. 'Dino,' I say again. Making the 'ee' sound long so she'll hear. Then I think maybe it doesn't matter so much.

There are two other kids here too, a boy and a girl. They talk a lot and I'm glad about that, because it means I can stay quiet.

She gave me some Lego to play with, and that's what I'm doing now, finding a sixer so that I can put the front wheels on properly.

She's just another person asking questions. I think she thinks if she keeps that silence going I'll fill it. I won't.

I drop a small bit, and I can't find it right away. I get down on my knees and have a look on the carpet, it's rough and worn. I find it, near the chair leg. I get back up.

I can hear the clock on the wall ticking.

I can wait. I can keep on waiting.

Freya and Dino drove back to the house. Most of their journey home was silent. She wondered how much of his time in the group had been the same – Joanna had mentioned to her, quietly, that Dino had seemed quite withdrawn. If only he could give a little – just enough so that she'd know where to start helping him – enough so that she knew what direction they were going in. Freya would get these glimmers, these moments of hope – like in the pet shop – and then he seemed to withdraw from her again.

When they arrived home, Dino went up the stairs and to his

room without saying a word. Freya took a deep breath, and went through to the kitchen to make herself some tea. This would take time. She had to be patient.

Joe came around after dinner, and the two of them sat in the garden and had a drink while the children played.

'How's it all going?' Joe asked.

'Slowly,' she said.

She glanced over at Dino, down on his knees, digging in the dirt. He was playing alongside Jessie, immersed in their joint task.

'The mindfulness group?'

'I don't know how much he's going to get out of it. I don't think he says a whole lot in there. But he's not refusing to go back, either. So I'm taking that as going OK.'

'And the rest?' Joe asked her, his voice soft. She appreciated his support. It meant a lot that he was there.

'Oh, you know,' she said. 'Leaving work was hard. You know all the groundwork I did to get in on that drama series – and now, when I do get back to work, I'll be starting from scratch all over again. But it is what it is. I made a promise to Sam, and Dino needs me here. It was too much for Mum to cover the childcare for both the kids, and I get that.'

'Is Dino still – you know?'

'Hitting out?' Freya said. Joe nodded. She still felt the sting of shame at those moments. The way she'd tried to hide the aggression, and its impact, because it didn't seem like something that should have happened in her home. She could see more clearly now that it was never anything to do with her.

'It's calmed down a bit. He still gets frustrated sometimes, but he'll direct it at a cushion, or a toy. I don't think he does it in front of the girls. I don't think he would.'

Joe looked relieved.

'I'm spending more time with him one on one,' she said. 'I think he's really benefiting from that.'

'That's good. Just watch that you don't get too involved.'

'What?' Freya said, with a flash of defensiveness.

'It's just, you've already invested a lot. Just remember that this isn't all yours to fix.'

Freya bristled at the comment. 'Not mine to fix?'

'That came out wrong. I just meant – you're not his mum.'

'He's a child, Joe. My nephew. Not a broken toy. By the sound of things my sister's let him down badly, and I'm not going to walk away from him – he deserves for someone to be there for him, for someone to be stable.'

'I get that,' Joe said. 'I'm sorry ...'

'Good,' she said, firmly.

'It's just – I see you sacrificing a lot. I know what your job meant to you. I'm not trying to dictate to you what you should or shouldn't do, Freya. I'm just looking out for you.'

'OK. Well, thank you, then.'

He looked at her directly, and put a hand on her arm. His hand was warm against her skin. It tingled at the unexpected contact. She hadn't felt that. Not for years.

'I love you, Freya, that's all. Three months ago, you didn't even know this boy existed. I want to know you're not going to get lost in all this.'

Chapter 16

I lie back and look up at the ceiling in the hostel – silently counting the poly-styrene tiles, the ones that are stained yellow, the ones that are loose. When I'm done (sixty-six) I turn on my side, and see that the woman in the bed next to me is restless. She's fidgeting and her face is lit blue by her mobile phone. I reach for mine, check my coat pockets. It's there – thank God. It's out of battery, but I didn't lose it like the other times. I'll probably have a dozen missed calls from Freya, when I switch it back on.

Some of the women around me are snoring. It's like being in a pigsty. It's so noisy in here. A toilet flushes, then another, somewhere else in the building. There are people in the next room laughing. It's not that genuinely happy laughter, it's the kind of laughing people do when they need to remind themselves that they once loved life. I saw those women earlier, pale and tired-looking. I can hear clear enough that they're laughing to remember who they were. You get the sense that there's a lot of dragging through the days that goes on in here.

I can't remember how I got here. I remember the beginning of the night, in the Wetherspoons, with Cassie and Al. Then they got together and I felt like a third wheel. We started arguing about something, Cassie and me. I can't even remember what. All I knew was, I didn't want to be around them, I couldn't go back to hers, and I sure as hell didn't want to go back to my own flat, with its blackened wall and all the reminders of how I messed up.

I got talking with the old guys in there, the ones that arrive when the doors open in the morning. Trying to fill that hole in the middle of me. The one that came when I thought about how Dino's skin feels, how soft it is. I don't need to be thinking that stuff, but it creeps up on me sometimes. I walked past a kid his age on the street yesterday. He was wearing the same hoodie, the one I got him from H&M last winter. He was the same height. Saw that and it cut right through me.

I know he's better off with her, not me. That's why I made all this happen – why I had to. Right now Dino'll be in a cosy living room with one of those big corner sofas like you see on the DFS adverts. It'll be one bought outright, not in instalments. One that they can't just come and take away like they did with ours that night just before Christmas. Dino was sitting on it when they came in. They were nice to him, to be fair. They had the decency to apologise, what with him being only a kid and everything, but they still took it out from under him, and the TV too. After they'd gone, I didn't know what to do, other than find us a Twix in the cupboard, sit on the carpet, and give him half. We didn't realise how much we watched that TV and sat on that sofa until the day they went. I got the TV back for us, in the end.

Dino never said anything much about anything, but he understood. An old soul, that's what Cassie calls him. When things go wrong, I'll make a joke of it, the small things, or make up a story. I'm good at that. I do it so that nothing is scary for him. They're stories, not lies, just so that he can think the world is a safe place. He doesn't need to know the truth – not yet – that good things don't always happen to good people.

I don't want to be here tonight, with all these sweaty, smelly old women and their socks with holes in them. I might not be in a great place, but I'm not as low as this. One night – that's it.

I can't remember how I got here. A siren, a light. Maybe it was for me – it wouldn't be the first time. But nothing ached, beyond the hangover that's throbbing in my temples. I normally know if I've come in that way. Maybe this time I just walked.

I wish Dino was back here with me. He'd give me his dog soft toy, his favourite one, the one he knows I like to hold when I've had a crap day, even though I'm meant to be the grown-up. He didn't have that many toys, but he'd give me every last one. Somehow I made a boy that's ten times the person I am.

That's kids for you, though, isn't it? That love that spills out of them, even when you don't deserve it. Even when all you were ever going to do to their little hearts was break them into pieces.

The way it looks with Dino isn't the way it was. I planned it. I wanted a baby. It was so easy getting pregnant that I never figured that the rest – the birth, and most of all the whole when-they're-here thing – could be so damn hard. There's no one around you to show how not to mess it up. I was never expecting Dino's dad – Kieron, he was called – that much I remember, and not much else – to stick around. I'm a lot of things but I'm not naïve. So I left. I wasn't going to give him the chance to be the one to leave me.

I never had anyone I could go to, apart from Cassie. Once I left Dorset, that was it. No going back, not for anything. I just relied on me. And it worked OK, for a while.

I wish they'd go away, the thoughts of Dino. They get in my head and I can't push them out – but I can't fix things and get him back either. I can do numb, that's about it. Last night it was the only time in the hostel where I actually wanted there to be more noise than there was. There was too much time to think. To picture Dino. To miss him. I've hurt him a lot, I know that. I've not meant to – but I have. I've messed up. I've done enough to show him that the people he loves can let him down. But have I done enough to damage him? That's what rings in my ears at night. That's what won't let me sleep, won't leave me alone. Have I done enough to break him?

*

135

I'm back with Joanna. It's fifty minutes that I need to stay on this side of the door, while Freya and Jessie are on the other. The other kids are playing and chatting, but I'm just waiting for it to be over.

The room has a digital clock, so it's easier to tell the time and count down exactly. Forty-eight minutes isn't that much. I'd rather be playing Uno with Jessie, but I can be here. It's not that bad, sitting here, in this room. But it's not that comfortable either, so when it flicks to forty-seven minutes, forty-six, I like that.

'Dino,' Joanna says, gently. She still says my name funny – Dy-no. I did put her right at the beginning, but I guess she's forgotten.

She asks us all to build something, and the other boy, Cassian, makes a garage. Joanna is talking with the other girl, who's sad about something.

'Is that your house?' Cassian asks. 'Is that your mum?'

I look at the figures. I don't think any of them are my mum. It's not that I don't miss her because a big bit of me does. I'm OK with that part. That's the right way to feel. But somehow, today, the other side is bigger.

When I feel it, I feel bad, and I want to curl up and never see anyone again. Not Mum, not Freya, not Jessie, definitely not this boy, or Joanna. Because it screws up my whole heart, and most of all it makes me not-good. Not human, almost.

Because this is the truth. I feel better. Away from Mum, I feel better.

Freya was sitting and waiting for Dino to come out of the Community Centre room. She wondered what they were doing in there. She could hear soft music playing, and the occasional burst of laughter. She knew that she needed support for him, but Joe's words kept coming back to her. Was she taking on too much – and was she trying to be his mum, when she wasn't?

There was still radio silence from Sam, and Freya felt as if she might almost have imagined the whole thing – the contact with her sister, the promise of the two of them being reunited. It seemed such a strange, bold hope now. This situation wasn't sustainable – she knew that much. If this went on, she would have to get Social Services involved – it wasn't optional; she had a duty to Dino. But maybe they could do this for just a little longer. Maybe there was still a way for her to keep her promise to Sam to not involve anyone else.

She just kept hoping that the next time she called, her sister would pick up.

Dino came out of Joanna's group at the Community Centre and made his way over to Freya.

'How was it today?' Freya asked him, as they walked out to the car. She didn't always ask, but for some reason today she felt she could. There was something different about him, more open.

'Good. I did some Lego.'

'OK,' Freya said.

'We talked a bit.'

He looked slightly distant then. She didn't want to push him. She knew he would close up completely if she did.

'Then we painted. I painted a picture. It's still in there, drying. I don't know if I got it right.'

Freya took his hand in hers and looked at him square on. 'There's no right or wrong, love.'

'It was nice to paint.'

'What did you do?'

'I was painting the lights.'

'The lights?' Freya asked. 'Which lights are those?'

'The ones you can see from our flat. The lights from Dreamland.'

It hit Freya, right in the chest.

Dreamland.

Margate.

*

When Freya got home, she put a TV programme on for Dino and dashed into the kitchen so she could be on her own to look at her phone. Her heart was beating hard in her chest. She knew. She already knew. But she had to be sure she'd got it right. She searched online for Dreamland, and images of the Margate amusement park filled her screen. She brought up a map, and zoomed in on the streets facing on to the area.

A few hours up the coast. Practically on their doorstep.

That was where they lived.

That was where Sam was.

He'd handed her the answer – just like that.

This was it. This was what he'd been talking about. He hadn't meant to tell her – he'd just let it slip. But in that one word he'd given Freya everything she'd needed. Everything she'd spent years hoping for. She wanted more details – she wanted to ask him question after question to narrow it down, so that she'd know just which door to knock on. But she didn't want to drag him into this, to make him tell her things he might not want to. She would take the little that she had, and find Sam with it.

She looked at the network of intersecting roads on her iPhone screen. These streets – this had to be where Sam was.

Freya dropped Louisa round at Joe's, and then drove to her mum's house with the younger kids in the back, feeling that she couldn't waste another minute. While Jessie and Dino were in the other room, she explained what Dino had said – the clue he'd given her – and she saw her mum's eyes brighten with hope. She assured her that she'd be back for bedtime.

She drove over to Margate, listening to an audiobook on the way to try to calm her racing thoughts. She parked at the station and walked out in the direction of the sea.

The motivation to find Sam got her moving at twice her usual speed. This time she had a clue, and she held it so close – this precious new thing. This time she wouldn't give up, she wouldn't be deterred. Because this time she had a real chance. This wasn't just about Sam any more. It was bigger than that. She wanted to find her sister, as she always had, but she also needed to understand more about Dino's life, so that she could help him.

She neared the water, the tang of sea-salt hitting her nostrils. Just looking out at that wide expanse of water gave her a rush of energy. The light here was brighter. As she walked towards the Old Town the rattle and beeps of arcade games met with the squawks of seagulls. She saw a couple walking, bickering with one another, empty-eyed. This town that had absorbed her sister, enabled her to vanish for years, was an easy place to disappear in.

Freya had a picture in her handbag: a photo of Sam, a month or so before she'd left. Her hair was twisted up into a topknot and she was wearing a checked lumberjack shirt. It was how Freya remembered her – and she hoped upon hope that someone else might recall her too.

I need your help.

The words her sister had said pulled at Freya's heart. Had her sister, deep down, been asking to be found?

She looked at the people crouched on damp sleeping bags in the doorways, bowls of dog food and yellowing paperbacks beside them. They might be the ones to know. She showed them the photo, and asked, but they looked back blankly. Shivering. Shook their heads. She left money beside them and went on.

I get in the shower at the hostel. The hot water feels good. I use one of the soap samples to get myself properly clean. I know they're donated, just like a lot of the stuff here. People doing their weekly shop at Waitrose chucking a few donations into the food bank bin. I never thought I'd be relying on charity, but hey, there's a lot I didn't predict about how life panned out.

I don't care. I'd rather be clean than not, and the water is so good and hot. I've got used to it, showering rarely and quickly, to keep money on the meter. But I never get really clean. There's that layer of grime on my skin that I can't seem to get rid of. It's coming off now, really coming off, until my skin feels like it used to, a long time ago, before I got dirty like this in the first place.

Freya walked down the street in a daze. Samantha – Sam – was the name that their parents had chosen for her, and one Freya had called out hundreds of times, in the playground, when she was waiting to use the bathroom, when she was calling her sister down for dinner. But nowadays, if she was here, she might have a whole new name.

She found the network of streets that were facing on to the amusement park, wondering where to start. The task felt daunting. She reminded herself that she was doing this for all of them. If she could find Sam, she could find out more about Dino. She couldn't go on like this, trying to understand a boy about whom she knew so little. He had a whole history behind him that seemed to be affecting him now, and yet she was entirely without the tools to help him. She came to a road of terraced houses. If you looked from a distance they might look like an appealing place to live, but as she drew closer she saw that they had metal shutters covering the doors and windows. This was an abandoned street, the kind where they sold property off cheap – but still, if you were the first to move in there you'd be living alone.

This, she saw now, was a place her sister could lose herself in; this was a far cry from candyfloss and seaside postcards. She walked past a house where the top floor looked blackened by smoke damage. Outside, beside the red front door, there were the remnants of burnt furniture. It sent a chill through her wondering if anyone had been inside.

As she walked down the street, her pace quickening, one of the doors, one of the few that wasn't shuttered, opened up. A woman, dressed in combat trousers, with colourful rags twisted into her dreadlocks, walked out and called something back into the house before closing the door behind her. She caught Freya looking at her, and took in Freya's trousers and smart jacket.

'You lost?'

'Not exactly,' Freya said.

'It's just, you don't look like you live round here, that's all.'

Freya forced herself to ask. 'I'm looking for someone. Actually, I'm looking for my sister. Sam.'

The woman stopped still, and took a breath. 'Your sister?'

Freya's heart caught. There was no mistaking it, the connection. She was close.

'Do you know her – Sam?'

The woman turned towards Freya, her stare cold. 'You want me to help you find your sister,' she said. 'But what if what you find isn't what you're hoping for?'

Freya's heart raced. This could be something – this could be it. 'I know she's had problems. I know she still does. But I need to find her. I'm looking after her son, and—'

The woman paused for a moment. Freya saw it in her eyes. She knew Sam. She knew Dino.

'Listen – I'll do anything. Please just help me find her.'

For a moment Freya was sure she was softening, but then the door slammed shut. 'I'm sorry,' she said, shaking her head. 'You're on your own.'

Jessie pulls out a green crayon and passes it to me, so that I can finish my drawing. 'You don't have to use that colour, but this type is the best. They twist up, see, so they never really go flat, and you can keep on using them.'

I take it, and go back to colouring. I'm drawing a staircase.

'What's at the top of the steps?' Jessie asks.

I shrug. 'I don't know.'

'You should draw a door,' Jessie says. 'I think every staircase should lead to a door. Then you can think about what's behind it. There's always something good behind a door.'

I didn't know about that. 'Is there?'

'Yes,' Jessie says. 'You know – they find the princess to rescue, or the cat that's been lost, or it leads you to Narnia, or it takes you out of the house into a different world, or . . .'

I draw another step, and another. What she said sounds silly. But then, she is only six.

'You could draw it now,' she says, gently.

'Maybe it could be the door to my old flat,' I say. 'It was red.' *I try to remember it as it was, before it all got burned and black.*

'OK, do that.'

I sketch it out, but it looks all wrong, so I scribble through it. 'My steps are going to keep on going.'

Jessie chooses a new piece of coloured card for herself, and pulls out a glitter pen. 'I'm going to do you a door,' she says. 'Behind it is going to be all the things you've ever wished for. What do you want in there?'

'I don't know.'

'A bike?' Jessie says.

'I've never had a bike. I don't know how to ride one.'

'I could teach you.'

'Maybe.' *I don't know, though. I don't really have stuff like that.*

'Anything else?' Jessie asked. 'A big scooter? A skateboard? A tree house?'

'Nothing, really.' *It stings. Because I've never had any of those things. I never will have any of those things.*

'Nothing?'

I shake my head. My heart hurts. 'I don't want to play this any more.'

'A ticket to Legoland?'

142

'Stop it, Jessie,' I say. She's annoying me now. I feel angry inside. I want the feeling out. 'I said no.'

Freya had knocked on door after door in the streets around Dreamland, showing people the photo of Sam, and getting nothing. She had walked until her legs ached and her voice was hoarse with asking the same question. No one remembered Sam, or recognised the photo. One woman had shown a glimmer of recognition when she'd mentioned Dino, but then said she couldn't be sure, there were a lot of kids around there.

She felt despondent, but wasn't ready to give up. She decided to check out the homeless hostels. She Googled where they were located, and could see one on the corner – there were people milling around outside it. People who looked like she didn't want Sam to look. But she didn't care. Nothing mattered apart from finding her sister.

I put my dirty clothes back on. I wish I had some clean stuff with me.

I want to take these layers off me and never put them on again. I want to take them somewhere – throw them away, burn them on the beach. I want them gone. Those layers, they are what have dragged me down here – they're the reason I couldn't be a better person, a better mother, even though I wanted it this time. I wanted it so much it aches. I still do.

I don't look at the other mothers, the other parents, at Dino's school. I never do. I guess that's one thing that I have. I'm never compared myself to other people because I know there's no point. My brain's wired differently, I guess. It turns out my superpower is just to trip myself up, however well things seem to be going. I could sit here hating myself for it, or I can get up. Try again. I have to put on these old clothes again. But they don't have to make me act the same. I can be different. I can be different today. I want to cast off those layers so I can start to be someone better, someone new.

I'm not coming back here again. Whatever it takes. I don't care if

I'm messed up. I don't belong here, with all the down-and-outs. This isn't who I am.

I need Dino to see me as the person I want to be. So that he can be reflected back in that. So that if he sees me, more sorted, he'll know he can be like that too. He deserves that.

At least Dino isn't here to see me now. At least Dino can't see me sink this low.

Freya walked towards the entrance of the hostel. She breathed in; she breathed out. She knew this was a long shot.

The urge to see her sister again filled every part of her body: a cellular yearning. She didn't care if Sam was the same as she used to be, or if time had changed her. Seeing her sister again would put Freya back together. She was sure of that. However imperfect, it would make her whole again.

I'm leaving the hostel, and I'm more than ready. I know this place well enough to know you don't go out the main entrance on to the square, where everyone can see you. Where all the suits on their way home from work can cast their judgements. I won't be the person who makes them feel better about themselves, no way. I slip away through the side exit instead, and do the best I can to become invisible. I'm going to be a better person for Dino, and for me.

I just wish I wasn't doing this alone. I have Cassie, but God knows she's as much of a mess as I am most of the time. To have someone by my side, who could make me feel stronger – to have someone I trust to tell me I can do this, even when it seems hard – it would just make it all easier.

I haven't even got a home to go back to – the flat's still burnt out from the fire. It'll be at least another couple of weeks until the landlord sorts that, given how long it normally takes him to fix anything.

And – well, I guess this is all of it, really – wherever I am, Dino won't be there. Even on the bad days – in fact maybe on the bad days most of all – it was him who made me feel I'd come back home. The way he'd bring me a painting at the school gate, some glitter-covered thing that he'd be crazily proud of, or a volcano made out of papier-mâché, whatever. And I'd be thinking, Where the hell are we going to put this in our flat? – but also I'd know that without him – and without those things of his – there wouldn't be a home there at all.

Before I had Dino there were days when I felt like I didn't know anything at all. I'd see these people, you know, on the TV, with their university degrees, and their City jobs, and I'd think – well, I never got that far. I only own a couple of books, ones I picked up at the book exchange at the train station, and actually the only one I made it all the way through was The Alchemist. *I started* Eat, Pray, Love *and God I lost patience with that one – this woman thinking she'd lost it all just because she broke up with someone, but she has the money, and the freedom to travel the whole world 'looking for herself' and for the things that make her happy. Who does that? Who has that?*

Anyway, then I had Dino. And we'd spend a lot of time sitting on the sofa in the flat, or in the park. There's no children's centre round here, and I wasn't about to spend a tenner we didn't have so he could bang a tambourine and get under a parachute or whatever it was those other mums did. So we'd play with the pots and pans that we had in the kitchen, pour flour through the sieve, and I'd talk to him about the things I knew in the world. In the park I'd find him a woodlouse or a beetle and he'd look at me – those big wide eyes – as if I was bringing him some golden treasure. Because you can think you know nothing – and that's how I've felt almost all of my life. But when I showed him an oak leaf, or a daffodil, and he'd say the words after me, it made me see that I did know some things that mattered, after all.

After a good day – because those happen too – I used to love getting back to Dino. But most of the time there was just the guilt that I'd left him. This mess I am right now isn't sucking anyone else into it, and I'm good with that.

Freya went into the hostel and up to the reception desk. She thought for a moment about asking for her sister by name, and then realised she didn't even know which name to give. She looked around the entrance area instead, scanning faces, searching for traces of Sam in the eyes of these strangers.

'Are you looking for someone?'

It was an older woman, in her sixties maybe, or perhaps that was just how old she'd begun to look. Her hair was scraped back into a bun, and she was wearing a hoodie with stains on it.

'Yes. My sister. Sam.'

The woman smiled. Kinder than the other woman Freya had met, she thought. She looked like she was willing to help. 'Maybe she's by the seafront: she sits on the sea wall sometimes. Or at The George, that pub.'

'The George, you say?' Freya said, with a rush of hope.

'Sam, Sam, Sam,' the other woman sing-songed, and she laughed, a hollow, empty laugh. The atmosphere changed. The woman's voice sent a chill through Freya, but right now these pointers were the only thing she had, so she forced herself to stay and listen.

'Or wait here,' said the woman, 'and she'll be back soon enough. She can't beat them, you see. Your sister's got demons she can't beat.' Then she turned and walked away.

Sam. As Freya walked out of the hostel, a memory that had detached itself from the rest came into her mind. Her sister as a teenager – shouting at the dinner table, arguing with their dad about how they should all be vegetarian, and that the only answer to what was wrong in the world was to overthrow capitalism. Their dad would ask Sam why she couldn't be like other girls her age. Normal. Freya had found Sam's outbursts embarrassing. Disruptive. Awkward. She'd wanted for there to be peace in their house, and with Sam around there never could be. Her sister churned up the sediment daily. Freya had found it exhausting. But now she saw things differently – thought how right her sister had been, not to always accept the status quo. Sam had been right to question, to challenge. Sam hadn't just been difficult; she'd been brave.

She headed down towards the seafront, hoping that she could trust what the woman in the hostel had said to her. She saw a woman heading in the direction of a pub – The George. That was the name, wasn't it? Freya was sure. That was the place the woman had mentioned. Her pace picked up. Freya crossed the road after her. She couldn't see the woman's face, but instinct told her to keep going, to catch her up.

I'm almost at the seafront, and that's when I see her – pulling her coat around her, strands of her dark bob clinging to her face, wet with the damp sea-air – she's looking around. Oh, God. My heart is in my throat. Freya can't find me – she can't.

For a moment I think how it would be to be happy. How it would be if seeing Freya was a good thing. How it would be if she was a sister who could be there for me, while get I well again. If she could sit with me, make me tea, hold my hand while I get through the rough bits. I think about that and for a second I have this warm feeling, and then I'm reminded that that'll never be how it is. Not for me, not for us.

She thinks she knows what she wants, but she doesn't know the half of it. Whatever happens, I can't let her find me.

She's out of sight, and I breathe out. I lean back against the wall and relief washes over me. She's gone. I peek around the corner again, just to be sure.

Freya was just a few feet away from the woman when she was distracted by a beggar in the doorway. 'Miss,' the older woman in a headscarf called out. 'Miss, please help me.'

Freya stopped.

'Could you spare something for a sandwich?' the woman asked.

She searched in her wallet, gave the woman a couple of pounds, and looked back to see where the woman who looked like her sister had gone. The pavement was empty. She went to the pub, looked inside, but Sam wasn't there.

I get back to our flat, and let myself in. My heart's slowed down now, but only just.

She nearly found me. She came so close. Too close.

I know I can't let this run on much longer.

I'm here again. This place might be a mess, but it's my mess. And it's the best chance I've got of getting well.

I go to the kitchen cupboard and get out the artwork from Dino's tray, the stuff they gave me on the last day of term, before I sent him away. In there is a photo of him, one they printed out in his class, and decorated with sequins and stuff. He wrote a story around it, about the moon landings.

I go over to the fridge and take down the picture of young me. I'm never getting back to her. I can't. Maybe I don't even want to.

I put the photo of Dino up with magnets.

This is about him. My son. I'm going to do this for him.

Chapter 17

Freya got back to her mum's house at ten p.m., much later than she'd planned to – on the journey home from Margate she'd spent hours in traffic, with too much time to think. About Sam, about coming back empty-handed. Jilly took her up to the spare room, where the kids had fallen asleep.

'I let them play together for a while up here. They wanted to wait for you to get home, and when you didn't they just curled up together and fell asleep on the sofa there,' Jilly said, affectionately. 'They look sweet like that, don't they?'

Freya looked at the soft heap of limbs and hair, draped in the heirloom quilt she used to have on her own bed when she was younger.

'I'm sorry, Mum,' she said. She meant about being late, letting her down when she'd promised to be home to put the kids to bed. But the apology was about so much more than that. She'd gone to Margate thinking she could bring some word of Sam home, and yet she was coming back with nothing. She felt as if she'd let everyone down, not least Dino. Her heart was heavy. Why had she thought, even with the clue Dino had given her, that she'd manage to locate Sam in one day? But she'd had that hope – believed the impossible. Now she was sinking down. She was back in Fern Bay, without her sister. All she could think about was Sam – the traces and shadows of her she was sure she'd touched, and how they had led to nothing tangible at all.

Her mum reached out and draped an arm around her daughter's waist. 'It's not your fault, love. You know that, don't you?'

'But I let you think I could track her down . . . '

'And you might have done. You did what you could, with what you knew. That's all you can do, Freya. This time wasn't the right time. But I'll never stop believing that one day we'll find her.'

Freya tried to fight the fading of her own optimism. She had to stay positive.

Her mum held her a little more closely. 'Stay here tonight, love. I don't think we should move them, do you?'

'Sure,' Freya said. 'Yes, you're right.' She went over to Jessie and Dino and adjusted the quilt so that it was covering more of their legs.

'The bed in your old room's made up.'

Freya walked down the hallway through to her old bedroom. On the vintage wooden desk there was a pile of shells, the ones she and Sam had collected years ago, when they were both living there. They brought to mind the summers of their childhood. Those days when she and Sam went down to the rock pools together, and walked on the stones, those dark rocks slippery and covered in barnacles.

She remembered the day they'd sat up there and watched the sun go down, eating the Haribo from the local Woolworth's. A bag of Haribo had fallen into Freya's schoolbag, without invitation. Sam had caught her eye and given her a wink. It was the only time she'd ever shoplifted. She hadn't meant to go along with it; it had just happened.

Sam had held her sister's hand, on the rocks. They'd looked out at the horizon and the sunset, feeling the cling of their wet dresses on the tops of their legs, but determined to wait it out until the sun dipped down into the sea. The sea they knew so well that its rhythms were inscribed on both their souls.

'You're part of me,' Sam said.

'I know.'

Freya felt it – as she always had.

Sam was a part of her.

She'd returned to that memory, time and again, over the years. The closeness they'd shared.

But as she stood in her old room now, she remembered how it had felt to have those sweets in her bag. She hadn't wanted to take them. It hadn't felt right to take them.

The memory took on an edge.

You're a part of me.

Those words were meant as a gift from her sister, she was sure of it.

But the uncomfortable truth was that they hadn't felt like a gift – not then, and not now. They were a weight she bore.

Freya heard Sam's voice in a different way, resounding through her memories.

Those words: *You're a part of me.*

Sam won't ever let go.

I put on the radio, and they're playing 'Shotgun', one of Dino's favourites. I dance around the kitchen to it, like the two of us would do together after school sometimes. I look at that photo and I dance to the song and if I shut my eyes I can imagine him there. He's dancing with me, and he has this silly smile on his face, and he's laughing. And I am too.

Then I open my eyes and there's no one there – just me.

And I feel terrible, because there's nothing in the house. Not even any alcohol, nothing. And I know that I need to keep going, push on through. But it hurts so much to feel this empty. It hurts so much to know that I am broken. To not be able to block that out with anything feels too much. It hurts so much to see this empty room and not be able to fill it with my family again, because I'm not enough to make that family safe.

The song's switched, something else – Ariana Grande, I think. I'm sitting on the floor, and the picture of Dino is in my hands now, and I'm on the cold tiles and there's nothing. Nothing to help me get through this.

The next day Freya drove with the children back to her own house. The sunlight she'd held so briefly in her soul was almost gone.

Disappointment sat with her, heavy – a half-feeling, a poor relation to anger, to fear. That was how she'd always thought of it. It sounded lightweight, trivial, easy to find your way through – but it felt nothing like that. It sat in her like the heaviest stone. She'd pictured stepping back in through her front door with news for her mum, and for Dino. With news of her sister – what her life was like and when she would come. When she'd heard Dino's clue and come up with Margate, she'd thought she was so smart. She'd thought that this was possible – to find Sam on the strength of this one lead, to do something that the police hadn't managed in almost two decades.

She'd wanted so badly to be able to find Sam and talk with her. Perhaps even persuade her to come back home. She'd wanted it for herself, and she'd wanted it for Dino. Freya desperately wanted to be able to promise him an end to this – and to be able to tell him he had a future and what that future might look like.

Instead she was back here in Fern Bay, empty-handed, and a little empty-hearted. But she wouldn't give up.

Freya held Jessie and Dino close to her that night, as she put them to bed at home. She didn't mention the trip to Dino – there was nothing to tell, after all. She hadn't managed to bring him even a step closer to his mother. She carried that with her, determined to keep pushing, keep looking and get something more next time.

Freya felt, deep down, that she didn't deserve for any of this to be easy. Maybe, after the way she'd acted that summer, the things that had happened, she didn't deserve to find Sam at all.

Freya did what she could to refocus on the day-to-day. Making food for the kids, helping Jessie practise her gymnastics, and keeping Dino's daily appointments with Joanna's group.

Louisa was seeing Matt every other day or so, going into town to meet him and his friends. Freya could hear them talking on the phone in the evening, and hear her daughter laughing. Perhaps it should have made her feel more relaxed to hear Louisa happy, but she still didn't feel that entirely. She was trying, each day, to trust her elder daughter, and to let go of the reins a little, but it wasn't easy. There had been something about Matt that had put her on edge, and she couldn't shift that feeling.

Freya told herself to just keep going. There were times in life you just had to tread water for a while. They would all move forward, in one way or another, when the time was right, she told herself. She tried to let go of the things that she couldn't control, focus on what she could. There was nothing to be gained by trying to get to the truth of her sister's life, when Sam and only Sam was living it. Her sister had always been stubborn. She'd made it clear, even when they were kids, that no one would tell her what to do, not shopkeepers, teachers, or their parents. The very last person she'd take it from would be Freya.

Sam didn't want to be found. That much was clear. She might be in a mess – Freya was getting that impression – but she was still expert in covering her tracks. She seemed to have erased her connections to Fern Bay, to the Jackson family, to anything she'd been before she left.

Maybe there was nothing to be gained in finding her before she was ready, anyway. If she didn't feel strong enough or ready enough to see Dino, then there was no benefit in forcing it. Dino had already been unsettled enough. Hopefully, by her giving Sam the space she needed, he could go home to a place, and a parent, who was solid. Who could be there for him in the way that he deserved, and who could be there this time without wavering.

If they did get to meet – and Freya was still driven by the hope that they would – the key would be giving Sam space: the space to come to her own decisions; the space to feel that whatever she was deciding came from her and her only. The only way she was going to be able to get anywhere in this game – get Dino the best place to be – was by doing this slowly, and doing it in a way that would stop Sam running. Because Sam had shown that, time and time again – if you pushed her, she would run. It was the power that she had.

Their dad had always said it. 'Your sister's got one foot out of the door, always has. She was even born quickly; I had to run red lights to get your mum to the hospital on time. Always in a hurry to get out. I wish I could understand why.'

He had seen it coming maybe earlier than all of them: that one day she would go and not come back. He'd spent years suspecting that one day they'd feel this pain.

Freya had never really been able to understand how, when it finally happened, he could have decided to loosen and pull apart the fabric of their family just when they needed the remaining parts of it to stay intact. He'd retreated into his own world, barely talking to Jilly and Freya. Then he'd died.

But maybe it was this: he'd lived through the loss of Sam so many times already, anticipated the pain of losing Sam in flashes. So, when it actually happened, he didn't have the energy, or the drive, to keep waiting. By then, he just wanted to be somewhere else, and try to forget.

He wasn't here to search any more, but she was.

Freya took a deep breath. This wasn't over. It couldn't be. She'd hit a bump in the road, that was all. A fresh wave of determination came.

This wasn't the end. It was just the beginning. She was going to have to push for more information, but do so gently. When she was by herself in the evening, she sent one more email.

To: blackbirdsinging

Sam. Listen, I can do this. I'm not going to let you down. Dino's doing well. He's OK. But me? Maybe I'm not. I need to know how you are, and how long this might all last. I can do this but I need more from you. I can't do it if you won't talk to me.

She pictured her sister, wherever she was in that network of seaside streets. She must be there, somewhere. She decided to push it just a little more.

I know you told me you didn't want anyone else involved. No police, no Social Services. But if I don't hear from you I'm going to be left with no other choice, Sam. I can't do this all on my own.

After a couple of minutes, a new message came through on her phone. Her heart-rate picked up as she read it.

I get that, came the reply. And I'm sorry. I'm really sorry I've been quiet lately. I haven't forgotten about Dino, or about you.

Sam. Sam's words. Sam was here again. Her spirits lifted. Everything made sense again. She wasn't alone in all of this. She was doing this with her sister. And nothing was hard when you saw it like that. Freya waited for another message. Something more.

Quiet . . . Freya thought. That word didn't fit. Didn't fit with the huge echoing silence that was always there. No matter how loudly Jessie and Dino were playing, no matter how she turned the volume up on the music in her car. Her sister had come into her life again and then uttered barely a word to her.

What's going on with you? Freya asked.

Then a reply.

I'm OK. Look, I appreciate what you've been doing. I really do. How is he?

He's doing well, Freya typed. He's doing really well. But he needs to know, Sam, when I can bring him back. And I think I need to know too.

Dino shouldn't have to be the bridge between her and her sister, she knew that. But in a way he was.

He's a good kid, isn't he?
    Yep. He's a great kid.
    I miss him, you know.
    I'm sure you do.

And us, Freya thought. Do you miss us at all?

It's not been as easy as I thought. Getting straight.

OK. Freya thought. She could be patient. She would be patient.

156

I need more time.

OK, Freya typed. OK.

Thank you. A couple of weeks. That's all. Then I'll be there - for Dino. For you. For Mum. I promise.

Chapter 18

I hadn't planned to go out. Not until I'd done three days, at least. Seventy-two hours. The worst of it is done by then. The muscle aches, the sweat, the racing heart, the cramps. I've been there before, just never made it all the way to the other side. It's getting to me this time, though, and I need to get out.

I've only got through a day before I get restless, rattling round in the flat on my own, with nothing to distract me. I need some fresh air.

Outside, the streets are full; it's the weekend so all of East London is up here, going into the vintage shops and buying overpriced shirts. I breathe in the sea air. It fills me up. I feel something close to good. I go into the shop on the corner. I normally duck in and out of here quickly, because I've nicked stuff from here a couple of times before and I feel bad about that. But today I get the milk, bread and some pasta, and I stand up straight, and I look the guy in the eye. He's about fifty maybe, with grey hairs in his black beard.

'How are you today, miss?' he asks.

He's never asked that before. It feels strange. But good-strange. I guess maybe he never realised about me taking things before. 'I'm OK, thanks.'

'And your little boy?'

It stabs a bit in my chest. But it's nice that he's asked.

'He's staying with family,' I say. 'He'll be back soon.'

'Bit of peace and quiet for you, then,' he says. He has a nice smile. I haven't seen him smile before. He's usually focused on the schoolkids, trying to stop them all coming in at once.

'Something like that,' I say.

I hate the quiet. Anything but the quiet.

I take the bag and say thanks.

I feel something close to normal.

A couple more weeks. That was what Freya had promised her sister, and it was a promise she would keep. She called Joe, to let him know how it had gone in Margate. She told him about what Dino had said about Dreamland, and the places that information hadn't, in the end, led. Joe was kind, and supportive. When that conversation came to an end, though, there was an awkward silence.

'Is everything OK?' she asked.

'Yes,' Joe said. 'Yes, everything's good.'

She sensed a certain distance in his voice.

'Is something going on with you, Joe?'

He coughed. All right, this was serious. You didn't know a man for as long as she'd known Joe without developing a sixth sense for when there was something on his mind. Joe was never quiet, unless he had a reason to be nervous about what he was going to say.

'Yes, I suppose there is. Listen, Frey, I've been wanting to talk to you about this for a little while.'

This was it. This was the thing, the conversation she hadn't even realised she'd been waiting for. The one that would change the good thing they had, their status quo, into something different. She could tell it instantly from his voice – this wasn't just about the two of them any more.

'You've met someone, haven't you?'

'Yes. Yes, I have,' he said.

'Right,' Freya said, letting it sink in. She felt suddenly vulnerable, surplus to requirements almost. It wasn't that Joe shouldn't be dating. He was entitled to do whatever he liked – as was she. It was just that she hadn't, for some reason, *suspected* that he was.

She roused light-heartedness, friendliness, from somewhere; it was the least he deserved. 'Well, that's good. So what's her name? What's she like?'

'Lily.'

'And?'

'She's great, Freya. She's not like anyone I've ever met before.'

That stung a bit. Not like her, that had to mean, right?

Lily and Joe had met on one of the apps, he explained. They'd had so much in common it had surprised them. Their birthdays were just a day apart. They'd only gone for a beer, but they'd ended up playing crazy golf down on the seafront, and the sun had set without them even realising. It was one of those *connections*. It might have started on a phone screen – but it was real now. So real. And of course Freya was happy for him, and of course he deserved this – but God, how she wished Joe would stop talking about her. Each word hurt.

Freya checked herself. This wasn't about her, or her pride. The only thing that really mattered was the impact this would have on the girls. Whatever shape it was, they needed to hang on to the family that they'd built so lovingly together.

She knew Joe would've chosen well. Responsibly. And she'd considered dating herself, a few times. Just never really got around to it. So why did she feel like this? As though the rug had been pulled out from under her.

She wasn't the most important person in Joe's life any more. The support he gave her, the focus he put on her – there was no way that wouldn't be disrupted by this. But it was the way things were supposed to go. It was exactly what should happen. When she'd suggested that they part ways, that they live apart, she must have been thinking it would come to this, at some point. But she'd never – not really – ever got quite this far in her mind. And, if she was completely honest, maybe she never truly believed that he would be the one to find it first.

'You want to introduce her to the girls, don't you?' Freya said.

'I'd like to, yes.'

After I leave the newsagent's, I walk down to the pier. Just a bit more of a stroll, to clear my head, and then I'll go back. I'm not done yet, with getting clean. I need to keep focused.

Then I see him – in jeans and a black T-shirt, with a cap on, crossing the road, without really looking. Neil.

OK, this – him – I don't need.

I duck into a bookshop, and wait just inside until he's out of view. I don't want to see him. Not today. Not today when a tiny seed of hope that I can be someone better, someone stronger, is starting to grow. I walked away from him once, and that was hard enough.

He catches my eye through the window. My heart thuds, and the flight instinct kicks in. But he carries on. He can't have seen me, after all.

Just this glimpse of him and it all comes back. It's like that whole fantasy I had in the newsagent's, of being a proper person, falls away. I remember that I'm me – messed-up me – and I'll never be anything other than that.

Being with Neil wasn't easy. It had never been easy.

I always thought I was the strong one – when we got together I was so sure he was the one with the problems, the ones I was going to help him fix. But it's me, it's me that's hiding from him now.

I watch him walking past, and down the seafront. I know where he's heading – The George – and I know the friends, if you can call them that, that he'll be meeting there.

He always said this: 'You see me for who I really am. You're not like the others – you know me. You get me.'

That evening, Freya sat in front of the TV with the girls and Dino. She felt slightly dazed after the conversation she'd just had with Joe.

This was the two of them moving forward, she told herself. This was exactly what they should be doing. There was no unfinished business between her and Joe; there were no what-ifs, there was nothing to rekindle – that was the story she'd told herself for months. But now, she started to doubt it. When she thought of Joe, her mind flooded with memories – of the holidays they'd had on the continent when Louisa was young, when they had stretched out on picnic blankets in front of fields of sunflowers, and eaten croissants until they thought they'd never be able to eat another. The day when they brought Jessie home from the hospital and introduced her to her big sister, and their family felt so overwhelmingly *complete*. The way that, for years, the clock would be at eight, and the oven would be on, and Freya and Joe would sit and eat, and then walk those same steps to the sofa, and one of them would choose a programme to watch. And some days it had felt so quiet that Freya had wanted something more – more excitement, maybe. That there was something they needed to shift, move on from, something they needed to disrupt in order to keep them both feeling alive.

But now, knowing that Joe was in another woman's arms, Freya questioned all of that. Because what had once seemed quiet, and too safe, now seemed a very, very good thing that she'd somehow let slip away.

Neil and I are walking up the beach, talking. I found him in The George, where I knew he'd be.

162

I tell him how it's been. He reminds me there are ups and downs in getting clean, and that I'd been clean once and would be again. He tells me he's two months in, and has never felt better. He goes to the gym now, every day. He's making some money online. Spread-betting, he says.

We walk, and I feel a surge of hope. Maybe I don't have to be alone in this, after all. Maybe Neil can be my strength.

He reminds me of the good times we had – because, despite all the rest, we did have those too. We wouldn't have stayed together all that time otherwise. By the time we get to the jetty, he's talking about that time we ran out of a late-night café without paying, and I'm laughing, a lot. It's a real laugh that wells up from right inside me. I'm laughing so hard that tears are coming from my eyes and damn, I feel like me.

He doesn't ask about Dino, and that's OK. Sometimes I like the space to imagine – only for a bit, don't get me wrong – that it could be just me. That I could have a simple life, like I did once, no responsibilities. Maybe he thinks Dino's with Cassie. I don't have an answer for him so it's easier that he doesn't ask. He was never bad to Dino, but he was never really interested in him the way, when we first met, I'd hoped he would be. But you can't expect it to be like in a film – that's not real life. Right now I'm with this man, this man who gets me, who sees me, who accepts me just as I am, and he's kissing me and my head's spinning in a good way, and I'm also thinking – I'll have somewhere to be. I want something familiar. Neil's place is familiar. And Neil is familiar.

Later that evening, I'm in Neil's bed, the duvet and sheets all messed up. I feel good. Content. This afternoon I'm remembering every other afternoon we spent like this, wasting time in the best way. He brings me in a cup of tea, and we lie for a while like this. Chatting and laughing and it's – I don't know – it's easy. It's easy to be with him again. I know every inch of skin on his body. I know where everything is in this flat, this flat that might be my home for now. And God knows I need that.

He kisses me on the top of my head, then ruffles my hair.

163

'I've missed you so damn much, you know,' he says.

And it's everything that I've been thinking too.

I've missed that glimmer of mischief in his eyes. I've missed the way he touches me. The way he can bring so much pleasure into my body, get me to these heights that make the edges of the rest of the world softer even when I've come back down. He fits with me. That's what he's always said, and it's as true now as it ever was. I can calm him like no one else, he says. I know that. It's one of the few things, I guess, that I know for sure I'm really good at.

We never used to fit together – the three of us. But now. There's space to be just me and Neil. And I want to be like this for a while.

Chapter 19

I'm staying here in Fern Bay for two more weeks, that's what Freya says. That's what my mum told her. It's not long, really.

I can wait. I feel better, just knowing. It won't be long now, until school starts again, and I want to be back for that.

Freya's just brought me in some new swimming trunks, and a rubber ring for me to blow up, for the pool. Today Jessie and Louisa are going out with their dad, to meet his new girlfriend Lily, she says. She looks a bit sad in her eyes when she says that part. Then she gets brighter – she says, 'And you and I are going to have some fun.' My heart feels sort of bigger, then.

Freya had a good time with Dino that afternoon, at the pool – it was exactly the distraction she needed. She'd gone on the water-slides with him, again and again, and played in the wave machine, before finishing up with hot chocolate in the café. When they got home, he'd been elated but tired, and had gone up to his room to watch something on her iPad. In those moments of quiet, the first she'd had that day, she found herself wondering how the day with Lily and the girls had gone. They'd taken the news seemingly in their stride, especially Louisa. It seemed as if they had been expecting this more than she herself had.

Joe dropped Jessie and Louisa home at seven, when Freya was clearing away dinner. Jessie came bounding through the hallway and into the living room, before jumping into her favourite armchair.

'Good day?' Freya asked. It certainly looked that way.

'Yep,' Jessie said. 'It was great.'

'Yes?' Freya said, leaving space for them to say more, if they wanted to.

Louisa slid on to the sofa and curled her legs up under her. 'Come on, Mum, you can just ask, you know.'

'What?' Freya said.

'You know. It's obvious that you're dying to know what she's like,' Louisa said, laughing.

'Is it?' Freya said. She felt her cheeks flush and wished she could make it stop. She thought she'd hidden her curiosity better than that. She hoped that Joe hadn't picked up on it when they'd met at the door.

'Of course it is,' Louisa said. 'It's written all over your face. *How old is she? Is she prettier than meeee?*'

'Oh, stop it,' Freya said crossly. 'It's not like that. Stop teasing me.'

'All right,' Louisa said, raising an eyebrow. 'But in case you *were* wondering – about thirty, a bit older maybe, and no. Quite plain really.'

Freya smiled. 'As long as your dad is happy, that's all that matters.'

'He looks happy,' Jessie said. She was smiling, and she seemed calm.

'And you guys are happy to spend time with her?' Freya said.

Jessie shrugged. 'Sure.' She pulled a cushion up on to her lap and hugged it.

166

'She was nice enough,' Louisa said. 'She asked me questions about films I like, and stuff. Played with Jessie. She made an effort.'

'Well, I'm glad your dad's found someone else,' Freya said. 'He deserves it.'

'Really?' Louisa said, sceptical.

'Yes,' Freya said. 'Really.'

I liked this afternoon, with Freya. It was just me and her, and I stayed in the pool until all my fingerprints were lost in the raisiny wrinkles.

They are all downstairs, and up here it's quiet. Freya's left her phone in the bathroom. She hasn't been back upstairs for a long time – no one has.

I know her phone passcode. It's 1509, which is Jessie's birthday – the fifteenth of September. Jessie told me that yesterday, and I can still remember it. 1509. It's stuck in my brain like the names of the continents and the capital cities, and the addresses of the places Mum and I have lived since I was little.

I know I shouldn't do it. I try and block out the passcode and make myself forget it, but it's still there. I want to speak to Mum so much that it makes me ache in my chest, and that ache doesn't seem to go away.

I pick up the phone. I go through Freya's contacts and find the name: Sam.

I call the number and wait, and my heart is beating really fast.

It's still beeping, and I think Freya might come up the stairs soon, and I get scared. But I don't want to put it down, just in case now is when she answers.

'Hey. Who is this?' It's Neil. I recognise his voice.

I feel small when I talk to him. I don't know why. I always do. I whisper really quietly. 'It's Dino. Is Mum there?'

'Oh, hi. Hi, mate.'

I can hear my mum's voice in the background. I can hear her ask a question.

'Your mum's busy. But she sends her love. She'll call you another time.'

I go to say something, to explain that she can't call me, because Freya doesn't know I'm doing this, and maybe she'd be cross that I'm on her phone,

I don't know. I go to say a lot of things, but the words get lost in my throat and don't get as high up as my mouth.

'See you,' Neil says. He puts the phone down.

I can hear Freya coming up the stairs.

My heart's beating hard now.

I wish it had been her at the other end. But it was just him. And I feel worse, now, than if I'd never called at all.

Freya went up to the landing and found Dino sitting on the stairs by the bathroom. He was hunched over, his head in his hands. She realised she'd let herself forget about him, when she had been caught up talking to Louisa and Jessie downstairs.

She sat beside him, quietly. Just close enough so that he'd know she was there. He started to rub at his eyes in that way he had, as though he wanted to scrub away the pain.

'What's up?' Freya asked. 'I thought we had a good day together today. Has something happened?'

'We did,' he said, quietly. 'It's not about swimming.'

'You seem really upset. Will you let me help you?'

He shook his head, not meeting her gaze.

'Are you missing your mum?' she asked.

He started to scratch at the skin on his forearm, digging the nails in a tiny bit, and without looking up, he shook his head again.

Chapter 20

French toast with honey. Tea with two spoonfuls of sugar — Neil had remem-
bered. Yellow tulips, bright and happy-looking. I sit up in bed and put the
tray on my lap.

'I've got the morning off today,' he says. He's sitting on the bed with me,
already dressed in jeans and a polo shirt. He's had a shave, and he looks
really smart. I don't really know why he's here with the chaos of me. But he
is. 'Thought we could spend it together.'

I take a bite of toast. It's good. I haven't been that hungry lately, but today
I could eat this a hundred times over. 'What's all this for?' I ask.

'Just glad to have you back,' he says.

'Well, thank you.'

'And I want to help you get stronger again.'

This is what I've needed. Someone who's with me in this. Who can help
me. Remind me why I'm doing this. What's waiting for me at the other end.

Freya gave Jessie and Dino breakfast. They read out the facts
on the back of the cereal packet together, Jessie laughing. Dino
wasn't quite smiling, but he seemed more relaxed than he had
the previous night. She'd wanted to hold him then — comfort him,

get to the heart of what he was holding and help fix it for him. But she followed his lead, being there but also giving him space. Today she would do what she could to distract him from what he was missing.

'Here,' she said, passing Jessie a five-pound note. 'We need some more milk. Louisa will go out with you. Could you guys get us two pints? You can spend the change on some vegetables, if you like.'

Dino laughed. 'Vegetables?' he said.

'It's code,' Jessie said. 'She means sweets.'

Jessie and I are walking to the corner shop – the owner is called Steve, she says. Louisa's way ahead, on her phone, not really paying attention to us. She waits outside while we go in. Jessie gets a Freddo and one of those hard round lollipops, and I get a handful of those jelly snakes, the green ones that have yellow foam on the bottom and a see-through green bit on the top. There isn't enough for a magazine or anything, and Jessie says she wants one, but I tell her she can save up next time. She says 'harrumph' in that way that always makes me laugh, with her nose all scrunched up, and then she cracks up too, and I think she forgets about the magazine.

Steve, the shopkeeper, says to say hi to Freya for him, and he winks, and when we're outside the shop Jessie says she definitely will not be telling her mum that. She says when her mum and dad broke up Steve started acting all weird around her mum, and it creeped her out. She says she doesn't mind if her mum gets a new boyfriend one day, just so long as it's not Steve. I think about Neil, and how he's with my mum again. I don't want to think of her being with him. I tell Jessie about Neil, because that part is OK to say, I guess. I tell her how my mum says it's hard being on her own, so maybe it's better that she's not – but that Neil gives me that weird feeling, in my stomach.

I don't think Jessie really gets it. 'My mum says it's easier now that she and Dad aren't together. But I think she's still hoping they might get back together. I think him meeting Lily is making her want that more. Anyway, no way am I letting her go out with Steve. She's way too good for him.'

Freya's pretty different from Mum. She just sort of gets on with things. Mum finds a lot of stuff hard. It doesn't matter to me, except that I don't like it when she's sad. The things I love best about Mum are that she's warm, and that she wears colourful dresses. When Neil's around I don't get to cuddle her as much, and she doesn't wear those dresses.

I know that Freya is kind, and that she's there for me. She's always saying that – that all I need to do is tell her, and she's there for me. But there are times, like last night, when I could hug her, and I want to – but I know, deep down, that she's not my mum. She belongs to Louisa and Jessie. Not to me. So I can't start believing too much that she's there for me.

Jessie's playing with an old phone that Louisa gave her. It says Samsung on it. It doesn't do anything, I don't think she's even got a charger for it, but she gets it out sometimes, and plays pretend.

She's walking along, pretending to text, like Louisa's doing a block away, and then, not looking, she pretends to bump into a lamppost. It makes me laugh. Jessie acts like a bit of an idiot a lot of the time, and I guess I never realised that could really be a good thing. Because when she does stuff like that it makes this laugh come out of me that I haven't really heard before, and it makes my sides hurt in a good way.

We pass a house that's half falling down, or at least it looks that way from the outside. It's the same sort of bungalow that Jessie's grandma Jilly lives in, but it isn't as well looked after.

'Dare you to go in there,' Jessie says.

'No,' I say. Because she wouldn't say that if there wasn't something weird about the place. And I can tell that by looking at it, anyway.

'Go on,' she says. She has this cheeky look on her face, like this is going to be fun. But it's not.

'You go first,' I say.

'Sure,' she says. She shrugs like it's nothing, but I can tell she's scared, just a little bit. 'How far?'

171

'Up to the door and back,' I say. I don't even really want her to do it, I just want to get away from this place really.

But she's brave enough, Jessie, that I know she'll do it. She walks up the path, and she only looks back at me a tiny bit, once. When she gets about halfway up, the curtains move, and I see a lady looking out. She's got grey hair, a dark dress and small eyes like a mole. Jessie looks back at me, and I can tell she's freaking out. She turns and runs, and when she's back with me we both run and keep running, until we're at the end of the block, out of breath and laughing with the relief of not being there any more. We're still checking back, but the woman hasn't followed us.

'Let's go home,' I say. We go home with Louisa, and when we get back Jessie realises she's lost the phone.

Freya was rearranging photos on the walls of the upstairs landing. Her gaze fell on one of her and Joe together with the two girls, when they were younger, in front of the leaning tower of Pisa. They had been happy that holiday. They had been really happy, once.

She ran her fingers over the glass, silently wishing she had the power to bring that time back. She'd thought she was at peace with the break-up, but seeing Joe move on had left her feeling empty.

She sat down on the step and got out her mobile. She scrolled to his number in her favourites, as she had a hundred times before.

'Joe, hi,' she said, when he picked up.

'Hey, you.'

For now, she was still *you*.

'I wanted to say ...'

She faltered, and the silence she'd created embarrassed her. She couldn't think now why she'd rung. What she was doing here, looking at a photo of a time that was long gone?

'I wanted to say that it went well, the other day, by the sound of things,' she said. She swallowed back the feeling that had brought her to call him. 'The girls really liked Lily.'

He gave a relieved laugh. 'Oh, good,' he said. 'God, you sounded so serious then, you had me worried. I'm really glad. I mean, I thought it went well too, but you can never tell, can you.'

'She must be special.'

'She is, Frey. She really is.'

Freya still felt tied to the Joe she'd fallen in love with, that young man whose heart had filled when he saw her. What they had shared – before children, during children – there was no one who could ever offer her that same thing. She knew that. And today – however unfair she knew it was – she longed to rekindle what they had so much it made her bones ache.

Joe, the man who'd come into himself as a father, earlier than either of them had planned or expected, and loved Louisa and Jessie with the most immense warmth. Joe, who belonged to someone else now.

That night Jessie crept into my room, after bedtime, and she sat there in the dark with me, and her voice was all sad like she might cry. I'm pretty sure it was about the phone, and how she'd lost it at that old woman's house. I told her I'd make it right, that she shouldn't worry. I would get it back for her. It would all be OK. She seemed a bit calmer after that.

Today I'm going back there, to the old lady's house. I don't feel easy doing it but I don't want to let Jessie down. I don't like seeing her cry, not ever, but especially not about something that's kind of my fault. I ask Freya if I can go to the shop, and she sends Louisa out with me. Louisa stops on the corner – that's where she meets Matt. She'll talk with him, and I'll go on on my own. That's what we've agreed we'll do.

The house makes me feel weird – it's creepy and run-down. I've walked past a lot of times but generally she's not outside. I guess it's warmer today.

She's crept out like a snail out of its shell. That sounds bad. I don't mean to be bad to her.

But she's there, sitting in her chair on the porch, looking like a whole heap of bad. I don't even know her. But there's something about her that makes you think if you cracked her open she might be all rotten inside.

Adriana's sitting in her wicker chair on the veranda playing dominoes. It's a warm day, and it's cooler out front than inside. She lays out the black and white bricks, and finds an order there. The boy walks along the pavement towards her house, and she sees he's on his own today. He's got a bag, a new one, and he's holding it by the strap so that it drags on the pavement. He's scuffing his feet along the ground, too. Freya's bought him some new shoes. Those aren't the ones he arrived in.

She remembers the bruise she saw on Freya's face. She'd tried to hide it with make-up, you could see that, but it was still obvious.

There he still is, she thinks. Taking his time walking by. Usually people walk past her place quickly, as if they're in a hurry to get by. Even the children. But this boy doesn't seem in a hurry.

He looks up at her. She wonders if maybe he felt her watching, somehow. He looks at her and she wishes he would just keep on going. He has that strange look – the one that tells her he's not to be trusted. His eyes seem to look right through her. Her skin prickles, and she feels nervous. She's all alone in the house. What if he were to do something? She's not sure what that something is, but she knows she shouldn't welcome it in. She knows he's only a child, but he would still be stronger than her. A woman on her own has to take care. The years have eaten away at her strength. She's not young any more. No point trying to fool anyone about that.

She sees that he's not just not hurrying, he's standing still. He's standing completely still, waiting at the end of her path, just looking at her. Her pulse quickens. Why isn't he walking on? He should just keep walking on towards the house where he lives. Leave her in peace here. She doesn't like being bothered by people, especially not strangers.

She worries that if she has to get up quickly she won't be able to. That she'll be trapped there, in her chair. Fragile. Vulnerable.

He starts to walk up the path towards her. He's slow, but he doesn't stop looking at her. Those who go on to attack you can act normal until the last minute, that much she knows.

He's closer now. His eyes meet hers again. There's something about him that's barely like a child at all.

She would be able to get up, she tells herself. She can still run, if she has to.

I decide I won't let her scare me. I walk on to her path. I scan around the front garden first. What I'm really hoping is that I'll see the phone and then I can just go, get out of there. But I can't see it anywhere. I figure she must've taken it, and kept it inside with all the other things. I can see the boxes in her front garden, and through the windows see how they're piling up inside.

'Can I help you?' she says. Her voice is sort of gruff. Like I've done something really wrong just being anywhere near her. It makes me jump a little. And it makes me want to get away from there really quickly. But I can't go, not just yet.

'I'm looking for something me and my friend were playing with. A little phone.'

'Oh, yes?' she says.

She doesn't offer anything. I don't know if I'm going to be brave enough to get the words out, but I think of Jessie and gather my strength until I can make them come out clearly.

'It belongs to Jessie. We live just over there.' I motion with my hand.

'I know,' she said. She doesn't move her body, not even a tiny bit.

'Can we have it back?' I ask. 'The toy?'

175

'Let me look for it,' she says. She gets up slowly. Like, really slowly. I think I hear her bones creak. As she's standing I can see that her hands are shaking a little. Almost like she's scared.

When she opens the door of her house, I see it's really messy inside. There are towers of stuff – boxes, papers. It's what our flat used to look like sometimes, before I started to tidy it up for Mum. I got into the habit of that, picking up after her. For a moment I wonder how she is now, and what she might be doing.

It takes the old lady a while to sort through it all, but eventually she comes back out. I can see she has the phone in her hand.

'Here,' she says gruffly. 'Take it.'

We stand there for a bit. I don't know what to say, but it seems rude to just turn and go, I guess.

'Thank you,' I say, in the end. I'm still clutching the phone.

I turn around, and start to walk away.

'Wait,' she says.

I feel scared, like I've done something wrong. But when I turn and look at her, her face looks softer, sort of.

'What's your name, boy?'

'Dino,' I say.

'Funny kind of a name.'

'I guess so,' I say.

'I'm Adriana.'

Chapter 21

I thought me and Neil spending the day together would make things better. Make us solid. Make us a real couple. But now I'm not so sure. Maybe sometimes it's better to spend less time together, rather than more.

Since we went out, had lunch, saw his friends, he's been getting irritated by me. I think he's remembering the things about me that he never liked so much, the first time around. The way I leave a trail, sometimes, of tea mugs, or damp towels, or laundry that hasn't found its way right into the basket. I try to be tidier, but it's just that sometimes I forget. I don't see it as clearly as he does. When he points it out, I can see how much it's stressing him out, and I know I need to make more effort. That I have to change.

*

I go out with Louisa again, and she stops on the corner with Matt, like before. I don't go as far as the shop – which doesn't matter, because there's nothing in particular that Freya needs today.

I stop outside the old woman's house. I don't know what makes me stop. I see her sitting on the veranda, just like yesterday. She's playing dominoes, on her own again. I look at her, and she looks at me. She still looks scared, but perhaps a little less so this time.

177

I walk closer, going up the path. I see her start to get restless. I need to say something because if I don't I feel like maybe she's going to get jumpy.

'What do you want?' she says. She says it quietly, though. So if I were any further away I wouldn't hear it at all. Her voice is softer than it was the last time. She's not shouting. Jessie told me she shouted a lot, but she's not shouting now.

I walk towards her really slowly.

I don't know her. But I know what it's like to be alone. Long days, all alone.

I ask her if I can sit and play dominoes with her.

Her eyes go big, like she can't work it out. Why I'm here, why I've said that.

Then she pulls out a little chair for me.

'OK,' she says. 'One game. Come and sit down.'

*

Neil's raging at something, slamming a can down on the kitchen counter. He turns and glares at me. Just take it in, take in as much as you can, so that it burns out quick. And so, when Dino comes back, none of it ever has to reach him. I'm strong enough. He's raging and raging at me tonight, accusing me of things I've never done and would never do – talking to other guys, stealing from him. Mad stuff. It doesn't matter. I know who I am, and that I haven't done those things. I can take this. I stay calm, don't flinch.

It'll pass, just like any other storm.

His anger peaks. It's like the temper tantrums Dino had when he was a toddler. I can almost set my watch by the different stages. What changes is how far he'll take it. Will he block my way out of the room this time? Will he call me a liar? My heart is thudding but I make myself look at the kitchen clock, remember that it will burn itself out. At least this time I don't have to hide what's happening. I don't have to hear the CBeebies theme tune from the other room, knowing Dino's in there and could walk in at any minute. I don't have to worry about anyone else but me. And I'm strong enough.

He sits down at the table and a heavy, sullen silence settles over the room. Until bedtime, this silence is going to last. It's not comfortable, but it's relative safety.

I take a step away.

Then I realise he's not sulking. This is worse, this is harder.

This is the part that chips my heart. I can feel it coming.

He looks down. His head falls to his hands.

'I'm sorry. I'm sorry.'

It breaks me, because then I start to love him again.

Neil's flat doesn't seem like such a great place to be, but leaving doesn't feel like a choice. He needs me. I remember how strong I had to make myself last time before I could go.

Chapter 22

The doorbell rang as Freya was getting Jessie ready for bed. Her daughter was fresh out of the bath, wrapped in a towel, and Freya told her to wait a minute and she'd be right back. She went downstairs and opened the front door to find Joe standing there. Her heart lifted when she saw him.

'I'm sorry – it's not a good time, is it?' Joe said, awkwardly.

'Well, I mean, it's bathtime ... ' Freya said.

She'd thought this was a social call, that maybe he'd come around because he wanted to see her – but from his tone she could tell that wasn't the case. 'Do you want to come in?'

He glanced back towards his car. There was a brunette in the passenger seat, looking at something on her phone.

'Is that Lily?' she asked.

He nodded.

The silence between them made her feel uncomfortable.

'I won't stay,' he said.

He had a brown envelope in his hands. Freya looked at it, confused. 'Is that for me?

'Yes,' he said. 'Freya ... ' He paused, and she sensed it was something important.

The step they hadn't taken. The one that hurt, even to think about.

'I met with a lawyer today. About us getting divorced.'

'Wow,' she said. This felt sudden. Maybe it wasn't sudden, but it felt it.

He nodded. 'These are some details about where we go from here.'

The envelope felt heavy in her hands. She wanted to put it down, somewhere out of sight.

'Is this because of Lily?' Freya said.

'No,' Joe said. 'I mean Lily's part of it, yes. But it's bigger than that, you know it is. It feels like time, Freya. Don't you think?'

Freya looked over at the car, and at the woman waiting there. She felt humiliated, before they'd even met. 'Was it really necessary to come round with her?'

'Sorry,' he said. 'We were on our way home, and . . .'

Home. Their home. Tears came to her eyes but she fought them back. She should have, perhaps, but she hadn't expected this.

'Mu—uuuuuuuuum,' Jessie called down the stairs. 'Who is it?'

'It's your dad,' Freya shouted up. She took the emotion right out of her voice, and felt a dash of pride at that. 'He's not stopping.'

'Come back up!' Jessie called.

'Listen, I'm sorry,' Joe said, quietly. 'I thought if I waited for a good time there might never be one.'

Freya put the envelope on the side. 'Sure. OK.' She felt empty and sad, and this all felt shittier than she'd imagined it could.

'Nothing's going to change,' Joe said.

Freya looked again at the car and wondered.

'Does it have to be now . . .' Freya started. She stopped herself, because as she looked at Joe, as she took in the detail of his face, she saw that, while the pieces might look as though they'd fit back

181

together, they never truly would. They would never be able to regain what they'd once had.

She dug deep. 'You're right. There's no going back.'

Joe's face softened with relief. 'I still love you, Freya.'

'I know. Me too. Perhaps it would be easier if I didn't. But you're right. This is right. It's just knowing we need to move on doesn't make it easier.'

Joe hugged her, and they stood there together on the doorstep. It was only a couple of seconds. Not long enough, really, to say goodbye.

'I'd better go,' Freya said. 'And it looks as if you should too.'

He walked away, and she closed the door after him.

'It's time for bed, Jessie,' she said, when she got back upstairs.

'I saw Daddy give you something,' Jessie said. 'What was it?'

There was a lump in Freya's throat and she didn't trust herself to speak. She just shook her head. Bought herself some time. Long enough to breathe, and calm her nerves.

'It was just a letter. Nothing for you to worry about, love.'

I go back to see Adriana. I sit with her out on the porch and we play Blackjack. Freya lets me go with Louisa, like she always does, and Louisa never asks questions about where I go. I don't think she really cares. I didn't know that game before but Adriana's taught me it, and now we are playing it together. She says she likes being by herself usually and mostly I believe her but I'm starting to not believe her so much, because these days when I come around to visit she doesn't seem to want me to leave so quickly, like she did at the start.

I look over at the sun and see it's getting low in the sky. I forgot to wear my watch today but I can tell by the light when it's time to be getting back. I tell Adriana I need to get back and have my supper, and she nods. She gathers the cards back in towards her, and I pass her the packet.

The corners of her mouth turn up a tiny bit. It's like a smile. Not quite, but closer than I've seen before. Her face looks a bit softer. She doesn't look away quickly. The hard parts of her – I haven't seen them for a while.

I pick up my rucksack and get to my feet. I brush myself off because it's kind of dusty outside on her porch. Next time I'm here I'll sweep up a little bit. I could do that.

'Freya will be waiting for me to get back,' I say.

Adriana nods. She gets it, I think.

There are nights when Adriana can't sleep. It has always been like that, since she lost the first baby. She let herself cry, but still kept enough inside that it disturbed her dreams. Then she lost the second, then the third, and she balled the emotion up tight until it had nowhere to go but to show itself in the night, wrestling its way into her thoughts and denying her any rest. She tried again, held another foetus in her womb for a few weeks, and then, cruelly, it slipped away and her home and her heart were back to feeling empty, and the ache that had become so familiar to her returned.

Then it had all got too much for Graham, and the only man she'd ever loved left too. She didn't blame him. She'd had nothing to give him, and she'd let their love fade away. She'd only been half-there. She'd been so full of the sadness of it all that she'd had nothing to give. She'd saved herself up to love each one of those children, and then, one by one, they'd slipped away and left her alone.

There's no point dwelling on it – the way things are is the way it was destined to be. She'd wanted to be a mother, but that alone wasn't enough to make it happen. It was never her fate, and perhaps it's as simple as that. She's made her peace with it now, mostly. But there is still the occasional night, when the dark thoughts creep in, and this night is one of those.

She puts on the TV to drown out the thoughts, but tonight they won't stay silent. She switches it off. It's a nursing chair, the one she's sitting on. It has never been used for anything other than simply rocking, the way she is tonight, back and forth. The road is dark, usually, but tonight there's a big, bright moon, bright enough. In the cluster of cottages you could forget about the forest, but when you look out, really look, you can see that it's all around you. The black shapes seem different at night. She watches the road that leads out of town, but few cars pass along it.

Her mind starts to race, memories flood back of a night that looked just like this one, and she knows that only one thing will help. She gets up, and goes downstairs. She pulls on her jacket. She'll walk for a while, until she's tired.

Maybe it's the babies that have held her back from saying anything, all of these years. She knows what it's like to have someone take hope away from you. She's had it time and again.

Chapter 23

Freya gives me a long list of things to get from the shop this time when I go out with Louisa. It means I'll need to be quick getting them, but I am quick – and there's time to stop at Adriana's house on the way home.

This time she smiles when she sees me. She usually looks sad. And today she still does – but it's a small smile. Definitely.

And I don't know why but seeing her smile – her crumpled sort of face, it looks better. She looks not-so-old for a minute. It makes me feel better too.

'I thought you might come by again,' she said. 'I had a feeling.'

Two glasses of something are out on the table already. I don't know why they are already out.

'I made lemonade,' she said.

I really, really like lemonade.

I go up and sit beside her.

We drink the lemonade. It tastes really good. Way better than the lemonade Mum used to buy me from the shop, the R. Whites one. This makes me want to squeeze my mouth all up but it's also really sweet. It gives me a little shiver, the taste of it.

'I wasn't sure about you at first,' she says. 'You had a mischievous sort of a look about you.'

It hurts, kind of, when she says that. But it's not new. People say that about me. Teachers. I've heard it. I don't mean to be like that. I can't help having something inside that makes me want to hit out sometimes. It's a thing I can't always control. When Mum's around she gets cross with them and tells them they aren't right about it. They don't say it again after that.

Mum isn't here, though.

'But now I can see that you're a good lad,' she says.

And when she says it, her eyes go softer, sort of.

When she says it, I can almost believe it.

Freya sat down on the sofa and made herself open the envelope Joe had given her. She took out the printed sheets and scanned over them. There were notes about how they could go about formally ending their marriage, the timescales, and the kinds of costs involved.

When they'd got married she'd had such unquestioning confidence that they could and would make their marriage work. That she and Joe would grow old together, content, drawing on a lifetime's worth of shared memories. She'd thought it was in their control, whether their partnership worked or not – that, if they put the work in, it would. But they'd both tried. They'd tried for years, and somehow it hadn't been enough. Perhaps Freya had always expected too much from their marriage – expected it to heal something it was never capable of healing. It was a lot, to ask Joe and their love to fill the void her sister had left.

She put the papers back into the envelope, and put it to one side on the coffee table. She'd arrange a time with Joe to meet with the lawyer together, and they'd work through the steps until they were two separate people again. They'd do it, as they had everything else, with their focus on their children, and on being as kind as they could be to one another. A doubt crept in – that was how a lot of couples with children felt at the beginning of a divorce, wasn't it? That was how they all started out. Sure they could do it, pull apart their joint lives and finances, formalise custody arrangements for the children, and stay friends, stay kind. Freya wondered if the confidence she had right now was every bit as blind as what she'd felt on the day they got married – and that perhaps she couldn't entirely trust that, in spite of the odds, they would be the ones who could do this right, without anyone getting hurt.

Today at Adriana's there's no lemonade, but when she sees me she nods hello. She gets the chair out, and I sit down. She goes inside to get biscuits.

When the door's open I see the stacks of stuff again, boxes and letters and newspapers. She catches me looking. I think maybe she'll get cross with me for looking. For a moment she looks like she might.

We're just staring at each other for a minute. She puts the biscuits down on the table. Custard creams.

'It's messy, I know,' she says. Her face gets a little crumply, like thinking about it makes her feel sad.

'A bit,' I say. I shrug my shoulders. It doesn't really matter to me, one way or the other.

'It wasn't always like this,' she says. 'It used to be really tidy.'

'Do you want me to help you?' I ask. I think of our flat and that first time Mum went away, without telling me when she'd be back. By the time she did come back I'd put everything in order, super-neat. 'I'm good at tidying.'

I think for a minute that she's going to say yes. But then she shakes her head. 'It would take you a long time. And how would you explain that to Freya?'

'I could ask her,' I say. 'I'm sure she wouldn't mind.'

Adriana shifts a bit on her chair when I say that. Like it's not as comfortable as it was. 'It's OK,' she says, 'I'm used to it now.'

'Do you know Freya?' I ask.

'Everyone knows each other, around here,' she says. 'It's a small place,

Fern Bay. Especially when you've lived here as long as I have. But I don't know her well, no.'

I tell her Freya is kind, because she is. And that I like living with her and the girls.

She gives me a look, like she knows.

But she can't know.

There's no way she could.

'You know you can't go on like this, Dino, don't you?'

I feel sick. It's a bad feeling, deep down. It's not going away. I look down. I want to not hear her.

She says it again.

'You need to tell her the truth. She deserves that.'

When I get back to Freya's house, I think about what Adriana said. Nothing feels good any more. I don't feel good any more. There's this bad feeling rising up in me, because I can't do what I want to do – but I can't carry on pretending either. It's a sort of RAH! feeling that makes me want to shout. And I think back to Joanna and what she told me. 'When you feel like that,' she said, 'hold up your fingers for how old you are. Then blow those birthday candles out, one by one.' She says those deep breaths can take the anger away.

I lean back against the closed bathroom door and I do it, taking a deep breath and blowing those fingers out one by one.

But when my hands are all closed, into two fists, the feeling is still there.

Freya was sitting on the landing, silently praying that Dino would calm down soon. He'd come home in a fierce temper, and she had no idea why.

Louisa came down the stairs. 'Is Dino still upset?' she asked.

Freya pointed at the closed door. 'Sounds like it. I haven't been able to get inside – he's wedged the door shut with something.'

'God,' Louisa said. 'He's going crazy in there.'

'Was he OK when you guys went out?' Freya asked.

Louisa paused, biting her lip. 'Yep. Fine. I mean, he seemed pretty normal.'

Freya took in her daughter's dress and knee-high boots, her straightened hair. 'Are you coming to ask if you can go out?'

Louisa nodded.

Crash. Something else hit the door.

'Yes – Matt's taking me to the cinema. He's coming around in five.'

Another bang from Dino's room.

'Right,' Freya said, distracted. She wasn't quite sure how things had shifted from Louisa asking her if she could go out, to telling her it was happening. 'Bit of a last-minute request, Lou. Could you let me know earlier next time so we can discuss it properly?'

Louisa glanced downstairs, like she was eager to get down there. 'Sure, yes. Sorry.'

'Be back by eleven, OK?' Freya said.

'Eleven-thirty?' Louisa said, her eyes pleading.

It had gone quiet in Dino's bedroom, and it made Freya more rather than less concerned. She had to get in there and make sure Dino was OK. He didn't sound OK.

'Off you go, then,' Freya said. 'Eleven-thirty. Have fun. See you later.'

Louisa smiled, and went down the stairs.

'And Lou—?'

'Yes?'

'You look great, by the way.'

189

Chapter 24

Freya's eyes flicked open. It was dark, late. She had tried to stay awake until Louisa got back after her date with Matt, but she must have drifted off. She'd had a tangle of dreams, with echoes of the upset with Dino, and Joe, and thoughts about the divorce. When her eyes opened in the pitch-dark bedroom, it was silent. She checked the clock: 12.05. A hum of uneasiness buzzed inside her. She had a feeling that something was missing, something wasn't right.

She got out of bed and pulled on her dressing gown.

She hadn't heard Louisa get home – and the door usually woke her. It was half an hour after they'd agreed that she would come back. She'd definitely said eleven-thirty – that was what they'd agreed. She checked her phone: no messages. She went out on to the landing, and then up the stairs to Louisa's room. The bedroom was empty – she wasn't back.

Louisa had promised she'd be back home on time – and now Freya could have kicked herself for trusting her. She'd been distracted – worried about Dino – and she hadn't asked enough questions. She realised she didn't even know which cinema

Louisa had gone to, or what film she'd gone to see. Her mind raced. Going down the stairs, she opened the front door and looked out into the night – it was pitch-black, with no cars on the roads.

She still barely knew Matt. She should have insisted on meeting him properly.

She dialled Louisa's number. The call went straight to voicemail. *Hi, this is Louisa*, came her daughter's voice. But it wasn't Louisa – not really. Freya's heart was thudding hard in her chest now. She called again, but the voicemail recording kicked in again. She didn't even have Matt's number to call.

This was how it had felt that night. One minute Sam had been there, and everything had been normal. They had been normal sisters, in a normal home. So normal that she had just taken it all for granted. Images rushed through her head. Of her and Sam when they were children, playing together, of family Christmases, holidays spent in water parks and on horses, sneaking up into their mum's room and trying on her make-up when she was out. It hadn't ever been perfect – but Sam had been there – reliably enough that Freya had felt able to be irritated by her, frustrated. And then, in a moment, Sam had been gone, and all there was was emptiness. And she would have given anything to be with her again.

Freya's heart was beating even more furiously now, and she was struggling to breathe. Louisa was out there – somewhere. With an older boyfriend whom Freya barely knew. How had she let this happen, a second time? She should have trusted her own instincts.

The night that Sam left came back to her, as vividly as she'd lived it then.

Eliot and Freya had been sitting together on her bed, looking through one of her photography books.

'Barcelona?' Eliot said, pointing to a monochrome picture of Las Ramblas.

'I could do Barcelona,' Freya said, with a smile.

He flicked to another photo. 'Or Prague. Prague looks cool.'

She was sitting close to Eliot, her bare legs across his. She had one hand on the nape of his neck, touching the warm skin there. The territory of his body, which had once seemed so distant, was now hers to explore, and she didn't want to waste a moment when she could be touching him.

'Or we could just stay right here,' he said, turning towards her, and meeting her gaze. 'Because here is also good.'

'Here's just right,' Freya said. 'For now, it's enough. More than enough.'

He kissed her gently, and she felt herself dissolve into it. She wanted more and more, and drew closer to him, but he pulled away.

'Give me a minute. Don't move. Don't go anywhere.'

He got up to go to the bathroom. She was only wearing a T-shirt and, feeling the cold, she brought the duvet up around her. She could hear the water running in the bathroom, and then the sound of voices. She got up and went over to the door and opened it a crack. Sam and Eliot were standing by the doorway, talking to each other.

'I didn't realise you were still here,' Sam said to him.

'Yup. I am.' His voice wavered. Sam might not detect it, but to Freya it was obvious that he was nervous at being caught out in her room.

'I thought you'd left ages ago,' Sam said, sounding unsettled. 'I was—'

'Upstairs, with Echo,' he said. 'I know.'

'Yep, we're up there chatting, she's having a hard time at home, you know, with her dad—' Sam seemed jumpy. Freya could hear it in her voice. Was she trying to make sense of why Eliot was there by her sister's room? To work out where he'd been?

'I'll come up,' Eliot said. 'I'll go and get us some more beers, and then I'll be up.'

'Cool,' Sam said, but her tone implied it wasn't. 'Sure.'

Freya closed the door, so that her sister wouldn't catch sight of her. She pressed her back against it. That was too close. She wasn't ready yet to explain what had been going on with Eliot. She wasn't ready yet to ask for forgiveness. She hadn't worked out how to.

She and Eliot had talked about what they'd do, if this happened. He would act normal, hang out with Sam just like before, pretend nothing was going on. But they hadn't been careful enough tonight. Why else would he have left Sam for all this time, only to be found by Freya's room? They'd been so caught up in each other, and in the moment, that they'd forgotten to be careful.

She felt a pull, as if on an invisible thread. She knew Eliot would want to come back in to see her, just as much as she longed for him to. But they'd agreed they had to handle this the right way. She heard Eliot go downstairs. She lay in bed, read a little, knowing he might not be back. Eventually she must have fallen asleep. The sound of the front door closing woke her.

She went up to Sam's room and found it empty. She checked the wardrobe, drawers – she'd taken clothes and quite a few of her things with her. She called her mobile – nothing. Panic rose inside her. This time was different. This time it wasn't about an argument with their dad.

She called their parents, and they drove home right away. They went out to search for Sam in their car, hoping they'd find her at the nearest bus shelter, or trying to hitch a lift on the A-road. Freya was left behind. They insisted she stay in case Sam had a change of heart and returned. They wanted to pretend it was all going to be

OK, even though it was already clear to all of them that it wasn't going to be – nothing would ever be OK again, after that night. As soon as they were out of the door, Freya searched the house for a note. She told herself Sam couldn't just vanish, without a word even to her, but deep down she knew that it was just the sort of thing Sam would do. Perhaps she'd always known it – that Sam had always had one foot out of the door, ready to run at any point. Finding out about Freya and Eliot had tipped her over that line.

Freya tried not to think about what she'd done. But she knew that Sam must have worked out what was happening, and felt betrayed by her, the one person she should have been able to trust. In the coming weeks, the search for her sister had yielded nothing but emptiness, and silence. This search was her penance – and it felt fitting. She accepted it.

Freya had her phone in her hand, ready to call Joe. It was 12.20, and Louisa wasn't back. Somehow it had only been fifteen minutes since she'd woken, that she'd been waiting for her daughter, but it had felt like hours. Her mind was racing with possibilities, and she wanted Joe there with her, to share the burden of worry.

Just as she was about to make the call, a car pulled up in front of their drive. She recognised it from the night of the prom – it was Matt's. She breathed a sigh of relief. She could see Louisa on the front seat, and she raised a hand to her chest. Louisa was back, and she was fine.

Matt and Louisa got out of the car and walked up the path towards her, both looking slightly sheepish. Freya couldn't hide her annoyance, and didn't try. She'd trusted them, and they'd both let her down.

'You're late, Louisa,' she said firmly. 'We said eleven-thirty and it's past midnight.'

'Sorry, Mum,' she said, looking down at the ground.

'I've been really worried about you,' Freya said. 'You weren't answering your phone—'

Matt spoke up. 'It's not Louisa's fault, it's mine. I encouraged her to stay out later, and I should have brought her home. I was driving – she couldn't come back home without me.'

Freya couldn't tell if he was covering for Louisa or not, but it didn't really matter. He was right – this wouldn't have happened if he hadn't been around. Louisa had never been late home before. Freya didn't ever, ever want to feel the way she'd felt this evening again.

'You broke our rules,' Freya said, looking from Matt to Louisa. 'This relationship isn't OK – my gut feeling was right and I should've listened to it.'

'Sorry, what? What are you saying, Mum?' Louisa said.

'If you're not responsible enough to stick to our agreements, then you're not grown-up enough to be going out with Matt.'

'You can't do that,' Matt said, his face falling.

'You're really not in any position to tell me what I can and can't do, Matt.'

'But Mum—' Louisa said, aghast.

'Get inside, Louisa,' Freya said sternly, 'right now.'

Freya sent Louisa straight up to her bedroom. She berated herself – she had been complacent, too relaxed, and that had been a risk. She wasn't going to be that parent any more. Louisa needed firm boundaries.

She could not – would not – let history repeat itself.

She recalled the void Sam had left – instead of her sister, all there had been was the search, and the search had become her everything. Looking for Sam had become Freya's life – the frustrations of it, the raised and dashed hopes. Those highs and lows that defined her days, even now.

Back then, in the weeks after Sam's disappearance, she'd spoken to Eliot only once – to ask him what had happened that night after he'd left her room. He'd told her he'd stayed about an hour longer, drinking with Sam and Echo, then left and gone home on his own. After hearing the facts she needed, she'd ignored Eliot's calls. Guilt had crept in, a hostile visitor that refused to leave, and it told her that if Sam hadn't worked out what was going on with her and Eliot that night, she wouldn't have left. The uncomfortable feeling lodged itself somewhere in the bottom of her gut, gnawing at her. There were days when she could quieten the insistent voice, but there were others still, during the endless, sleepless nights, when the noise of her transgression was loud in her ears. Freya had betrayed Sam's trust, and now Sam was gone.

Freya's need for redemption had driven her. She led the search for Sam, pushed the police for answers, spoke to the cameras, pleaded for information. It burned, this need in her – to find Sam. She wanted her sister back, more than anything – but also she had a duty to make things right. When Sam was back, she'd make it up to her – they'd return to their proper positions, as the sisters and daughters they'd always been, with their own comfortable dynamic. Sam was the one who messed up, let people down. Not her. Not Freya. Right now nothing made sense.

Eliot kept calling, and she blocked his number. There was nothing good that could come of their being together, she could see that now. After the police completed all their interviews, she heard he'd moved out of town.

She and Joe had got together, and it seemed as if she was getting something right. She put what she'd felt for Eliot to the very back of her mind. With Joe she was calm; her feelings were steady. She welcomed it. She enjoyed Joe's company, but never too much – never so much that the sides of her would blur, and never so much that she became unsure of herself. Never so much that she became volatile, and could cause damage. The guilt of what she'd done drowned out anything that might have been good in the way she'd felt about Eliot. Freya had the certainty that, deep down, her desire had led all of this to happen.

She'd committed completely to being with Joe, and to the search, and to being the person she wanted to be. But the truth was that Eliot's touch, and the way it had made her feel – vibrant, alive – never really left her.

On the handful of occasions she'd seen him since then, the guilt had weighed heavy as cement. That part was easy – she'd been ready to carry that. She'd expected to feel bad, almost welcomed it. What had always been less comfortable was the light that seeing him brought into her heart. The bright glimmer of that secret she held. When she saw him she was revisited by the flicker of possibility that she could be someone very different from the person she had always been.

She'd never told anyone. She'd just held it close over the years. Told herself she was wrestling with the guilt of it, but really she was nurturing the memory, feeding it, so that she'd never forget that she could be someone else – that being herself, the Freya everyone else knew, was a choice.

Now, sitting at the kitchen table, Freya poured herself a glass of wine, and when the faint beginnings of numbness came she was grateful for them. It was what she needed, a habit she'd fallen into – something she did whenever she recalled how things had been with Eliot. The more she could get towards feeling nothing, the better. It was feeling deeply – feeling as much as she had for Eliot – that had caused her to let her sister down. She'd churned up the earth in allowing herself to think back over that summer, and it had brought with it everything she'd felt for Eliot.

She'd never told Eliot directly that she couldn't see him any longer. And even when she was married to Joe, Eliot would come into her mind, in unsettling flashes. She'd remember the curls that fell into his eyes. The way he'd looked at her that first night he came up to her room. She would do what she could to distract herself, to remind herself that the past was the past and her life wasn't there. But he'd never really gone away. It was unfinished. She'd been the one to cut off, but she hadn't been able to bring herself to say the words to tell him they were over.

The thoughts would come, when things were busy, when things were quiet, when she felt alone or when she thought things were finally OK. What was he doing now? Did he ever think of her, the way she thought of him? She shouldn't care. But she did. Every part of her did.

She couldn't go back and fix things – she could never redeem herself. She was stuck, and always would be, in the morally murky waters of having let her sister down, betrayed her, been a less-good person than anyone had expected, than she had even expected of herself. Freya knew she had to keep this all locked tight inside her. Because if she let it out – the truth of what she'd done – what else might pour out with it? What else might be made visible, about the person, and sister, that she really was?

It was hard to let go of something your heart wanted. To let go of wanting to be with someone who made you feel alive. Her only option was to try and feel less, of everything. To keep busy, try not to feel, and control whatever she could.

When she'd finished her glass of wine, Freya went upstairs to her bedroom. The alcohol hadn't helped; if anything she felt more unsettled than she had before, even with Louisa back home. It didn't make any sense, but she still had that feeling that something wasn't right.

She passed by Dino's room, and sneaked a look through the

door. The room was dark, but she could make out the ruffled bedclothes, and the Tigger toy that he had taken to sleeping with. It felt good, comforting, to see that her nest was full.

She looked in on Jessie after that, opening the door as quietly as she could. She saw the familiar shape of her daughter in bed, a heap of duvet wrapped around her. She felt the draw to go and sit with her, watch her sleep as she used to when she was younger. She went softly on the carpeted floor, then perched on the edge of the bed. She touched the duvet – and, as her eyes adjusted to the dim light, she saw Dino's shoulder, Dino's dark hair. He must have got scared and come in with Jessie, she reasoned. She lifted the blanket, looking for Jessie's sleeping form beside him, but there was no one else there.

Her eyes went to the floor, the beanbag, searching. She got up, went back into Dino's room, and checked his bed – it was empty. Her heart was racing now. Something was wrong. She dashed up to Louisa's room, and saw her teenage daughter sprawled out on her bed. There was no one else in there.

She'd felt it. Something *was* wrong. But it wasn't ever about Louisa.

It was Jessie. Jessie was gone.

Chapter 25

Freya called Joe, waking him up. Their conversation the previous evening about the divorce seemed irrelevant, inconsequential, now. Her heart was thumping in her chest.

'Joe, I need you to come over,' she said. She did what she could to keep her voice steady, but she knew that it gave her concern away. It was one in the morning, she'd searched the whole house, and there was no sign at all of Jessie. 'I mean right now. It's Jessie. She's gone.'

'What? Christ! What do you mean? You've checked—'

'Yes, I've checked all the rooms—' Her voice cracked. 'Can you come over? I need your help.'

'Yes. Of course. God, yes. Give me a minute, Frey. I'm there.'

Freya went up to get Louisa. She was groggy and confused, waking from her too-brief sleep, but Freya quickly explained what was happening.

'Your dad's on the way. I think we need to get out in the neighbourhood and look for her. I'm going to wake up Dino,' Freya said.

In Jessie's room, Freya gently shook Dino awake. He woke,

200

disorientated, and for a moment he looked confused about being in the wrong bedroom. 'What's going on?' he said, huskily.

'Dino ...' She held him and looked him directly in the eye. 'I need you to tell me something. Do you know where Jessie is?'

He shook his head, not saying a word.

She laid her hand on his arm. 'I need to find Jessie,' she said, her tone serious. 'If you know anything at all – if she said anything, if you saw anything – I need you to tell me.'

Dino shook his head, then turned towards the wall, running a finger over the picture of a cowboy in the Cath Kidston print wallpaper. When he looked back, his eyes were glassy. 'I don't know where she is, Freya.'

Freya heard the key in the lock downstairs as Joe came into the house.

'Freya?' he called out.

'Dad!' Louisa called back. Freya could hear her running down the stairs.

'We need to go and find her,' Freya said, taking Dino's hand.

Downstairs, Joe gave her a hug. 'You haven't found her?' he said to Freya.

'No.' The strain was visible on his face. It triggered something in her, like a toddler with a grazed knee searching their parent's face for a reaction – if he was worried, this was real. This was happening. Their daughter was missing.

He grabbed a torch from the under-stairs cupboard. 'Lou – will you come with me and we'll search the block? See if she's snuck into anyone's front garden?'

'Sure,' Louisa said, putting on her coat.

He turned to Freya. 'Why don't you and Dino check the back garden and the shed? She's always hiding out there; maybe this was a game that's going on too long?'

Freya glanced back at Dino, standing in the doorway, and

willed what Joe was saying to be true. 'Come on, love. Let's go and see if we can find Jessie outside.'

A thought nagged at her, and she wished she could push past it. Dino had been there, hadn't he? In bed with her. Dino was the last person to see Jessie before she disappeared.

Adriana puts the custard cream packet back in the cupboard, and closes it. She puts on her slippers, and goes upstairs, avoiding the piles of papers and boxes, to get ready for bed.

She's liked having the boy here. She's grown used to his visits, and their card games. She will miss them. It has been a long time since people stopped by at her house, just because. She knows the children make jokes about her, and about her house – and that they're scared of her. It used to make her feel safe. But it has kept her alone. And perhaps no one, truly, likes being alone, whatever they tell themselves.

Dino won't be back. That much she knows for sure. He'll be gone soon.

Freya and Dino walked out into the garden, searching through the bushes with their torches, and calling out Jessie's name. Freya found she was checking Dino's face for clues, but it gave nothing away. It was blank, just as it had been the day he'd arrived with them. Even as he called out for Jessie, there was no sign of emotion.

The garden, which was usually the backdrop to the happiest of their memories – ball games and picnics and trampolining – now, in the moonlight, had taken on an air of threat. Would Jessie really have come out here, and stayed out here, even as it grew dark? She'd always been adventurous, but this didn't fit – none of it did.

It kept rushing back to her. The night that Sam had gone missing. Her search, increasingly frantic, through each of the rooms of their house. The gradual, terrifying diminishment of hope, as she found each room empty. She couldn't have it happen again, she *couldn't*. The memories ramped up the fear in her, and led her mind to places she didn't want it to go. She hated herself for mistrusting Dino, but something wasn't right – she was sure he knew more than he was letting on, and if she'd learned anything that evening it was to trust her gut feelings.

She unlocked the padlock on the shed door, and checked inside. She moved the rakes and brooms out of the way, looked behind the pile of garden chairs. She wanted so desperately to find Jessie in there, but there was no one in the dark spaces and shadows.

Reluctantly, Freya called Dino over and the two of them went back inside. A ball of fear grew in Freya's chest. She pictured Jessie's face – the sweet point of her chin, the way it jutted out when she was about to embark on some mischief or other. Her hair, the way she twirled a strand around her fingers absent-mindedly when she needed comfort, or sought sleep, and the way she sometimes ended up with tiny dreadlocks that Freya would have to unravel. The bounce in her step as she came out of school, brim-full of things to tell her mum and sister. Jessie, their sunshine. The one who brought them all together, with her tricks and jokes and laughter. Freya's breath came raggedly, and her heart ached. This couldn't be happening. They couldn't lose Jessie. She couldn't lose her little girl.

Joe and Louisa came back in through the front door. She could see enough from their faces – tired, drawn – to know what the result was without having to ask. 'Nothing,' Joe said. 'I woke the neighbours on either side and checked, but they hadn't heard or seen anything. We might need to wait till morning to speak with the others.'

Louisa's eyes were shiny with unshed tears. Joe took one look at

Freya and saw her, as he always had – he could see her thoughts were spiralling and she was in a dark place.

'Don't, Frey,' he said. 'Don't do this to yourself. This isn't it. We're going to find her.'

She felt lost. She'd slipped away into a place where hope had gone. An empty hole of desperation and loss, somewhere she knew she couldn't afford to go and yet nonetheless she could feel taking her in.

'Freya.'

For a brief moment the voice seemed to come from her past – she felt locked into that night, when she'd been alone in the house waiting for news that wouldn't come.

'Freya,' Joe said again, louder this time. 'Don't go,' he said, touching her shoulder. 'We need you here.'

She forced herself to come back into the present. 'We have to call the police,' she said. 'Jessie's only six – we need to let them know.'

'You're right,' Joe said. 'I'll phone them.' He went into the kitchen to make the call.

'It makes no sense,' Freya said to Louisa. 'She's been so happy. What reason would she have to run away?'

'Maybe she didn't,' Louisa said. Dino was sitting on the sofa beside her, and he shifted position, seeming uncomfortable.

'Don't say that, Lou,' Freya said. 'Please don't say that.' Every disappeared child in the newspapers flashed through her mind then – children snatched from their beds, on their way home from school, from their gardens as they played. She tried to see everyone in the world as inherently good, and yet in the light of some of those stories her faith was tested. There was no sign of forced entry, no one but their immediate neighbours had their keys – but these things happened, didn't they? No home was ever completely secure. Had she missed something – a window that should have had a lock, the loose back gate . . . ? The possibilities swirled in her head, tormenting her.

Damn. Her mind wouldn't cease circling back to Dino. He knew something – she was sure of it. What was family, if it wasn't trust? But she didn't trust him. Not completely.

Would Dino be capable of hurting Jessie? He'd certainly proved himself able to hurt her, Freya. There was an anger within him that had startled her – he was unstable, unpredictable. Could he have done something to put Jessie at risk?

She went into the kitchen.

'They're on their way,' said Joe, hanging up the phone. He sucked in his breath and let it out slowly, and Freya could see how much he was keeping his own anxiety inside. 'They said, with Jessie's age, this is a priority for them.'

'I don't know what to do,' Freya confided in him. 'I feel like Dino knows something. He knows more than he's telling us.'

'Dino? What makes you think that?'

'My gut. He knows something about why she's gone.'

Joe put his arm around her, and brought her in close to his chest, calming her.

'I'm scared, Joe,' she said. 'I don't think I've ever felt so scared.' His touch, his closeness, made her feel stronger.

The doorbell rang. 'That must be the police. They got here fast,' Joe said. They went through into the hallway together.

When they opened the front door, Jessie was standing there. Her eyes were wide, her cheeks red-raw and puffy with tears. She was standing on the doorstep in her unicorn-print pyjamas, the top and trousers blackened in patches. One of their neighbours, Jean, was beside her.

'After Joe had gone,' she said, 'Dan thought we'd better check the back garden. We found this little one in the shed, curled up there.'

Tears of relief flooded down Freya's cheeks as she pulled her daughter towards her and into a hug. 'Jessie!' Joe knelt down beside them, and touched his daughter's tear-stained face. 'You're OK,' Freya said, smoothing her ruffled hair. 'God, Jessie. You really gave us a scare.'

Joe said softly, 'You're back. You're safe.'

When at last Jessie's sobs subsided, Freya pulled away for a moment, smoothing her daughter's hair back from her face so she could see it clearly. 'What happened?' she asked. 'What on earth happened?'

Jessie's heart. Freya was still holding her closely enough to feel it racing. Jessie looked blank for a moment, then glanced across the room. 'I ran away. But then I got scared, I didn't know where else to go.'

'But why – why would you do this, and in the middle of the night?' Freya said. 'We were so worried about you.'

'I don't know,' Jessie said.

Jessie was safe. So why was it that Freya didn't feel the complete sense of relief that she should? She could see Dino out of the corner of her eye, sitting on the stairs, close to them but saying nothing.

A chill went through her. He was some part of this. *He'd known.*

206

Chapter 26

The next morning, Freya was bleary-eyed after barely any sleep, but nothing mattered other than the fact that her whole family were back home – Joe, Louisa, Jessie and Dino were sitting around the kitchen table.

She made blueberry pancakes and dished them out. It felt good, being here in the kitchen, her family returning to calm domesticity. Her daughters sitting side by side at the table, as they had done their whole lives, from when Jessie was in a high chair. There were cracks in their lives, in their family – Freya couldn't ignore that, and she didn't want to. But, just for this one morning, it felt good to try and smooth over them and make things more normal.

Jessie ate her pancakes as if she hadn't eaten in days. Last night had crystallised a truth for Freya – when it came down to it, she and Joe were parents together, devoted to their two girls, and they always would be. Married or not, this was their family.

Jessie still looked shaken, and there were dark circles under her eyes, her skin pale from the late night – but she was here. Not shivering in some unknown back garden, or wandering the night-time streets, disorientated, or, worse still . . . Well, there had been so many – too many – worse stills that had gone through Freya's mind the previous night.

'Here you go,' Jessie said softly, passing some syrup to Dino.

Dino nodded, and poured the syrup on his pancake.

'You sure you're OK?' Freya said.

'Yes,' Jessie said. 'I'm fine.'

'Do you feel ready to tell us any more about what happened?' Freya asked tentatively.

Jessie bit her lip. 'Nope.'

'We were really worried about you, Jessie,' Joe said. 'You gave us a real scare. You're far too young to be out there on your own; you could have been hurt.'

'I know,' Jessie said, looking down at her plate. 'I'm sorry.'

Freya and Joe exchanged a look. After Jessie's silence the previous night when they'd put her to bed, they'd agreed not to push it. She would tell them when she was ready. They would have to wait.

They fell into silence.

Louisa turned to her dad. 'Did Mum tell you what else happened last night?'

'There's more?' Joe said, raising an eyebrow.

'She went ballistic at Matt.'

'No – hang on, Louisa . . . ' Freya said. 'You broke our agreement. We said eleven-thirty—'

'And I came home a bit late, big deal.'

Joe shot her a look. 'Yes. It is, actually.'

'Such a big deal that she's said I can't see Matt any more?'

Joe rubbed his brow. 'God, it's never just the one thing, is it?' he said. 'Well, look, Lou. If you think I'm going to go against your mum on this one, you're wrong. If she's made a decision about what she thinks is right, then I back her on that.'

'But she totally overreacted,' Louisa said, exasperated. 'I've only just been allowed to start seeing Matt again, and now this. I'm sixteen, I'm not a kid any more.'

'You're sixteen,' Freya said, 'and he's nineteen – and the more I think about it, Louisa, the more I'm not sure it ever was a good idea. He doesn't seem to respect our boundaries. I'm sorry, but I'm standing firm on this one.'

That evening, Freya sat with Jessie as she drifted off to sleep. She didn't want to leave – in that moment Jessie felt almost intolerably precious to her. Freya wondered if she'd ever felt more grateful to have her younger daughter there with her. Maybe that first night they'd brought Jessie home from the hospital. She'd held her tightly, cared for her, done everything in her power to keep her safe every year of her life. And yet, somehow, she'd failed her. Jessie had wanted to run away from her family.

Joe was downstairs, tidying away the dinner things. He'd stayed around the whole day, to make sure the family was OK. She went into the kitchen to join him. They sat down opposite each other at the breakfast bar, and Freya opened a bottle of red wine.

It was like a pressure on her brain, this thought she couldn't let herself think. The fear, that, once she'd voiced her suspicions, they would have to lead to action. Her head throbbed. There was too much at stake.

'Neither of us really knows what happened last night,' Freya said. 'But one thing's clear – and that's that Jessie isn't telling us everything.'

'I just don't understand why she'd do this,' Joe said. 'She has everything she wants here.'

'I know,' Freya said. 'It's not at all like her, is it? Something has to be going on.'

'You're still concerned about Dino?'

'Aren't you, Joe? I know it sounds terrible. He's only seven.' It wasn't just that, though. It was the love Freya had come to feel for him. She didn't want to admit to herself or to anyone else that she might have misjudged things, got it wrong. 'Did you see how he wasn't surprised when we found her? He didn't come over to comfort her, check she was OK. It was weird.'

'You did say it always takes a while for him to talk, to show his feelings, step forward ...'

'I know.' She wanted to believe it.

'But it's also true that we know he's capable of lashing out,' Joe said, reluctantly. 'It's possible he did something that made Jessie want to run.'

Freya thought back to the time he'd hurt her. The sting of her cheek that time Dino had struck her, accidentally, she'd thought – it felt fresh again. She had been so sure that they'd moved on from that moment, so sure that Dino's aggression was something they could consign to the past, but perhaps she'd been in a hurry to believe that. In a way, what Joe was saying was the only thing that made sense.

'I think we need to put our daughters first,' Freya said. It stung to say those words.

'We'd never forgive ourselves if something happened to Jessie, or Louisa,' Joe said. 'Our promise – the first one we ever made – was to care for them and to protect them. How can we say we're doing that if we can't be sure that Dino's not a threat?

They didn't know the whole of him. That was a simple fact. She'd wanted to know him, she'd begun to love him, but she didn't know the whole of him.

They didn't know what fired up his rages. They didn't know how bad his emotional damage was, or what had caused it. How his being hurt might lead to him passing that hurt on. There was no way Freya or Joe could predict how far he would go.

'We can't let things go on as they are,' Joe said. 'We're talking about the wellbeing of our kids.'

His resolve had strengthened, and Freya felt something inside her harden too. Dino was an unknown, a risk. She'd brought an unknown child into their home, and perhaps she'd got it all dangerously wrong.

'This has gone beyond whatever promise you made to Sam, Freya. Seeing Jessie's face last night . . . I think we need to talk to Social Services about Dino, and get to the bottom of this.'

Freya's pulse quickened. She knew once they started down that path they would never be able to turn back. 'Let me try Sam and see if she can help us.'

As she sat with Joe, she got out her phone and sent Sam a message:

Sam. I need to talk to you, about Dino. About where we go from here. Things have happened that I need to understand. You promised me you wouldn't go quiet on me. I need you to get in touch.

That night, Freya couldn't relax. Not after what they'd all been through, after the conversation with Joe. It was the worst feeling, knowing that, even with Jessie under her roof, she couldn't be completely sure her daughter was safe.

Freya had learned to rely on order, structure, and facts – and, when Sam had left, those things had become even more important. She didn't take risks. She didn't take chances. She didn't trust her instinct. Instinct had led her to places before that she knew weren't right. All that had changed when Sam had come back into her life. She'd got that message from Sam, and let everything she was sure about fall away. She'd turned her back on the things that she had learned were important.

211

She'd let herself rely on instinct, the instinct that told her that she needed to be there, for her sister, for her nephew, no matter what. No matter that it would disrupt all their lives, including her daughters'. And now she was starting to question that. Had it in fact been selfish to bring another child into her family? And after all that the years had taught her – to stick to plans, to create schedules, to think about the future – had it really been the right thing, to let that all go?

The following day, the strangeness of Jessie's brief disappearance hung in the air inside the house. Freya hoovered and scrubbed the floors, sprayed and wiped the windows, wiped the sinks, got to the cobwebs up high with a long feather-duster. But it remained – there was something contaminating in the body of the house.

There had been no word back from Sam, and Freya's commitment to Joe weighed on her mind. If she didn't hear back soon, and if they weren't able to find a way forward, she would have to take other action. She needed to know more about Dino, at the very least, to be reassured that there was nothing he could have done to cause Jessie to run away.

Freya couldn't shake the feeling she'd experienced when she had thought her younger daughter was gone. It might only have been an hour or two, but in that time Freya's mind had raced ahead – she'd lived a lifetime without Jessie, flashed ahead to days when her daughter would not be there, where life would be empty, and the imprint of that on her mind, and on the house, was still there.

Freya thought of Jessie's tearstained face as she'd arrived back at the house. She'd been a different child, in that moment, and, while over the course of the next day she'd brightened again, something of that child still lingered. The whole house felt more silent than usual. Louisa sulked in her room, still harbouring resentment about not being allowed to see Matt. Dino, too, was quieter, more subdued. Freya longed to be able to put the pieces in place, but, with neither of them opening up to her, it felt like an impossible task.

As the afternoon turned to evening, though, and without Freya doing anything much at all, the atmosphere in the house started to lighten. The kids began to jostle with and annoy each other in a reassuringly normal way. By evening, at dinnertime, Jessie was jabbing her elder sister in the ribs as she ate.

'Stop it,' Louisa said.

Jessie kept doing it.

Louisa narrowed her eyes at her sister. 'Stop annoying me,' she snapped.

'*Stop annoying me,*' Jessie copied her.

Dino smiled, the tiniest bit.

'Argh,' Louisa said. 'You're driving me nuts, Jess. Maybe you should have run away a bit further.'

Freya drew in her breath sharply. 'Louisa!'

'What?' Louisa said defensively. 'She probably only did it for attention.'

'That's not true,' Jessie said.

'Is so,' Louisa said.

'I hate you,' Jessie snapped. She pushed her chair back, the legs scraping on the floor, and then got up and ran away from the table and upstairs.

Freya gave her elder daughter a stern glare, then followed Jessie upstairs. She found Jessie in the fairy-lit wigwam in her bedroom. She had built herself a den in the corner, and blocked herself in with cushions. Her mother could still just about squeeze in beside her.

'What's up, love? You seem upset.'

Jessie was an open book. Her flushed cheeks . . .

'Is it what Louisa was saying? You know she can be unkind sometimes. She doesn't really mean it.'

'Kind of. But it's not only that.'

'What do you mean?'

'It's just … I don't know.' Jessie toyed with the threads on a cushion.

'Jessie. I'm so glad you're here, and that you're safe. You know that nothing could change how much me and your dad love you, don't you?'

'Yes, I know that.'

Now. Freya needed to do it now.

'There's something I need to ask you. Believe me, it's not easy for me to ask. But I have to.'

'OK.'

'Did Dino have something to do with you running away? Did he know about it?'

Jessie looked at her for a long time, her mouth slightly open, saying nothing.

'You can tell, me, Jess. You can tell me the truth.'

'Yes,' she said, softly.

The words hit Freya in the chest. She'd been right. She'd so desperately wanted to be wrong. But she'd been right.

Chapter 27

Freya stared at Jessie. Her heart was in her throat.

'What did Dino have to do with what happened last night?' Freya asked.

Jessie fell silent again.

'You've got to tell me, Jess.'

Jessie shrugged.

'This is important. I need you to tell me the whole truth. Did he hurt you in some way, or make you feel scared?'

'No, he never hurt me,' Jessie said, shaking her head. 'He wouldn't do that.'

Freya inwardly breathed a sigh of relief. Her worst imaginings had been avoided.

'But he did – he was part of it,' Jessie said.

'How?'

'I don't want to say. I don't want him to get in trouble.'

A shiver went over Freya's skin. What was happening here? What was happening right at the heart of her family, that she didn't know anything about? 'Jessie,' she said softly. 'You don't have to do this. You don't have to protect him. Please, Jessie. Tell me what he did.'

215

Jessie chewed on her bottom lip nervously. 'I told him I wanted to run away, and he helped me to pack my bag.'

Freya waited for more, but nothing came.

'That's it?' Freya said.

'Yes. That was it.'

OK, maybe she hadn't got Dino wrong after all. Freya's head ached with the confusion of it all. The urge to leave had all come from Jessie, in that case.

'Where were you even going?'

Jessie shrugged. 'I thought maybe Grandma's house, but then I couldn't remember the way through the back gardens, because that's different from how we usually walk there.'

'But why?'

'I saw Dad give you that envelope,' Jessie said.

The divorce stuff, Freya thought. Oh, God. Of course.

'You came upstairs, and you were acting all weird. Sad, kind of. That evening I found the envelope on the table, and took it up to Louisa. She told me some of what the papers said. Then she went really quiet.'

The pieces fell into place in Freya's mind. Jessie had been so strong and happy through the whole separation, and it had lulled Freya and Joe into a false sense of security. Of course she'd be upset and unsettled, deep down, especially with the way that things were progressing.

'I can see why you're upset,' Freya said. 'I should have talked to you about it all properly. Divorce is a hard thing, but it's nothing to do with how much we love you, Jessie.'

'I knew you weren't getting back together,' Jessie said. The rims of her eyes grew red. 'I just didn't realise, really, the forever-ness of it. I know Lily is with Dad now – but I didn't realise she was going to take him away.'

'She hasn't,' Freya said. She drew her daughter into a hug.

She had an overwhelming urge to comfort her, protect, make all the pain that she was feeling go away. 'Lily's making your dad happy right now, but she's not the reason we broke up, Jess. That happened long ago.'

As she said the words out loud, they sank deep into her soul. There was the truth, in all its painful simplicity. There had been nothing, really, that either of them could have done to change the outcome they now had.

'I understand why you're upset, Jessie. But I still don't understand why you thought that running away was the answer.'

'Because I wanted Dad back here. I wanted you and Dad together – even if it was just for a night. I knew if I went missing then you'd have to look for me together.'

Imagining it all through a six-year-old's eyes, she could see how it might make sense.

'OK. I can see now what you were trying to do. I wish you hadn't done it – but it was us, it was the grown-ups, who got this wrong first.'

'Dino didn't want me to go. He just said if I was going to, I should have the right things, stuff that would keep me safe.'

Freya saw the whole evening differently, and a wave of guilt swept over her. In her hurry to find someone to blame she'd settled on Dino – and she'd missed what was really going on underneath.

'I'm sorry I did it, Mum. But it wasn't Dino's fault. Even before I found the envelope I'd thought about running away. Ever since we met Lily. Dino was the only person I could talk about it with. Everything felt too much in my head.'

'Why didn't you come to me about it?' Freya said.

'Because you were part of it.'

'Oh, love,' Freya said. How had she got this all so wrong?

'I want to go back to how I was.'

'Back to how you were?'

217

'I want it to be like before. When I could just be me, when that was enough. When you and Dad were together. Now I feel like me is not good enough any more.'

Freya's heart went out to her daughter. 'Of course you're good enough! You're my girl.'

Jessie started to cry, big tears falling on to her round cheeks.

'You're more than enough, Jessie.'

As Freya got into bed that night, the chat she'd had with Jessie was still going around in her mind. She'd been naïve to think she could keep the news of the divorce from her daughters. Jessie and Louisa were sharp, and they had always had a way of finding things out.

It hadn't only been about them, after all. She had missed so much of what was really going on with Jessie – the worries she had, the pressure she was feeling. It had been easier for Freya to put the papers away and try to forget about them. She was going to read them in time, of course she was. Formalising their separation wouldn't make any difference really, and it was the only way forward – and yet part of her was holding back. She and Joe had shared so much over the years – and their lives were still interwoven now. In recent weeks it had felt as though a little of what had once worked so well between them had come back.

Once they got divorced, things would change, there was no getting around that. There would be more space for Joe and Lily to grow as a couple, and with that happening, Freya would need to step away. That was all how it should be – and yet Freya was still resisting drawing a line under everything. This decision would cancel out any last chance they might have had. This was it.

The frame had shifted now, though, and what mattered most of all was the way that her actions had upset Jessie. She had allowed herself to get caught up in her own feelings, and that

218

wasn't right. She needed to reassure her daughters – and she wasn't going to bring anyone else into this, least of all Dino.

Freya went into Dino's room, where he was already asleep. She sat beside him and looked at his sweet head on the pillow, his chest as it gently rose and fell. This gentle boy, who had seen more than a boy his age should. This child who was a part of her sister, and therefore a part of her. His grandparents were her parents. The genes in him came from the people closest to her. She'd been wrong to doubt him. Her doubts had come from a place of fear, and she'd been wrong to feel that way. He was pure, and he was kind – when he'd acted out, it had been his hurt made concrete, that was all. There was no malice in him, she was sure of that now. She would do better – she would be better. She would put things right, and trust him more this time.

Jessie's back, and everyone is OK again. I hated her being gone. All I wanted was to tell Freya or Joe what her plan was, but she made me promise I wouldn't.

They were so panicky. I think they really thought she might have, I don't know, been stolen, or something. The kind of bad thing only grown-ups can imagine, I guess. But I'd promised Jessie, and that was a promise that I had to keep. Then, when it was night-time and she really had been gone a long time, I started to think maybe something bad had happened after all.

I've never been a good liar, and I don't like having to do it. It makes my chest go all fluttery, like a load of butterflies in there, and the skin on my face starts to itch. I used to have to do it at school, sometimes, when Mum would take me out for a few days to go on an adventure, and then when I got back the other kids would ask me where I'd been. Sick, I'd say. And they'd say I didn't look sick. I looked the same, because we'd never actually go on the adventure after all. What I'd done really was go to a playground or something while Mum sat with Cassie, or Neil, or that guy Al.

219

Anyway, Mum used to ask me to just stay quiet, and I'd do it. And she asked me to do it here, and I've done it. I've done it for a long time now, though, and it's time to stop. Lying gets tiring. I mostly try not to say anything, but sometimes I have to lie, and it's easy to forget what I've said.

I've never known what it's like to have a grandma, and now I – sort of – have two. I like Jilly, she's a good person, but when I'm with her I always feel second to Jessie and Louisa. And that's normal, that makes sense – she's known them a lot of years and me not long at all.

It's different when I'm with Adriana. I feel like I can be myself, with her. She doesn't ever ask questions so I never have to lie. I feel free there.

But it's strange: she's the one who never asked and yet she's the one who knows. I don't know how, but somehow she knows it. It's like she can see through me.

And that feels good, because it means I don't get to choose any more. She's told me to tell the truth, and now I feel like I have to.

Chapter 28

The next day Freya called Joe and told him about her conversation with Jessie. Later that morning, he came round to the house and they sat the girls down together and talked to them about what was going on. Freya set Dino up with the TV in the other room – he'd already been dragged into things enough. The papers from the lawyer were on the coffee table between them. Just pieces of paper. Yet somehow they'd unbalanced the whole house – unsettled Jessie to the point where she felt she had to hide away, and unsettled Freya too, far more than she'd even allowed herself to admit.

'We should have been more open with you guys about this,' Joe said. 'We've told you everything else, all the way along. So you shouldn't have had to find this out the way that you did.'

'I knew they were something important,' Jessie said, 'because Mum kept moving them from place to place, like she wanted them to go away.'

Freya felt her cheeks flush. It was embarrassing, because, while she hadn't realised it at the time, it was true. Perhaps unconsciously she'd hoped the papers might go missing that way, and she wouldn't have to think about or deal with them. She could continue to live in the same limbo she'd been comfortable in before.

Joe looked at her, and she glanced away. 'It wasn't like that, Jess. I just hadn't found a place to put them, that was all. I didn't want to forget to read them properly.'

'Forget?' Louisa said, raising an eyebrow, the trace of a smile on her lips.

'OK, look,' Freya said, 'so maybe this isn't the easiest thing in the world for me. Me and your dad were together for a long time. And, while the divorce won't change anything—'

'Really it won't,' Joe said, calmly.

'—it's still saying goodbye, to a time in our lives.' Tears came to her eyes. She willed them to disappear; they weren't going to help anyone here. But they wouldn't go. They stubbornly persisted, threatening to fall.

She'd told herself she needed to be cool and unemotional, but, faced with her children, and her ex, she found it was impossible. She realised she couldn't be that person any more, the Freya she'd once been. The one who boxed up her feelings and put them on a shelf to be dealt with at a convenient time.

'And that was a time when we were really happy,' Joe said.

'*Really* happy,' Freya said. The memories flashed back to her. The day they'd brought Louisa back from hospital, overwhelmed with love and the immense responsibility. The nights they'd paced the halls in turn, trying to get her to sleep. The day Jessie joined them and they introduced the two sisters. She recalled seeing the bond form between them – the slow realisation that she hadn't just given birth to another daughter, but to a sibling relationship that would take on an energy all of its own and, most likely, outlive both her and Joe. They had been happy, so happy. It was just that, no matter how they'd tried to avoid it, that happiness had been finite – it had come with an expiry date that had got stamped there, at some point, which they were powerless to undo.

'We love you, and love and respect each other just like before. This is just paper,' Freya told them, and herself.

'Are you and Lily going to get married now?' Jessie asked Joe.

Joe shook his head. 'We're still getting to know each other,' he said.

'But one day, maybe, right?' Freya said.

Joe nodded.

Louisa fidgeted, getting her phone out of her pocket. 'I get it,' she said.

'You're OK with it?' Joe said. 'Because if you have any questions . . .'

'I'm fine,' Louisa said. 'It's Jessie who got weirded out about it, not me.'

'I did not get weirded out,' Jessie said. Her cheeks pinked.

'Come on, Louisa, that was a bit mean,' Freya said.

Louisa put her arm around her sister and hugged her close. 'Look, sis. You get the idea. Mum and Dad are getting divorced, Dad's not coming home, but we knew that anyway. Dad's with Lily now, and she seems OK. Mum's having a bit of a mid-life about it but that's OK too. Things will carry on pretty much as they are now. So no more running away. OK?'

Jessie nodded. She went over to her mum and dad and gave them both a hug. Freya wanted to keep hold of her.

'Can I go out now?' Louisa said.

'OK,' Freya said. 'You're not—'

'No, I'm not. I'm meeting Ava. I'll stick to your stupid rule. But it doesn't mean I'm OK with it. Matt isn't either, he's really upset. I know you think he's this big ogre, but he's not, he's just a normal guy who happens to be a couple of years older than me, that's all. When my exam results come out – if I haven't messed anything up too badly – can we *please* talk about it again?'

Joe looked at Louisa, and Freya could see that he was softening. She felt almost frustrated that Louisa was being so reasonable. She could see that, while Joe was officially supporting her, he thought she was being too harsh. But she wasn't going to shift on this, not yet.

Louisa tells me to switch off the TV, so I do. I always do what she says. She's way bigger than me and she has this bossy voice that you know, you're not going to mess with that.

I can hear Freya talking with Joe downstairs, and Jessie saying goodbye to him. She told me they were going to talk to her today, about the divorce, so I guess that's what they've been doing.

She said before that she doesn't want her family to be broken. But I don't think she realises for a minute how all-stuck-together it is. Whatever she says about those papers, the ones that made her want to hide, so that her dad came back — those papers aren't going to stop her parents loving her.

I can't really tell her about Mum. Not much. I tell her that I love her. But I don't talk about how unstuck it all feels, a lot of the time. How people come and go from the flat. How Cassie is there, but sometimes she's not — it's like her eyes are different and they jump around.

I can't tell Jessie how good it feels to be here in her home, to know that each day, more or less, is the same. She wouldn't understand that. She wouldn't get how much I want to stay.

But I'm still going to do it. I'm still going to tell Freya.

Because Adriana's right. I know she is. I have to be honest, even if that means I have to go.

*

Neil is searching through my bag. My chest is really tight. I'm asking him to please not go through my things. Then I'm begging him not to. But it doesn't help.

He's emptying it out now, on to the floor — my hairbrush, my powder compact, which smashes.

'I know you've got something in here. I can tell by the way your eyes are. You're using something.'

He finds the zipped pocket on the side, in the end.

It's hard to breathe now.

He holds up the pills, waves them in my face. 'I knew it,' he says. His cheeks are red, and his nostrils are flared the way they get when he's really angry. 'You said you wanted to get clean. I trusted you.'

'I do,' I say. And I mean it.

'I wanted you back. Not a scabby addict.'

That's hard to hear. I can't argue back, though.

'Who got these for you? That bitch Cassie, I bet.'

I shake my head. 'No,' I say.

He leaves the flat, slamming the door behind him. I follow him out, but he's on his motorbike already. I text Cassie, and tell her to go away for a couple of days. She doesn't need this.

Freya watched as Dino toyed with his food over lunch.

After they'd eaten, she sent Jessie up to tidy her room and took a moment with Dino, alone.

His eyes were cast down, as they were when something was on his mind. She'd come to know the little quirks of him. The way his body moved when his thoughts and worries took over.

'Are you OK, Dino? What's up?'

He bit his lip. It trembled.

'What's happened?'

'You might get angry,' he said.

Freya took a deep breath. Whatever it is, she told herself, it will be OK. 'I won't be,' she said.

'It's a big thing,' he said softly. 'A really big thing. And I promised not to tell you. I promised my mum I wouldn't say anything about it to you, or to anyone.'

A chill ran through Freya. What secret had Sam insisted on

225

her son keeping, and why? It was clear that Dino was carrying a burden that was far too heavy for him.

'I don't want to break the promise,' he said. The tears were starting to come now, first a trickle, then thick and fast. He was sobbing. Freya held him until his breath turned to gasps. 'But I don't want to lie either,' he said, his voice barely more than a whisper.

'What is it, Dino? You can tell me.'

'I'm not who you think I am,' he said, looking up at her. His eyes were pools. She wanted to bundle him up into her arms.

Freya's heart went out to him. How had he come such a short distance in life, and yet he was full of self-doubt.

He pulled away. Covered his eyes with his forearm and rubbed away the tears.

I can hear Freya and Joe talking. I'm sitting at the top of the staircase, listening. Freya said she's worried about me.

They're confused, I think. Because, when I opened my mouth to tell the whole truth, only a little bit of it came. I don't want her to be worried, but maybe it's better than me having to leave. That's what will happen if I ever say the whole truth. I always thought secrets were good things, you know, like birthday presents hidden under the bed, not things like this that could make everything fall apart.

I think of Mum now and I get this scared feeling inside. My brain is telling me that my mum isn't safe.

Freya texted Sam, messaged her, called her.

Dino hadn't told her everything, she knew that. She didn't want to pressurise him, but she needed to know the whole of it.

No answer, no reply. No answer, no reply.

Whatever Sam was doing, she thought, fury rising in her, it was clearly more important than her own son.

*

226

I come round, wake up from the half-sleep I was in with the pills. The first thing I feel is Neil's weight on me. It's like being crushed.

He's so heavy on me I feel like I can't breathe. If I don't push him off me, I think I could die like this, here in his flat, with him on me, touching me.

I feel halfway to not being here already – the time out of mind has done that. But I know I can't have this. I don't think he even notices that my eyes are open, that I'm awake now. If he notices, then he doesn't really care. I'm wearing one of his T-shirts, and a pair of boxer shorts that I took from his drawer. When he's on me like this he's not the Neil that I like to be with, the one that makes me feel good inside. I say no. I say no. No. No. Like that. Not loudly, but loud enough for him to hear.

He pushes inside me, even though I'm crying hot tears and whispering for him to stop. When he does that, he's not the man I love, but he's something I know. The pain is something I know.

As he does it, I'm back at home in Fern Bay. I'm back in my room, fifteen years old. That guy locked the door – my bedroom door – behind him. It was my house, my room, and not his – he was just a friend of my dad's. An old guy I'd met once before. It was my room, he made it his. And even though it was my body, he made it his. I feel sick thinking of it.

So Neil isn't taking anything. Not really. Because I haven't got it to give. These bones and this flesh stopped being mine a long time ago. It hurts, what he's doing – it really hurts. But more than the pain, it's that, when Neil does this, he reminds me of how it's always been.

He reminds me that nothing – not the smallest part of myself – really belongs to me at all.

That evening, Freya sat with Dino up in his room. They played Connect 4 for a while. He was in his pyjamas, and Jessie was already asleep in the next-door room.

'What you said earlier. About how you're not who I think you are.'

Dino fidgeted, and moved away from her slightly, so he was

leaning back against the bed. He seemed scared, the way he had when he'd first arrived. He nodded.

'You know you don't need to be anything other than you,' Freya said. 'I love you, Dino.'

The words just came out, and, the moment they did, she felt how true they were.

'I love you just the way you are. I love the way you jump into bed with me in the morning. I love the way you make Jessie laugh, harder than anyone else can. I love that you've taught us all these card games, and now we do that instead of watching TV. I love that you draw things from your imagination that are bigger and more beautiful than anything a famous artist could do.'

He shook his head, then put his arms up around his knees and buried his face in them. She could hear his gentle sobs. She moved closer and put her arm around him.

His words came out muffled, but she could hear them. 'That's not it. That's not what I meant.'

'What is it, then?' Freya said. 'Because we are here for you, Dino. No matter what.'

'I don't think you will be,' he said.

'I will – you have my word,' Freya said, holding his hand in hers.

'It's my mum,' Dino said. 'She's not called Sam.'

'You mean she goes by a different name now?'

Dino shook his head.

'What do you mean?' Freya said, confused, her pulse racing now.

'It's not that. It's the thing she made me promise.' He rubbed at the skin on his arm with a single finger, as if there were something he was trying to scrub away.

'You can tell me,' Freya said, prompting him gently.

'She's from here, from Fern Bay. But my mum is not your sister.'

Freya's breath caught in her chest.

What was he saying? This couldn't be happening.

'And she told you to keep that a secret?'

'Yes,' he said. 'She said it was a white lie. That it wasn't such a big thing really. She was going to be your sister, just for a while.'

Freya's head throbbed. *No.* 'What's her name, Dino?'

'I can't tell you. I'm not allowed to.'

This could not be happening.

This was not real.

Sam couldn't disappear again. No.

She wanted, with every cell in her body, for what Dino just said to be a lie. But, when she looked into his eyes, fearful and innocent, she knew that it wasn't.

Part Three

Chapter 29

Sam. Sam. Sam.

Freya was struggling to get to sleep. There was too much silence. The only sound was that single syllable reverberating in her head, the person she had lost – not once but twice. She wanted something to distract her – if Joe had been sleeping beside her, he would have reached out an arm to pull her closer in the night. She remembered how Jessie would pad-pad into the room in her pyjamas, and then clamber into bed between her and Joe, asking for a cuddle. She wouldn't have minded the disruption, not tonight. She longed for anything, anyone, that would stop her from thinking of what Dino had told her. She flicked the radio on to the World Service, but then, unable to settle with the news, she switched that off.

As she moved restlessly in bed, she pictured her sister's face. The scattering of freckles. Her intense green eyes, a faraway look that meant she always seemed half in one place, half in another. She had thought they were close – almost close enough to touch. And now that had been snatched away from her. Why would another person want to do this to her – offer the mirage of Sam, let her believe that her family, and her life, might soon regain its missing piece – and then for it all to be a lie.

Freya thought of the ups and downs she'd experienced over the years, as she'd searched for her sister. The false leads, the hopes dashed. Could this really have been just another of those? A nothing, after all, when it had seemed so much like everything?

Her heart ached. She couldn't be left like this, with a handful of nothing. She couldn't go back to the emptiness she'd carried in her before. She wanted to push back on believing. She wanted to resist it, because it didn't serve her at all. All it did was disrupt everything she wanted. She wanted, more than anything, to be given back the gentle lie that she'd soon have Sam back in her life again.

Neil goes out to work this morning; he's got some shift work as a security guard at a shop in town. We don't talk about what happened. He kisses me goodbye. I don't move my mouth back but I don't think he notices.

'We're OK,' he says. It's not a question.

It's easier for him to pretend I wanted it, and that it was normal, even though I'm pretty sure he knows it wasn't like that.

I don't want to do anything much today. Just draw the curtains. Sit in the quiet. Today isn't good, but tomorrow can be. Tomorrow will be.

Cassie texts me, asks if I want to go to hers and hang out. It's only a couple of blocks away but it feels further. Too far. I could just about get there, and then what? She'd see it, wouldn't she? She'd take one look at me, and she'd know. And I don't want that. I want to scrub it out. I tell myself again and again that maybe it didn't happen, or maybe it didn't happen like I remember it, that maybe I was more willing, or made it look like I was, so he didn't really know. The thing is, I'm glad he acted as if nothing happened, because to look at this closely cuts me so deep I can't go there. When he left without saying anything, he gave me a chance to forget it, to picture it all again, differently. To make it more right, in my head.

*

The following afternoon, when the kids were out with Jilly, Freya called Joe and asked him to come over when he was free. When he arrived, in the evening after the others had gone to bed, she filled him in on what Dino had told her – the news she had barely taken in herself.

'Dino and I talked last night. You know he'd mentioned earlier in the week that there was a secret he couldn't tell. But God, Joe, I wasn't expecting this.'

Joe's forehead creased in concern. 'What did he say?'

'That this is all a lie.'

'Sorry?'

'His mum isn't my sister. Sam isn't back. His mum is someone else altogether.'

'What? Who?'

Freya shrugged. 'I don't know. Only that she's not Sam.'

It felt both better and worse to say it out loud. She was grateful to have someone to share it with, but it brought her no closer to the truth.

'She told him not to say anything. She made her own child lie. And I don't know how to make any sense of this, Joe, I really don't. I feel sick. Now I look back, it makes sense – we mostly communicated by email ... and the one phone conversation we had, I could barely hear her, the reception was so bad. How could I have been so stupid?'

'Come on, Frey, don't be hard on yourself. How could you have known there was someone out there who would try this?'

'I guess so,' she said.

'You're sure it's true, what Dino said?'

'He's got no reason to lie. And he seems really upset about it all.'

'Have you spoken with his mum – whoever this woman is?'

'She doesn't answer the phone when I call. It just rings out.'

'So what do we do? Have you told the police?'

'No. Not yet,' Freya said. 'I think I have to get my head around it first. Why would anyone *do* this? I just feel so confused. Those emails – there were details in there that sounded so much like her . . .'

'Maybe whoever it is did their homework,' Joe said, softly.

'I was clutching at straws, wasn't I? Seeing what I wanted to see? I've wanted to find Sam so badly—' Freya's voice caught.

Joe drew her in close to him, the way he had when they were still together. He held her for a while, neither of them speaking.

She wanted to cry. Wanted to feel some kind of release, not just this emotion balled tight inside her.

'I just wanted to believe she was coming back,' she said.

Letting go of hope – it was like her own soul leaving her body. She longed to be full of dreams again, but the longer they stayed in her, the more bruised and damaged they became.

'I know how badly you wanted her back,' Joe said, softly. 'I know.'

Freya drew on all her strength, and pulled back, composing herself. 'I have to forget about it now, though, don't I? Forget about all of it, and just think about Dino.'

Joe nodded. 'I'm with you, Freya. I'm right here with you, whatever happens. Where do we start?'

'We have to find out who he is,' she said, the resolve firming up in her. 'And where he's come from.'

Freya dialled the number she had for Sam. For Sam or – that bitter sediment in her stomach – whoever it was who was pretending to be her.

She imagined for a fleeting moment that her sister might pick up. That all of what Dino had said could prove to be a misunderstanding. A mistake. But the tone rang out, and her heart sank.

It rang just as it had every other time. It rang and rang, and gave nothing away.

Freya needed Sam to be there. She needed to believe that there wasn't someone out there who could do this terrible thing – toy with her feelings, and her family's feelings. That there wasn't a mother out there capable of this lie – and of leaving their own child to be cared for by strangers. If Sam picks up, she bargained with a God she'd never previously believed in, I will do anything. She didn't care how much help her sister needed – she would be there for her. Give her everything she could possibly need.

She hung up the phone. It had rung too long.

She remembered again what Dino had said. *My mum is not your sister.*

She hadn't always trusted him. But now, just when he was telling her not to, she realised she trusted him to his very bones.

And what reason on earth would he have to lie?

She sent an email, to the address she'd always thought was Sam's.

Hi, she wrote. No name. Whoever you are, you're not Sam, she thought. *Hi. I know you're not my sister.* I feel so much in the dark I can't see my own hands in front on my face. *I need to see you. We need to talk.*

Gently, slowly, she would get to the truth, and she saw now that if she went in too hard, too quickly, it might slip out of her grasp for ever. She needed to know what was happening – who had been messing with her, and why. But, more than all of that, she needed to know how to take Dino back to where he'd come from, and where he belonged.

I read the email from Freya.
    Dino's said something, he must have.
    She's worked it out.
    No. No. No. No.

237

I'm not ready. My breath is getting all fast. Neil asks me what I'm panicking about.

I guess Dino couldn't lie any more. My boy was always too good. Too good for any of this.

I don't know where to start explaining. And I don't want to. Not to Neil. Not after what he did to me.

I know I need to find a way to leave Neil. But whenever I build up a bit of strength it all seems to go again. It's just like it was last time.

I don't want Dino here. I don't want him to see this, or to see me like this. But I know how bad it got last time I left.

A message came through on Freya's phone.

Freya. I know you don't owe me anything – but could you just keep Dino with you until the weekend? We can meet then, and talk. I'll explain.

Freya bit back her frustration. This woman – whoever she was – was talking about Dino as if he were a dog that needed homing. She wrote back.

Dino will be safe here with me.

It wasn't a hard thing to promise. There was no way she was going to send Dino back to a complete unknown.

But we can't go on like this. I'm going to speak to Social Services, and the police – this has gone too far now and Dino needs proper support.

The reply came back almost immediately.

Please don't. Please, Freya. Just meet with me. We can make a decision after that. But please meet with me first. Give me a chance to explain.

Freya breathed deep and tried to keep her calm.

Who are you?

Fury welled up in her.

And why have you done this to us?

She saw the three typing dots appear and disappear, once, twice, three times. She began to wonder if any message would come at all.

I did it because I had to.

Freya bristled. *I find it hard to believe that.*

Let me explain. Give me one chance.

Freya thought about stopping there. Getting on the phone to the police and putting an end to all of this. But something stopped her. The boy who was upstairs, singing softly to himself.

OK, but I'm doing this for Dino, she typed. *Not for you.*

I get that. You're a good person. Come to Margate and I'll meet you at the station – Saturday, 11?

Freya shook her head. This didn't feel right, but she was beginning to accept she had no alternative.

OK. One chance. I'll be there.

She put her phone down. In two days, she might have some answers. The ones she needed so badly. Two more days in this limbo of not knowing, but two days that would ultimately lead her to the truth.

She would go to Margate again, and this time she'd be meeting a real person, not chasing an illusion. She didn't want to do this, but she needed to.

She opened the back door and sat on the doorstep, looking out at the garden. It was close to midnight, and dark, but the moon and stars were bright in the sky, like the drawings in a children's book. She remembered other nights like this, during the summer that Sam went missing. How it had felt to lose herself on nights like this. Then how it had felt to lose Sam.

Her thought escaped as a whisper, lifting up and out into the night air.

'Sam, if that wasn't you, where are you?'

Chapter 30

There were times in Freya's life when two days might have flown by, in a whirl of school runs and work emails and rushed dinners – but now the hours stretched out in front of her. They meant living in a limbo where she would know nothing more about what had brought Dino to her, and his future would hang, uncertain, unspoken about, in the air between them.

Freya had to find a focus, and that focus became filling the days for the children. None of this was Dino's fault, and he shouldn't be the one to suffer – keeping him distracted and entertained was her mission. Once she had that, her determination grew, and shifted away from her own gnawing loss.

She tried hard to not see Dino differently now, but something in the energy of the house had already shifted. There was a boy living with them, and he wasn't her nephew, or any relation to any of them. He wasn't a bridge to her sister, and he never had been. She didn't know who his parents were, or anything else about him. He was a mystery to her, and to all of them. They didn't know what had happened to him in his life, and in what ways he might have been affected by those events.

As she saw it, Freya had no option but to tolerate that uncertainty. But her mind was full of questions. Who was Dino's mother, and why had she chosen Freya? She found she couldn't focus too much on the questions or her head would start to spin. Because the one certainty that she did have was that none of it had been his choice, and none of it was his fault.

Freya was going to fix this the way she always fixed things: by trying to control the things that she could.

'We're going on a trip today,' she announced over breakfast.

Louisa shook her head. 'No, thanks,' she said. She was still trying to punish Freya for the fact she wasn't allowed to see Matt. Freya felt it in each small distance Louisa created. It saddened her, but it did nothing to dent her resolve.

'All right,' she said. 'I guess that's your choice.'

'That's right,' Louisa said, coldly.

Freya turned to look at Jessie and Dino. 'Anyway, we, kids, are going to have an amazing time.'

Jessie smiled. Dino looked at her at if he couldn't quite believe he still had a place at their table, let alone that he was included in a family trip. That tugged at her heart, because even she couldn't promise how long that would last. But until she was able to meet with Dino's mother, and find out what was really going on, she would care for him just as she always had. Dino would be a member of their family, just like before. She would not let him feel that he was anything less. Whatever the circumstances were in which he'd arrived with them, they were not of his choosing.

They got the train up to London. They spent the day at the Science Museum – Dino and Jessie ran free inside the Wonderlab upstairs, watching magnetic fluids move, lifting pulleys and weights, and learning about electricity. They went in to see a show about explosions, and both jumped like children far younger than they were when one of the bombs made there exploded. Here, in this new and different place, the things that weighed so heavy in their lives seemed almost to disappear. Here – in this world of forces, of electricity, of planets, of moons – there was no time to think about the everyday or the earthly, however big, however painful. Freya gave in to the perpetual motion of the children as they ran between exhibits, ducking in and out of the small rooms. She let herself be caught up in the way they embraced the present, and found she was able to do the same.

It had been a long, long, time since she'd really done that. And now, just when everything seemed messier than it had ever been, she found she was able to. All of it mattered. It mattered hugely how her girls coped with their father's new relationship, and the divorce. It meant everything that Dino was safe, and could have the future that he deserved.

But this – the here and now, the laughter that Jessie and Dino let out, and shared as they ran with abandon – she got a glimpse of it – so bright and sudden – a certainty that somehow – somehow – there was a future that was right for all of them. And that together they could step out into it.

Back at home, Freya sat on the sofa, with Jessie curled up on one side of her and Dino on the other, all of them tired out from the day. Freya reached out and held Dino's hand in hers, felt the warmth of it. She brought him in closer to her. Who was this boy, who'd made his way so fully into her heart? Sometimes it bothered her so much, the strangeness of it, a child under her roof, with origins she knew nothing about. But then at times like this she felt the quiet beating of his heart against her side, and she knew it didn't matter. That this love could not be undone.

I'm with Freya and Jessie and we're watching Cat in the Hat. *When the adventure song comes on, the one they have in each episode, we all sing, and*

242

Jessie gets all the words right, but it's so quick that me and Freya stumble over them all and maybe get half between us. Freya laughs and normally I do but not today. I don't know, I feel weird. Even when Freya holds me close, which feels really nice, I don't know. And part of me wants to pull away and shout and I worry that maybe I could even hit again. Because why am I here still, really? It must only be because my mum doesn't want me back. So Freya has to keep me here. And I love Freya and Jessie and even Louisa mostly but I hate this. I hate never belonging anywhere. And not having a home.

Jessie had fallen asleep on the sofa, and Freya took her gently upstairs and lifted her into bed. Then she took her time with Dino, sitting and chatting with him as he sat in the bath, and letting him choose his favourite chapters to read at bedtime.

'I didn't mean to lie,' Dino said.

'I know,' Freya said. 'I know that, Dino.'

'I didn't want to come. I didn't know about your sister, that she'd been missing so long—'

The rims of his eyes were red, and tears started to well in the lower lids.

Inside, Freya broke. Dino had to understand that he wasn't responsible for any of this: the tangle that Sam had left, and which Dino's mum had stepped into; the tangle of her own conflicted feelings. If anyone was a true victim in this, it was this boy.

She reached out to him and brought him close to her. His tears came, and soaked into the shoulder of her T-shirt. She would keep soaking them up. She would be here for his sorrow until every last drop was out. Because he trusted her – and nothing was more important than that.

That evening, as Freya got into bed, she told herself she'd done the best she could. That day might not have fixed everything, but it had brought her back to what mattered most. Jessie had enjoyed herself and Dino, she hoped, had felt part of things. She longed to be able to give him promises. He deserved them. He should know who would be there for him, as he grew older, and where, truly, he could call home. She felt a quiet fury at the woman who had deprived him of those certainties, and who had lied to Freya herself. But anger was not going to help her here. She needed to convert that anger into determination. And she had a mission.

Tomorrow she would meet Dino's mother, find out who she was and why she had done this thing that had churned up the earth beneath her feet so that she could barely stand any more. She couldn't fix this, but she would get Dino the promises he deserved.

As she drove to Margate, Freya kept picturing Sam's face. The last time she'd travelled this route, she'd had in her heart the hope that she would find her sister. She'd been so sure that the clue she'd been given was enough to reunite her with Sam after eighteen years. Now, that was gone. She had to let go of finding Sam.

Jilly had taken Dino and Jessie to the park that morning, and they were going to the cinema in the afternoon. It was easier that Dino didn't know where Freya was going today, or why. She'd had enough of false promises, and she had the feeling he'd also had more than his fair share.

She walked from the car park over to Margate station, the place they'd agreed to meet. Freya scanned the entrance. She was, out of habit, still half-looking for her sister – that pale pink hair, the army jacket. She had to remind herself that it was another woman she was here to meet today, someone who might be a complete stranger. The area was busy with passengers who'd just disembarked, and Freya watched as the people thinned out. She felt suddenly foolish and vulnerable. She didn't even know who to look for – she had no idea who she was here to meet. Control. She'd kept such a tight grip on it over the years. It had been everything to her, to know that her life, her children, her house, were something she had a modicum of power over. That – like everything else, it felt like – was far away now.

Freya saw a woman waiting on a bench near the entrance, and instinct led her to make her way over. The woman had long, dark blonde hair up in a top knot and was wearing a big knitted jumper and tie-dye trousers. As she got nearer, Freya felt a prickle of recognition. She knew this woman, from a different time. The dark eyebrows, the nose ring. The defiant stare.

Echo's face was familiar to her – distantly, from that summer, from the few times they'd met at the house when Sam had brought her friends around. The two women – Sam and Echo – diverged in Freya's mind, became the separate people they'd always, of course, been. Freya couldn't see now how they'd ever become merged in her mind. She regretted letting hope lead her as far as it had.

'It's you,' Freya said.

'Yes, I guess it is,' Echo said, shrugging her shoulders. As if it meant nothing, who she was, and what she'd done. As if she wasn't the person who'd made this all happen – created a story and sucked Freya right into it.

Echo. The friend Sam had made that summer, and one of the girls who'd seemed to take her sister away. She hadn't liked Echo much then, and she was even less inclined to like her now. She had behaved ruthlessly. She'd lied to all of them, and, worse still, got her son to do the same.

Of course Echo would know the details of Fern Bay, she'd grown up there too. Freya's mind flicked back over their previous conversations, tied up the threads. Echo had known things about Sam's life, even what sweets she liked best, because she'd been close to it, part of it.

Sam was gone. The sister she'd imagined was nothing but a shadow.

There was still one thing that made no sense at all. The question that caused her blood to run hot. *Why?*

Why would Echo do this to her? To her own son? To Jilly? Why would she tear up their whole lives, knowing the pain it would cause?

Freya took a deep breath and buried her hands in her coat pockets. 'I'm freezing. Shall we go and find somewhere we can get tea?'

In the beachside café where they were sitting, Echo's hands were shaking as she got out a packet of rolling tobacco and cigarette papers. Freya saw how she had changed – the wrinkles around her eyes, her pale, washed-out skin. But it was more than that: there was a weariness in her that made it seem as if more years had passed than really had. She didn't seem to carry a trace of the wild energy she'd had as a teenager.

Echo looked up at her. 'You can't think much of me, doing what I did.'

'I'm struggling to understand it,' Freya said.

Her anger sat in the pit of her stomach, an unwelcome companion. She longed to let it out – to shout, to rage at Echo for doing what she'd done – for lying, for giving her false hope. But she couldn't. When Sam left she'd learned how to make herself numb, to keep everything in, and she realised she couldn't now undo it. She feared that if she let anything out, any part of that feeling, everything messy inside her would come tumbling out. All of the hurt and the fear, and the pain and the loss.

She stopped herself, kept calm, and told herself it was for Dino's sake, when perhaps it was more for her own.

Echo pulled up her hood and focused on rolling her cigarette. 'I know it was shit, what I did. You don't need to say it. If you hate me, I get it. I'd hate me.'

Freya thought about it. It wasn't hate, exactly. But something close to it.

'I did this for Dino, though,' she said. 'Not for me.' Her gaze flicked back to Freya, her eyes a piercing blue. 'I needed to get myself sorted. It was no good for him, like this.'

Freya took a breath, tried to stay calm. 'Couldn't you have taken a normal route to get help, rather than drag me into all this?'

Echo shook her head and laughed wryly. 'Maybe in your life that kind of thing would work out well,' she said. 'But in mine? No way.'

'Why not?'

'Are you kidding?' she said. 'What, you think if I went to my GP it wouldn't set any alarm bells ringing? You think they'd just help, and let me keep Dino?' She shook her head. 'I couldn't do that. I wanted to get myself clean – because it doesn't feel like anyone else's business but mine how I sort my family out. I just wanted to do that, then get Dino back when I was ready to be a better mum to him again.'

Freya tried to put herself in Echo's position. 'I can see that, I suppose. But what about your own family, friends – people Dino knows? Couldn't anyone else have taken him in?'

'Most of my friends here are as messed-up as me. I've got Cassie, and she's a good friend, don't get me wrong. But she's not someone you can rely on, week after week, you know. She's quicker off the rails than me, most of the time.'

'What about Dino's dad?'

'Nah,' Echo said. As if it didn't matter, was just a well-worn story she had to tell from time to time. 'We just hooked up once, when I was living in London. When I found out I was pregnant, I left. He gave me Dino and that's all. It would never have worked out.'

'And your family?'

She laughed. 'It's just my dad, and we're not in contact.'

In spite of herself, Freya realised she felt sorry for Echo – but her sympathy remained mixed with anger. 'Why did you have to lie to us, though? Couldn't you just have asked? Come to us – told us the truth . . . ?'

Echo raised an eyebrow. 'Me? You would have said yes, would you?'

Freya saw it now: the truth in all its ugliness, and judgement, and bitterness. It was difficult to think about, but she would have said no. She wouldn't have made space in her life for Dino, for another woman's child, let alone one she barely knew.

If it had happened that way, she would have missed out on knowing Dino, missed out on meeting this young person who had made her see the world in a different way.

'You're right,' Freya admitted. 'I never would have taken him in.'

'You get it now?' Echo licked the Rizla and twirled up the cigarette, putting it to one side.

'I suppose. Which, for the record, is not the same as thinking that what you did was OK.'

'I only wanted the best for Dino, I swear,' Echo said. Her forehead was creased, and it was clear none of this was easy for her. 'It made sense at the time.'

'And now?'

'It seems a bit messy.'

'You could say that,' Freya said, shaking her head at the understatement.

As much as Freya didn't want to push on with the questions, she had to – she wouldn't get all the answers she needed, but she had at least to get some.

'But why me?' Freya said. Fury and confusion rose in her.

'Why, of all the people you could have dragged into your life, did you choose me?'

'I left town the same night as Sam. I'm guessing you didn't know that.'

Freya shook her head. Why hadn't she realised? Why hadn't she heard?

'The thing is, when you're from my side of town, no one reports you missing. I'm pretty sure my dad was glad to see the back of me.'

Freya raised her eyebrows, involuntarily.

'You can't even comprehend it, can you? Lucky you.'

Freya felt frustrated, and bristled at the comment. Echo was the one who had lied, not her; Echo was the one who had let Dino down – and now the bitterness was coming her way.

Echo lifted her left sleeve with her other hand, revealing a tattoo on her forearm. A bluebird, blurred at the edges like an inked drawing left out in the rain. It was Sam's tattoo.

Freya squinted, confused. 'Why – how?'

'We got them together, Sam and me.'

'OK,' Freya said, taking it in.

'We did it to show we were serious. We were going to leave – together. Make a new start.'

Freya's chest felt tight. This – this was what her sister had been doing? 'You and Sam were both running away?'

'Yep. She said it was the only way she'd do it. She didn't want to come out in Fern Bay. Couldn't handle the thought of what your parents would say. What other people would say.'

Freya's head started to spin. 'You were . . . '

'We were together,' Echo said, with a shrug. 'I loved Sam. We were going to do this together.'

So that was it. Or part of it. Why Sam had always been pulling away, why she'd always insisted she was different, that she couldn't fit in as she was. Freya wished she had opened up. She could have been there for Sam, showed her that it didn't matter, that she was loved for whoever she was, whoever she loved. Her parents might have struggled to accept Sam's feelings, but Freya would have been right there beside her sister, supporting her until they did.

A thought niggled at Freya, something that didn't add up.

'But—' Freya thought of Eliot. Of the story she'd always had in her mind.

She thought of the scene, the night Sam left, how shifty Sam had seemed. Freya had always thought Sam was interested in Eliot, but now, as she scanned back through the memories, she could see that that was nothing more than a useful cover for what she had really felt about Echo. That night, Sam must have been worried that Eliot had worked it out – what was going on with her and Echo, and maybe even their plan to leave together. It was that which must have spooked her – not Freya's betrayal with Eliot.

'I went to meet her that night, drove home to get my bags, then came back to meet at the crossroads like we'd agreed – only my car broke down on the way. It was this crappy old Golf, really unreliable. I called Sam's phone but there was no answer. I left the car and walked up to the crossroads, to meet her on foot. But she wasn't there. Must have walked on to the train station. Changed her mind about us.'

'Why did you never say anything?' Freya said. 'To us, to the police? Something might have helped . . .'

'I just wanted to get out of there. Away from the hurt. We'd planned to come here, to Margate, but when Sam didn't show I couldn't face being here without her. I went to London instead. Then, ten years later, I felt the pull here. The pull towards Sam. The same thing that made me think of you, when I needed somewhere for Dino.'

It made a curious kind of sense, Echo finding her way back to their family.

'OK, I get that you were hurt. But do you have any *idea* what you've put us through? We thought we'd found Sam again! What you did was so selfish—' A lump formed in Freya's throat. She didn't want to cry. Not here. Not now.

Echo's eyes glazed over, as if she was shutting down.

'I thought I was talking to *my sister*,' Freya said, trying to reach her. Recalling it now, she felt raw. 'Can you imagine how it felt to have that taken away from me? I knew it wasn't going to be easy, but I genuinely thought that it was only a matter of time until I'd be with Sam again. And then – *poof* – it's gone. All an illusion. You broke our hearts all over again, Echo. Not just mine – my family's too.'

Echo looked down at the table. She scratched at it with a short, red-painted nail. She shrugged her shoulders. 'That must've been pretty bad,' she said. 'I didn't really think about that part of it. I don't know. I just ... I still miss her.'

'OK,' Freya said. On that level, if on no other, she could empathise with Echo. 'So that's why you got in touch with us.'

'Maybe,' she said. 'I don't know. I needed to reconnect with her. The memory of her. And being with Sam, being in your family home, Freya – that was the safest I've ever felt.'

Freya saw something change in Echo's eyes when she talked about Sam. There was a place she went to. Maybe it was the same place Freya herself went to. A place where Sam was still there – talking, moving, dancing, arguing. A place that was the only trace left of what had once been, when Sam was with them.

'I wanted Dino to feel that way too.'

Freya softened at the thought of him. She hoped that, even in all the mess of this, she had helped him to feel safe, for a while.

251

'Do you think you could have made it, you and Sam?' Freya asked.

Echo shrugged. 'I wanted it more than I've ever wanted anything. But I don't know. She never turned up. Maybe Sam never really wanted to come. Maybe the only person she was ever really in love with was the wind.'

It wasn't just that we didn't fit in, in Fern Bay, though of course that was part of it. Sam had always had a hunger for life – to get out of that place, to see the world. I told her we'd do it together.

She'd had enough of fighting with her dad – and she was sure if she came out to him he'd never accept it. She'd always known she was different, she told me. But it wasn't until she met me that she realised why.

I know Sam's parents thought I was a bad influence, that we all were, and I can tell Freya still thinks that – we believe what we want to. But Sam was the one to get me into drugs, not the other way around. When we were in that shop in town, she was the one who told me to put those designer sunglasses on my head and walk on out.

Freya's not perfect either. I guessed about her and Eliot, even if Sam never worked it out – she wasn't so pure after all. I'm not judging her – nothing is black and white – but if Sam's parents thought that either of their daughters were perfect, they were wrong.

The only person who ever loved me was Sam. Or at least that was what she told me. She told me she'd always love me. I wanted that to be true. Maybe we all believe what we want to.

Freya and Echo walked together through the back streets of Margate, away from the seafront and past the vintage shops and independent cafés in the Old Town, on the pavements where litter swirled around their feet. Closer to the train station, there were bingo halls and arcades, and a man walked past them, barefoot and bare-chested in the cold evening. Freya was out of her comfort zone, and she felt that – was embarrassed by it. They got to a road with a few large Victorian houses that looked like sheltered accommodation. Halfway houses, between there and here, wherever those two places were.

'Here we are,' Echo said, glancing up at a flat.

'This is you?' Freya asked. She noticed a man moving around in the front room.

'Yep,' Echo said. Her face seemed to cloud over.

Freya waited to see if she'd say anything more, maybe something about who the man was – whether he lived with her or not. But she didn't elaborate, and Freya knew better than to push.

'It's not for ever. Just until I get back in the old flat. The one I was living in with Dino, before the fire. The landlord's useless, but I've cleaned most of it up now, and Cassie's working on getting us some new furniture to replace the broken bits.'

They'd reached the end of their time together, of the day here. Freya couldn't put it off any longer. The reason she'd come. The reason they were both here.

'So, where do we go from here?' Freya asked.

Echo stayed silent, bit her lip.

'What do we do about your son?'

Echo looked at her at last, and shrugged. Her shoulders fell back into a slump. Every part of her seemed heavy, and sad.

'Are you off the drugs?' Freya asked.

Echo nodded. 'Yep. No going back now. No way.'

Freya tried to read her. Her eyes gave nothing away. They were calm, or weary, Freya couldn't tell. It was as if Echo couldn't quite be reached. Freya wanted to believe that her words were the truth.

'And would you be living here – with . . . ' Freya felt compelled to ask about the man she could see up in the flat.

'No, we'll be back at home. We'll go back home.'

'OK,' Freya said. Who was she, really, to keep Dino from his mother? No one. Echo had asked for a chance to get herself clean, and she'd done it. Her love for her son was obvious.

'I want Dino to come back here,' Echo said. 'I want him to live with me again.'

Freya got back home and put her bag down in the hall. Her mum had the kids, so her own house was empty. Freya didn't relish the prospect of telling her mother, then Jessie and Louisa, that Dino was not the blood relative they'd all believed him to be.

She'd done what she'd set out to do – she'd met Dino's mother, the woman who'd brought her into all of this. She knew who she was dealing with now – and together they'd made a decision. Dino would return to Echo, and Freya would let him go, and draw a line under this summer. Dino would go home, to his own family, and that had to be a good thing.

Her conscience nagged. Something didn't feel right. She should call Social Services – get them to check things out. Be sure that everything was OK. She thought of the figure she'd seen up in the flat. Echo had mentioned nothing about him at all.

If she called Social Services now, there would be no going back. Her call might cause Echo to be separated from her child for good. Was that the right thing?

The right thing, surely, had to be to help Dino get home.

I go back into the flat, and Neil's doing something in the kitchen. Cooking himself dinner, or making something for us, maybe – I'm not sure, but there's some banging of pots and pans that makes me not want to go in there. I don't know how his day has been, and it helps if I can get a sense of that. I'm not going in there just yet.

I close the door behind me, as quietly as I can. It clicks though, and he hears it and comes out.

When he looks at me, that intense look, I know that he's not had a good day. Someone has crossed him, or let him down. Something has gone wrong for him. Maybe I left the flat in a mess, I can't remember. I would've known better than to do that – but I was distracted this morning, knowing I was going to meet Freya.

My heart starts to race. I must have left a dirty plate out, or done one of the other things that he's told me he's tired of.

'Where have you been?' he says.

OK, what I've done is far worse, really, than leaving plates out on the counter, and I should know that by now. The panicky feeling starts up, in my chest.

I can't tell him about Freya. I can't tell him about what I've done. This mess I've created.

'Who have you been with?' he asks.

I don't know what to say, and I wait a minute too long.

Chapter 31

Freya sat with Dino in the garden. She thought of her mother's face as she'd broken the news to her, that the boy she'd thought was her grandson was no relation to her at all. Her face had taken on another layer of pain, and there was nothing that Freya could do about it. Louisa and Jessie, by contrast, had been confused, but accepting.

Dino was poking gently at the earth in the flowerbeds with a stick, and after a while a small frog hopped up. Dino smiled, and watched him hop under a nearby stone.

'Dino, love. You know how I met your mum, yesterday?' Freya said.

'Yep,' he said. He nudged at the earth again, his eyes fixed on the ground.

'She misses you very much,' Freya said.

'Good,' he said. There was a deep sadness in his voice. 'Is she OK?'

'She's OK.'

This was the part when she would tell him he was going back home. So why didn't she feel better about it?

She swallowed down her doubts. She had made a promise to Echo, and she would stick to it.

'She wants you to come home.'

He looked up at her, his eyes wide. 'That's what she said?'

Freya smiled. 'Yes, that's what she said.'

'When can I go?'

'Any time you like.'

He paused. His gaze returned to the ground.

'Do you want me to help you to pack?'

He nodded.

They went upstairs to his bedroom, and Freya watched as Dino packed up the handful of belongings that he'd arrived with.

Freya knew they had to take him back home. They had no claim over him; she had no right to try and keep him in their lives just because he had come to fit so well. He was far too young to understand the choice for himself and, with a mother out there who would love and care for him, Freya had no place trying to keep him in her own home and family.

He looked happy to be going back and that was what mattered. Freya felt as if she hadn't done enough for him. But when she saw him gathering up the dreamcatcher and some of the clothes she had picked out for him when he'd arrived, she reassured herself that she might not have done enough, but she had done something.

'I think I've got everything now,' Dino said.

'OK,' Freya said, swallowing back her sadness and trying to seem strong. 'Right. Let's go and say goodbye to the girls, then.'

Louisa hugged Dino goodbye, and gave him a long, hard squeeze. Jessie put some books into his bag, the *Faraway Tree* ones Freya had read to them both. 'One more thing,' Jessie said, going up to her room. She returned and gave him the Tigger toy he'd taken to sleeping with. 'This is yours now. You can keep it and remember us all.'

A lump came to Freya's throat as she saw the sadness in Jessie's eyes. 'Was there anything else you wanted to do before we go?' she asked him.

'Just one thing,' Dino said, his voice barely a whisper.

'Sure, what?'

'Can I say goodbye to my friend?' Dino said.

'Your friend?' Freya said, curious.

'Adriana.'

'*Adriana?*' Freya said. 'The woman on the corner? Do you really mean her?'

'Yes,' he said.

'What ... how?'

'I used to go there sometimes. Play dominoes with her. Cards sometimes.'

'Did you? When?'

'Er, Mum,' Louisa said, 'I think I can explain this one.'

'OK,' Freya said. 'Well, I'm certainly confused. But if you're friends then of course we should go and say goodbye to her.'

'We are,' Dino said. 'She told me to tell you the truth about my mum.'

'So you told her you weren't my nephew?'

Dino shook his head. 'I didn't have to.'

'What do you mean?'

He shrugged. 'She already knew.'

Chapter 32

The moon's lighting the road in front of me. I'm walking now, not running any more, and my rucksack feels heavier on my back. I have my headphones in and I'm listening to the White Stripes. I'll keep walking, a bit further. I don't get why Echo wasn't there at the crossroads. I've called her, and nothing. She's changed her mind, and it hurts so badly. The adrenaline's still coursing so I can keep going – but I'm starting to wish we'd decided to do it in the daytime now. It feels really quiet out here. Really quiet.

I'll find somewhere to crash until it's morning and I can get a train out of town, then another, further down the coast. I want to stay by the sea even when I'm far away from here. They are in my blood, these tidal ebbs and flows. The sea's the only part of Fern Bay that I really want to keep in my life.

Then the rain starts. It's the weirdest thing. That warm summer rain that seems to come out of nowhere. Days and days of no rain at all, and then, now, just when I need it not to, the weather breaks.

It's just drizzle at first, but quickly it gets heavier. My hoodie and my jeans are soaked through in a matter of minutes, and my backpack must be just as wet. I wonder if anything will be left dry inside. A car comes by, and another, the headlights bright in the dark night. I regret not asking Echo to come to the house now. I just want to see her, be with her. Why wasn't she at the crossroads where we said we would meet? I waited ages.

Then I see it. Headlights. Echo's car. My heart lifts.

It's raining so hard I can't see clearly. My eyes are blurry. I run towards the car.

The doorbell rang. So this is it, Freya thought. She gave Dino another hug, and together they went to open the front door.

Echo was there on the doorstep, a Transformer clutched in her hand. 'Hey, Dino,' she said. 'Hello, you.' She holds out her arms and crouches down, so that when he goes to her, and hugs her back, she can feel the whole of him.

'I brought you this one,' she said, passing him the toy. 'Figured you might be glad to see it again. It's been a while since you've had a chance to play with it.'

She smiled at him, an awkward smile, but Freya could see she was happy to see him again. Echo looked tired. She reached up and touched Dino's face, running a finger over his cheek. 'It's good to see you again.'

Freya passed Echo the bags, and then she stood back.

Jessie and Louisa went up to Dino and said their goodbyes again, tears in their eyes. 'Stay in touch,' Louisa said. Jessie pressed a bunch of her favourite scented erasers into the palm of his hand, and closed his fingers over them.

This was the right way for this to end, Freya thought. Dino was back where he belonged, in time for school to start again. Echo was in a better place, ready to care for him properly this time. Her girls had seen what it was to love someone new, and so had she. She could get back to work, and normality. This was what moving on felt like.

'Thank you,' Echo said. She was calm, appropriate. She seemed together enough. 'Thank you for everything, Freya.'

Freya nodded, so that she wouldn't cry. She touched Dino's shoulder one last time, and they shared a smile. It was time to let go.

Adriana had promised herself that if the boy told the truth, she would too.

It's time. This morning, she puts on a white blouse and a tweed knee-length skirt. She finds the matching jacket, and takes it off its hanger, ready to take downstairs with her. She glances at the rucksack at the bottom of her wardrobe. It's been there a long time. She checks her hair in the mirror and tidies some loose strands – the grey hairs are more unruly than when it was brown, decades ago. She checks her low-heeled shoes and finds a scuff. She gets out the shoe polish, makes it right, and then puts them on.

She takes a deep breath as she opens the door. There's no one around in the cul-de-sac, and she feels glad of that. She walks down her path, past the empty driveway. It'll be a good twenty-minute walk, but she can do it. She sets off along the A-road, towards town, and listens out for the birds in the woodland. She can recognise the calls of the wood pigeon, the blackbirds, the coal tits. Those woods are dense with wildlife, under the tree canopy. She used to walk in them every day, back when she and Graham had Bisto, their terrier. It's been years since she's gone in there, but she knows she'll be back later today, to do just that.

As she arrives in town, she sees from the clock tower that it's taken her exactly fifteen minutes, so her pace was a little brisker than she'd estimated. It feels like a small victory for her, today. She glances over at the post office, the library, the places she would normally go. She crosses the square instead, and walks up some stone steps into a building she's never set foot in before.

She walks up to the counter, adrenaline powering her on.

'Good morning,' Adriana says, to the police officer manning the desk. 'I've got something I need to tell you.'

Chapter 33

We're back in Margate. Mum brought Pokémon Top Trumps for the journey, and we played almost the whole way. She also brought a lot of snacks – popcorn, peanut M&Ms, Haribo.

When we come out the station I turn towards our flat, but she takes my hand and tugs it to show we're going in another direction.

'I've been living with Neil,' she says.

I get a heavy feeling in my stomach. I knew she might still be with him, but I didn't think we'd be in his flat.

'It'll just be for a couple of nights. Please, love. Then we'll go back to ours.'

'Can I go to Cassie's?' I ask, because I really don't want to see Neil. I don't want to hear the shouting. I don't want it.

Her face gets really sad then. 'You want to go to Cassie's?'

I try to say that it's not that I don't want to be with her, it's just that Neil gives me this weird feeling.

'It's OK,' she says, with a little nod. 'I get it. I'll call Cassie.'

Jilly opened her front door to find a police officer on her doorstep. Freya sent Jessie upstairs to play, saying that she and Jilly needed to talk to the policeman alone. As Freya did so, her palms gathered sweat. Something was happening. She could feel it.

This wasn't like the other times the police had checked in with them – she could see that much from the policeman's face. She went into the living room, where her mum was seated with the policeman. It was an older man, one whom Freya vaguely recognised.

'We've had some new information about Samantha,' he said.

Jilly grasped her daughter's hand and held it. Freya felt the prickle of goosebumps rising on her arms. This wasn't nothing.

It's over now. Adriana's done it. She doesn't know if she'll stop reliving that night over and over now. She accepts that probably those thoughts will always be there, and will always haunt her. That is her burden, and that's OK – it's no more than she deserves. In this, the winter of her life, everything good has gone, and all she can do is deliver truth. She can seek peace, but she cannot expect it.

In her mind's eye, she can still see the girl running towards her in the rain – right in the middle of the road. She can make her out through the rain on the windscreen, and she remembers the shock of it.

It was just a flash of her and then the bang, the shudder, of her body hitting the bonnet of the car. The flash of her face, then the back of her head as she flipped and it hit the windscreen. The blood. A lot of blood.

Adriana had stopped the car. She tells herself now, as she has for the past eighteen years, that she could have just kept on driving – some people might have done. She might never have checked what had happened to that girl and whether she could have done anything to change how things turned out.

But she did stop.

It wasn't until she got out that she saw that it was the younger of the Jackson girls, Samantha. There was blood matted in her pink hair, and on most of her face. Just a young woman, she could have seen that from her hands, if she hadn't already known. The blood from her head was pooling in the road.

If they'd both had luck on their side that night, things could have turned out differently. Adriana stopping the car and checking on Samantha might have been enough to save her life. If there'd been more breath in that girl's body still, then she could have helped her. She would have done all the right things. Adriana had been a nurse, once. She'd have been able to do certain things, to buy Samantha time. And then she would have taken her to hospital, called her parents – the Jacksons, Jilly and Harry, were known by everyone in Fern Bay – and stayed in the hospital waiting room until they all got the news that Samantha was going to be OK.

If things had gone that way, then Adriana could have gone back home, returned to her crafting, to looking after her roses. Her house would be tidier now, not a mess of papers and boxes that never properly covered the secret. When they'd first started looking for Samantha Jackson, she'd kept her curtains shut. But she'd still heard the whispers. That Samantha had always been running away. That since she was a teenager she'd been running away. Adriana couldn't help thinking – if only Samantha hadn't run away that night, putting herself at risk, everything would be fine.

Why you'd want to run away from a family like the Jacksons was something she'd never understand. They had a whole lot more than she'd ever had growing up. Some people weren't ever satisfied.

It makes Adriana feel sick to her stomach to remember the details of that night, but the police say she has to. The police officers make her rake through every second of it in that stuffy room. It feels undignified, sitting there, with the stupid, cold polystyrene cup of tea. The tea's no good. She knows she's chosen to be there, but it's too much really, for anyone.

It all sounds so ugly, when she says it out loud. They use words she wouldn't choose. They talk about her 'dragging' Samantha's body. Adriana was trying to lift her, do it in a way that was dignified, but the girl was too heavy. She was trying to get her to a place where the ground would be softer. Because she could see that life was drifting out of her, really quickly, and she didn't want it all to float away right there, on the A-road out of Fern Bay. So Adriana placed her in the shelter of the trees.

The night had been still and quiet. Not a single car had passed as she took Samantha off the road. When the girl's breathing stopped, Adriana had closed her eyes so that they weren't staring. It had been painful, watching that young woman fight for her breath, try to stay living, stay in the world.

The policewoman makes it all sound so intentional, as if Adriana is a criminal. But it wasn't like that. She might have seen better if she'd remembered her driving glasses, but anyone could have knocked into Samantha Jackson that night – she was the one in the middle of the road.

She doesn't think the police will understand the other part, so she decides not to say it. Once they were off the road, Samantha's breath came in ragged sounds, and there was the wetness of blood in that sound too. It had given Adriana the shivers. All she did was help Samantha to leave the world more peacefully, covering her mouth and nose with the fabric of her jacket. All Adriana knew was this – in that moment, it had been the right thing to do.

When Samantha stopped breathing, it was easier. Her pain was gone, and she looked younger, like a little girl. The way one of Adriana's children might have looked, maybe, if they'd ever had the chance to take a breath.

How could she have gone back and told Samantha's parents that she'd watched the life they'd given their daughter leave her body? Or that she'd got a spade from her house and buried their child? They wouldn't have understood how it happened without being there themselves.

The simple fact is that they had all had a part to play in what happened that night. If that girl hadn't run away from home, she never would have been walking on that road on her own. Her parents should have kept a closer eye on her. Then Adriana would never have had to be here, and everything – for each one of them – would have been better.

'We've had a woman come forward saying she knows something about what happened. She's a local resident who claims to have been involved in a collision with a pedestrian near here on August 22nd 2001, which you'll know is the night that Sam went missing.'

Freya's hand went to her mouth. Her breath caught.

'No,' Jilly said. The word escaped her, like a sigh.

'We don't know what really happened, not yet. But we have to take this confession seriously. The woman concerned has taken us to an area of woodland, and my colleagues are there with her at the moment.'

Jilly's eyes flashed. No one was saying it. No one had to.

'She's taken us to a particular spot, and we need to see if there are remains there.'

'You're looking for Sam's body,' Freya said, softly, more to herself than to anyone else there. She needed to make some sense of what she was hearing.

'Yes. As I say, the investigation is ongoing, but we've been led to believe we may have missed something when we searched . . . that Samantha's remains may be there.'

Freya was silent, but inside her mind roared. The information coursed through her, and brought with it noise, anger, confusion. This could not be.

'But – why there?' Jilly said, similarly uncomprehending. 'If you say she was hit on the road, why wasn't it reported – why have we had to wait until now . . . ?'

'Sometimes, confessions like can this lead to nothing,' the policeman said, hesitantly. 'But what the woman is claiming is that, when she hit Samantha while driving, she panicked. Instead of taking Samantha to hospital, or calling us, she chose to hide the evidence.'

After the police officer left, Jilly and Freya sat with each other, and with the fear that hung in the air between them, unspoken. Some things were better not said out loud. Freya pictured her sister leaving that night, as she had so many times before, and imagined her walking up the A-road out of town. The woodland the police officer was talking about was less than a mile from their house. It was practically on their doorstep.

Freya could see her mother lost in her own thoughts. Maybe they were similar, maybe they were worse. Almost certainly, like Freya, she'd been in those dark places before. Longed to find her way out of them but never had the facts to throw her a rope.

In the end it was Jilly who spoke first, and broke the silence.

'I want this all to go away,' she said. 'I want to undo it. Go back to not knowing.'

'It's been so long, Mum. We need closure, whatever the news turns out to be.'

Jilly's face was pale. She didn't react; she didn't say anything.

'We'll hear from them soon,' Freya repeated. 'And then we'll know.'

*

Cassie makes me hot chocolate and puts the TV on. We watch Horrible Histories *together, and she laughs every time the rat comes on. She always does that.*

She's set me up a bed beside hers in her room. She was happy to see me, and that felt nice. I had a lot to tell her, about the summer, about Jessie and Louisa and Freya, and the things we did.

I thought Mum might stay too, but she said she needed to go. I heard her talking in the hallway with Cassie, before she left. She said thank you to Cassie, and that maybe it's easier this way, for a while. Because Neil isn't great with kids. Cassie said something about how Neil isn't great full stop. Then she closed the door, and she was gone.

Later that week, Freya and Jilly got confirmation from the police that they'd found remains in the woodland and that they were Sam's. Forensics had established that much, though they hadn't yet been able to establish the cause of her death. They would keep examining, keep investigating.

When the police officers left Jilly's house, Freya excused herself, left her mother in the living room and went upstairs. By the time she got to the bathroom she was retching. She bent over the toilet, willing something to come up, something to come out of her that would make her feel better . . . but nothing. It was gone. The truth settled into Freya's bones like lead. Sam wasn't there any more – and she wasn't anywhere else. Sam was gone. And with that final, aching realisation came another cold truth. Freya would never, ever be able to make things right with her.

The certainty that Sam was not and never would be back was a pain worse than any Freya had ever known. It bored down to the very centre of her, leaving her breathless. They would have to wait for the details of what had happened that final night of her life, the slivers of information that might help them build up a picture. But the truth had already arrived.

For Freya the hours dragged, one after the other, the silent, empty, dark hours of night that carried with them the burden of uninterrupted thoughts. The end to one part of her life had come. The end to Sam's story. There was a metallic taste in her mouth. She got up in the middle of the night to make peppermint tea, and then drank some rum to see if that would help – but no matter what she ate or drank the taste stayed there.

She felt broken, but she was strangely OK with that. After so much time in limbo, she was finally – here. Somewhere.

She missed Dino – she missed his company, and she missed the distraction of him. She knew she should be relieved that he wasn't here while she was in this dark pit of grief, but instead she just missed him, viscerally. She would keep herself together, because there was no space here to fall apart. Dino might not be here, but her girls still relied on her.

Adriana had crashed into their lives, a familiar face and name, heavy with new significance. There had been a hole in both of them – in Freya, and in her mum – that had needed filling with an answer, but neither of them had wanted the answer to be this. That woman's name, and the news of what she'd done, had brought a shocked silence upon them. A whisper of denial.

But, even as she resisted it, Freya knew that somewhere, deep down, she needed it, needed whatever it might settle and turn into. An answer. The woman whose house they'd walked by for years, the one they'd sometimes avoided, had been at the centre of their lives all along.

The accident was one thing – but what she'd done in staying quiet all of these years, knowing the pain that Freya and her parents were suffering – that part, Freya found it almost impossible to forgive.

Adriana. She'd never been able to meet Freya's eyes. Had kept her door tight shut, hidden away, and now they all knew why.

There are things we can know, bone-deep, Freya thought, and still not let ourselves know. We busy ourselves, so that the pieces don't fall into place. Freya hadn't realised she'd been hiding from the truth until Dino had said those words. She'd put layers of wallpaper over wallpaper, welcomed in every story that fitted, in an unconscious effort to do one single thing – drown out her own intuition. She'd known Sam was gone. Perhaps she'd known it all along.

It was Dino who had somehow found a way to open that door a crack. If he hadn't come here, they might never have found out the truth.

Freya wished she could cry. But the emotion sat curled up inside her. Hard, fossilised, as dark and untouchable as night. She wasn't even close.

Chapter 34

I ask Cassie if we can go round and see Mum today. We walk the long way, so that we can be closer to the sea.

Cassie has called first, to make sure that Neil's not there. She says she doesn't like him, and she certainly doesn't want to bump into him today. When she says it, I feel like I can say it too. We make a pact and say we will try and get my mum to leave him, because she deserves someone nicer than he is.

We keep on walking, and she takes my hand, and swings it.

'You're a good kid, Dino,' Cassie says. 'I've missed you.'

Freya walked around to her mum's house, passing the woodland that had held the traces of Sam. She remembered, again, that Sam's life had ended right there, so close, and that she would never grow old. Those thoughts wore a groove. She would have them, she knew now, every day for the rest of her life.

She hugged her mum at the door. Jilly felt fragile in Freya's arms, her frame slighter than the last time she'd held her.

'You OK, Mum?' she said, holding her close, her voice just a murmur into her hair.

'Bearing up,' she said. 'The psychics are leaving me to it,' she said, with a wry smile. 'But the friends who matter have been here. They've all come by, with cake, and sympathy, and cards, and all those lovely useless things that make you feel like you're sick or something.'

Freya knew what she meant. She'd had the same. She hated the pity; it only made her feel worse. Only Joe had struck the right balance, being there when she needed him, stepping back to give her space the rest of the time.

Jilly's face had changed in the days since they'd found out about Sam. What shine she'd still had in her eyes had disappeared with the details of Adriana's confession. It pained Freya to look at her – to see her mother's loss of a child, and a reflection of her own grief cast in flesh. Freya applied her make-up each day, dressed in bright colours, styled her dark hair neatly, did everything she could to cover over the greyness she felt. But just a few moments in her mother's company unveiled her. Here, in her family home, there was no way of hiding.

'They've given us permission to go ahead with the cremation,' Jilly said.

'OK,' Freya said. 'That's good. We can move on. Draw a line under all of this, as we should've been able to do years ago.'

Jilly didn't answer, and Freya felt how hollow her words sounded. 'Do you think that woman's sorry, really?' she asked.

'They said she showed a degree of remorse,' Jilly said.

'*A degree of remorse,*' Freya echoed. It sounded so empty. Halfway to caring.

'She obviously felt something – enough to confess after all these years, when she would almost certainly have been able to take the secret to her grave, if she'd wanted.'

'But not enough to say an unmitigated sorry.' It wasn't enough, Freya thought. Her sister deserved more than this. More than any of this.

'That woman's not had an easy life,' Jilly said. 'I know that. Everyone round here knows that. But I never could have imagined that this was what kept her hidden away all of these years. I suppose she would have had to construct some story for herself, about why she wasn't to blame. Minds can be clever like that, can't they?'

'There are no excuses. I don't care where Sam was walking. She should have been able to avoid hitting her – and, even if it was an accident, then how could she excuse not telling us the truth, letting us go on hoping all these years?'

'The police say they're pretty sure she'll get a long sentence,' Jilly said. 'But it's hard to feel any kind of joy about that. She's an old woman, and I'm all out of energy to blame. I just want peace. The peace to be with my grandkids and to treat them with as much love as I possibly can.'

Freya took a deep breath. 'It's hard not to be angry, though, isn't it, Mum? Really hard.'

'I try not to have regrets, but I regret that Sam never had the chance to live the way she wanted to,' Jilly said. 'I wish she'd been honest with us, Freya. I wish she'd told us how she felt about Echo – I can't say I would have understood it right away, but I would have tried. I would have done everything I could for her to lead the life she wanted.'

Freya hugged her mum close. 'Don't do this to yourself, Mum. She was happy a lot of the time. Maybe it was never as simple as being in love, or even about being gay. We all know she was always a seeker, a yearner, a searcher. One of those people who would probably always have been striving for more. She was looking for it that night, and, who knows, she might have been looking for it for the rest of her life.'

'Maybe,' Jilly said.

The pain in her mother's face cut Freya to the core. She longed to take it away and keep it herself. It belonged to Jilly, and no one else. Just as her own pain was hers and hers only to bear. 'I'm just glad this is over now,' Jilly said. 'Now maybe I can move into a different phase of life, knowing that she's finally gone. But there's no worse feeling in the world, believe me. No worse feeling than knowing that a baby you brought into this world has left it before you.'

I'm in the bathroom. Cassie and Dino left about an hour ago, and now Neil is home.

He starts banging on the door.

'Who's Anya?' he says.

I spit out the toothpaste and open the door. 'Anya? Why?'

He holds up my mobile, so I can see the missed call.

I didn't hear the phone ringing, so I guess he did and picked it up. I try to take the phone from him, but he pulls it away. Neil likes to know who's who in my life. Anya is from the time before him, and he's never met her.

I didn't even know that Anya still had my number. She's only called me a handful of times since I left Fern Bay. Neil isn't happy. He's not happy often, lately. I try and I try to get him to relax, to ease the pain he seems to be in. But none of it makes any difference.

'She's a friend from Fern Bay,' I say. 'She's a woman, Neil. There's nothing for you to be suspicious about.'

'Can you blame me, after the other day?' he says.

I tell him he's being unfair, and take the phone off him. I close the bathroom door tight shut and return the call. I know it's about Sam, before Anya even says it.

Anya tells me that they've found some remains in the woodland near Sam's parents' house.

I feel sick.

'But what – how . . . ?' I say. The words trip out of me. I have no control over them.

'They're Sam's,' Anya says. 'She was buried in the woods – in an area overlooked in the initial search.'

It hits me, hard, like a punch in the stomach. I pretended to be a dead woman, to get what I wanted. I stirred up all this pain for Freya, for my own reasons.

'What?' I say. It escapes as a whisper, because I don't have breath left in my body. Or at least that's what it feels like.

I made this happen, somehow. Because, before I sent Dino over, Sam wasn't dead. She definitely wasn't. And now she is.

Even when Anya tells me the details of what happened, it doesn't really change anything. Because I know, in my soul, that I was responsible in some way.

Sam died on the night she left, she said. Hit by a car, and the driver – an old woman now – has finally confessed. She'd got scared and covered the whole thing up.

I hate myself for what I did to Freya, and to her mum. Like I said, this horrible truth didn't exist before I came along and made it true.

I didn't mean for that to happen. I didn't mean to hurt anyone. But damn, what was I thinking? I hit my head against the wall, because that pain makes me feel what I deserve to feel. I do it again. The pain blocks out room for anything else. For the bad feelings.

I've done a bad thing, and this has happened. And I know I can't go on like this.

The news of Sam's death had changed the colour of everything. Everything around Freya seemed muted, a sepia filter over it. Over the years she'd always imagined that her sister was out there somewhere, filling the world with light, and now that light she'd pictured had gone out.

At home, Freya got out a family photo album. With the certainty of Sam being gone, she knew she had to go back, even if it was raw, and painful.

She looked at the photos of her and Sam as baby and toddler, out in their back garden. Family picnics – Freya cradled in her mother's arms, and a two-year-old Sam on her dad's shoulders. Birthday parties as they went into school, and the holidays that had given their childhood colour. Their parents were smiling in all of them, and so were they. It hadn't been a lie, that they'd had good times. Freya had wanted more than anything to keep that family together.

She looked at another photo, of Sam and Freya in front of her university halls in Bristol, on the day her family had dropped her off there. It was one of the last photos of them, and one where they looked happy.

There were things she'd experienced that Sam had never had the chance to. But Sam's days had been her days. The ones she was given. She might never have felt a baby grow in her womb, but she might never have wanted that anyway. She'd known love, and there was the mercy that she'd never woken with the empty heart of a woman who had lost it. She'd not found the job of her dreams, or got her driving licence, or flown to a faraway country. But she'd also never known the pain of losing a parent, getting ill, or losing, truly and for ever, a sister.

What Sam had known was the sweet release of laughter, the sensation of toes in sand as she walked into the surf. She'd known the warmth of friendship, and the pleasure of completing a Rubik's cube and getting to the final level of *Super Mario*. She'd seen the wild poppies bloom in their garden. She had felt the comfort of sharing a blanket in a tent with her sister on a rainy night out in their garden. She'd known the softness of their fox terrier's fur underneath her fingertips.

Who decided what the measure of a life well lived really was? If Freya could have lived fewer years and never had to feel the pain of losing Sam, might she have chosen it? The kids were the only part that made it make sense. If Sam had lived longer, her life might have been beautiful – or it might have been like Echo's. Hard, with each day and week something to get through.

Freya imagined what would happen if Sam – Sam as she was – were to appear at her door, a smile on her face, dark liner on her eyes. What would she say? What would Sam say about the life Freya had made?

The Sam that Freya pictured in her mind would stay forever on the cusp of adulthood, that fearless time. That Sam, if she were here now, would look around the living room, at the framed prints, and the glass coffee table. And Freya knew just what she'd say. This life, these daughters, you're trying to keep a tight hold on, Frey – let go a little.

Sam was at peace. Adriana had given them all that. Freya saw that filtering out the colour from her own life wasn't a duty, it was a habit. What she owed Sam was this – to appreciate and feel grateful for every day that she had on earth. She was going to fill them with light, and with love, no matter what it took. She wasn't going to push away joy – she was going to fight to feel it. She would live life for the both of them, in the best way she possibly could.

Louisa came into the room, and Freya was abruptly pulled back into the present. Here was her eldest daughter, and today was a big day – Louisa had been to get her exam results. Freya made herself bring her full attention to the moment and tried to read Louisa's expression; her smile looked forced. It didn't look good, but it didn't look entirely bad either.

'How did you get on?' Freya asked, nervously.

Louisa passed the papers over, and Freya scanned the results. 'These look great,' she said. Then she got to the final one: a D in Biology.

'I knew I'd messed it up. I wasn't feeling well that day, do you remember?'

'Yes, love. I do,' Freya said. 'Listen, we can work this out. You did well, Lou. You tried your hardest, and you can still do it, we'll just have to go a little further to get there.' Freya drew her daughter in towards her for a hug. 'You'll be fine, I promise.'

'Thanks, Mum. It feels kind of crappy right now, but I'm sure it'll look better in an hour or so. I just want to forget about it for now.'

'OK, I understand.'

'What have you been up to?' Louisa asked.

Freya's gaze drifted over to the family photos of Sam.

'It must be really hard for you, Mum,' Louisa said.

'Yes, Lou. It is.' Freya wiped away a tear that she'd once thought she might never shed. 'It breaks my heart to think that for Sam it all ended that night. That she died on her own, so close to where I was. But we know now. We have the truth, and I wondered sometimes if I'd ever get that – so I'm grateful for it.'

She put her arm around Louisa's shoulder, and her daughter hugged her tightly around her waist. The distance that had built up between them over the past weeks slipped away. Freya took a deep breath.

'I think I got it wrong with you, Louisa. I tried to hold you too tightly. I'm not saying it was OK for you and Matt to come home late that night – it wasn't. But the way I reacted wasn't only to do with you. I was scared. I was scared that if I let you be with Matt, you might never come back to us.'

'Mum!' Louisa said, shaking her head. 'That's not true.'

'I know. I can't control what happens to you, or stop you from getting hurt, any more than I could protect Sam that night. I need to start trusting you to make your own decisions.'

'Even if that means making my own mistakes, too?' Louisa said.

'Yes. Even then.'

'Are you saying what I'm think you're saying?' Louisa said.

'I trust you. And that means trusting you to be with the person you want to be with. Does Matt make you happy?' Freya said.

Louisa nodded, and the flush in her cheeks deepened. 'Yes. He makes me happy.'

'Well, that's the best start you're ever going to have.'

'I think I've started to get what everyone's been going on about all this time,' Louisa said, beaming.

'Just like you, Lou, to bide your time, and wait for someone who is worth it.'

'Hardly,' Louisa said, with a laugh. 'Just that no one ever looked at me before. Well, not like Matt does, anyway.'

'You deserve to be happy. And I'm sorry if I've stood in the way of that.'

Neil's shouting. He's telling me he knows it was a man calling. It doesn't matter that Anya's a woman's name – that's the oldest trick in the book.

Sam's dead. Somehow, way back or just now. And it's because of me.

It should have been me.

It should always have been me.

Her family kept looking. Her family has never stopped looking. Her sister, her parents.

I tried to make myself her.

I did it for Dino but maybe I also did it for me.

All that time, I told myself she was on a beach somewhere. That someone as lucky as Sam was always going to hit her happy ever after. That was what people like her were destined to do.

But all the while, she was dead.

And I'm here – but I'm only half here. I'm not here for the people that matter.

I keep trying to be here, and I just can't be.

It should have been me.

He starts to hit me, across the face. I shield myself. Then I drop my hands from my face and just let his fists go in hard. When I'm on the floor, I don't even bring up my knees when he kicks me in the stomach. I just let it happen, again and again.

Chapter 35

Today was the day they would finally say goodbye to Sam. Freya and Jilly made their way into the crematorium together. At the end of the service, Freya took a deep breath and squeezed her mum's hand. Louisa, in turn, reached for hers and did the same. As Freya exhaled, she felt a sense of release. Her daughter had seemed more distant, now that she was seeing Matt again, but today she was here. They were family, and in the midst of the pain there was a solidarity that would get them to tomorrow, and the next day, and next year.

Freya looked around at who else was there. Friends, relatives, neighbours. People who'd checked in on her and Jilly over the years, who'd always been there. It was a good turnout. She smiled as she saw Anya with a small baby strapped to her chest – the kind of sad smile that comes out at funerals when there are babies and toddlers there. She glanced around, looking for Echo. Freya had told her about the funeral, but it looked as if she had decided not to come.

The service passed in a blur. Freya heard the kind words others said about Sam as if they were about a stranger. When her time came, she walked up to the podium on autopilot, read from her prepared speech, and played the songs that she'd wanted to play for Sam. But she felt barely present. Maybe she was insulating herself from the pain. Or maybe she'd just said her goodbyes already, without even having realised it.

After the service, the back door to the crematorium opened and people drifted out slowly, in silence. A man got up from the back row, and as he turned to go their eyes met briefly. Freya's breath caught. A woman she'd once, briefly, been was suddenly part of her again, and the shift was so abrupt it shook her. Eliot. The man who had undone her once. There he was.

She gravitated towards him. He looked at her, those blue eyes she'd pictured a hundred times. 'Freya. I'm so sorry.'

She nodded, thanked him. Sorry was what people said when someone died. But from Eliot it meant something. He saw her, saw everything she was, and everything she'd been through. And, because of that, the words meant more.

She wanted to reach out across the distance between them. She longed to be held by him. Eliot was the only person who really knew, really understood. What it had been like to be with Sam that summer, and to lose her.

'If you ever want to talk, Frey – I'm here.'

They hadn't wanted a wake. Freya and Jilly had both found the news reports, the attention in town, and the funeral itself draining. They would find their own ways of remembering Sam, as they always had – they didn't need sandwiches and a house full of concerned neighbours in order for that to happen. Freya just wanted to get home, and get back to normality. When she arrived home, Joe was in the living room with the girls, who he'd driven back after the funeral.

'Freya, is it OK if Matt comes around?' Joe said. 'Louisa's just spoken with him.'

Louisa nodded. 'He said he wants to be here with me.'

Freya hesitated. She didn't feel much like company, but perhaps it would be the distraction they all needed.

Joe caught Freya's eye and held her gaze for a minute, silently nudging her to agree.

'Sure,' she said. 'It's nice of him to think of it.'

Half an hour later, Joe welcomed Matt inside. They all stood slightly awkwardly in the kitchen and Freya tried to think of a way to break the silence.

'Beer?' Joe said.

Matt nodded, and then smiled. Joe got them one from the fridge.

Louisa and Matt stood next to each other, and Freya saw him reach out for her hand and take it in his.

Louisa had known, after all, Freya thought. Louisa had known far better than her what kind of a man he was, and what it was she needed.

Jessie came in, riding a unicorn hobby horse and sprinkling glitter behind her. The melancholy of the morning had lifted quickly for her, and Freya felt grateful for the swift change of children's moods.

'Jessie,' Freya said, taking the glitter off her. 'I've only just finished hoovering up the last lot.'

'Is this Matt?' Jessie said, stopping to look at him. She set her hobby horse to one side and gave Matt a huge smile, her white teeth gleaming. 'Are you Louisa's *boyfriend*?' she sing-songed.

'I told you this would be embarrassing,' Louisa said to Matt. Her cheeks flushed pink.

Matt laughed, and glanced over at Louisa before looking back at Jessie. 'Yep. I guess that's who I am.'

*

When they'd said goodbye to Matt, the girls had gone to stay over at Joe's. Freya sat back on the sofa – the house seemed too quiet, all of a sudden. The evening had gone well – Matt had been easy to get on with and when they all sat down for dinner together his nerves had eased and she'd got to know him a little better. It had all been a welcome relief from the heaviness of saying goodbye to Sam. Louisa had been glowing in his company, and was talking pragmatically about how she'd manage her studies for the re-sit. When Freya and Joe crossed paths in the hallway, they'd shared a moment of whispered pride about the girl they'd raised together. Joe had joked about how Freya had been giving Matt the third degree. She'd eased her hold, yes, but she still wasn't about to give Louisa up to just anyone. They could both see, though, how caring Matt was towards Louisa, and how gentle he was in his way with her. His bright sense of humour had started to emerge, and reminded Freya of how Joe had been when they'd first met.

Freya felt relieved. Letting go of her control over Louisa's life had been easier, in the end, than she'd anticipated.

The buzz of her family around her had been a welcome distraction from the darkness that had consumed her over the past days. But now they were gone, she felt herself slipping back into that place. She didn't want to go back – she wanted to go forward. She wanted to do something she hadn't been brave enough to do before, but which she felt ready to do now.

When she'd stepped out of her usual role during those warm summer evenings with Eliot before Sam left, she'd felt the plates in the earth shift, and it had unnerved her. It had shaken her so deeply that she'd feared ever doing it again. It had led her into being with Joe. She'd seen that Joe was safe, and with someone safe maybe she'd be able defuse the desire that had derailed her before. But it hadn't worked that way. The desire had never gone away.

284

She took out her phone, scrolled to Eliot's number, and texted him.

Are you around tonight?

She waited for his reply, her heart beating outside of her chest.

I can be.

They met at a pub close to the East Cliff. Eliot was sitting in a booth by the window, and Freya went over to join him. When he saw her, his eyes lit up. He smiled at her, as though he couldn't help it.

'It's good to see you,' he said.

She nodded, unable to raise a smile, and sat down.

'Are you OK?' Eliot said. 'Look, just say if this is too much.'

'It's OK.' She didn't want him to go. 'Listen, I'm sorry. I'm a bit of a mess right now.'

'Understandable.'

They went quiet for a moment. 'Let me get some wine,' he said, going over to the bar.

Freya watched him across the room. She wanted this. She wanted him. She wanted him so much it ached. But she wasn't sure she could get this right – wasn't sure that there was room for this good thing alongside all of the bad.

Eliot came back, and passed her a glass of red wine. 'Listen, we can talk about whatever you want to talk about. I can talk to you about films, or the joy and pain of making and selling furniture, or my trip to the Isle of Man for the bike race, if you want distracting.' He smiled and his eyes crinkled at the corners. His company jolted her awake, and yet she felt calm and safe at the same time; he made her feel good, accepted, whole.

Freya smiled. 'I think I just want to talk about Sam, if that's OK,' she said. 'It's pretty much all I can think about.'

'I'm here for that,' Eliot said, softly.

'She deserves so much more than what happened.'

'That's for sure.'

'It just makes me so sad that this was how it ended for her. So early. Alone.'

'It must be a lot to take in,' he said.

'And then all of this stuff with Echo, with Dino . . .'

'I heard about that. I mean – seriously – I knew Echo was intense, she was always intense. But what she did—'

'She's in a bad situation,' Freya said. 'That's the only way I can make sense of it.'

'Yep. You're right,' Eliot said. 'I mean, Echo had a tough family life, we all knew that. She didn't go into details, but she was always looking for a reason to avoid going home. Your sister was the best friend she'd ever had – and she told me that the nights she stayed at your house were the ones where she felt safest. I don't think Echo ever really got over losing Sam. Maybe in some twisted way this was all a way to feel closer to her again.' He shrugged. 'Who knows? Echo's Echo. She was always out there. Too out there for me.'

'Did you know they were together? Echo and Sam . . .'

'What?' Eliot said, his eyes widening.

'They were in love,' Freya said. 'That's what Echo said – matching tattoos, planning on a future together – they were running away together that night. Only Sam never made it that far.'

'Christ. Nope.' He seemed startled. 'No idea. I was with them that night, I mean, you know this already. That night, after I left you, I went up to Sam's room. But I only stayed long enough to make things normal, like we'd always said we would, right?'

Freya nodded.

'I didn't realise anything was going on between them.'

'All these years I thought it was seeing the two of us together that made Sam run,' Freya said, shaking her head, and smiling in spite of herself. 'I got that one wrong.'

She had to say it. Years had passed, too quickly. She might not get another chance. 'I'm sorry I shut you out.'

He looked at her. He looked at her the way he'd looked at her that night, as if he could see right into her soul.

'You did what you had to do,' Eliot said. 'But it was hard. I wanted to be there for you, Freya.'

Freya felt her phone vibrate in her pocket. She took it out: UNKNOWN CALLER.

'Sorry,' she said to Eliot, picking up warily.

'Freya, hi.' A female voice, panicked. 'It's Cassie, Echo's friend. I found your number in her phone. I need to talk to you.'

'What is it?' Freya's heart raced. 'Is it Dino? Is he OK?'

'Don't worry, he's with me. I've been looking after him since he came back.'

'What's happened?'

'It's Echo. She's in hospital. Shit, Freya. He's put her in hospital.'

Chapter 36

There were lights. But not like the ones on the wall, the ones that Dino and I used to watch. Blue lights. Blue lights. Those lights have flashed in and out of my life a lot of times. I can't think straight. I see Dino's face. I remember the warmth of his hugs. I see his green eyes, his long lashes. I remember the day he took his first steps, in our living room. The way he used to curl up in bed with me when he couldn't sleep at night. I get a flash of that height chart on our kitchen wall. I could barely keep up. As those legs got so long and nursery turned into school. I see his birthday cakes. The one with the 2 on it, the one with the 3. And I see the school photos. I didn't have much. We've never had much. But I'd save up to buy those. Those things mattered.

The next morning, Freya got in her car and drove towards Margate. She and Cassie had spoken on the phone for a while the previous night, after she'd said goodbye to Eliot, and Cassie told her she'd been looking after Dino since he'd arrived back in Margate. Dino had wanted it that way, and Cassie said she knew why. Echo's boyfriend Neil had hurt Echo before, and this time he had beaten her until she was unconscious. One of the neighbours had found her and called an ambulance. Cassie said she couldn't go on like this: her anxiety was getting bad and the meds weren't working any more, plus she was running out of money. She was scared that the stress of it would rub off on Dino, and she hated lying to him so that he wouldn't worry.

Freya knew what she was asking, before she said it. Dino needed to be somewhere safe – and it looked as though the best place for that was with Freya.

Everything hurts. Every part of me hurts. I blink. Beep. Beep. I notice I'm rigged up to something, and there are tubes attached to me. There's a thin sheet over my body. My head throbs.

Then it hits me. I'm still here. I'm alive.

Oh, man.

I didn't think I'd still be here.

I didn't want to still be here.

Then I see someone beside the bed. I think I see him. I think I can see my boy.

Echo turned her head slightly towards Freya. She was looking right at her. Her face was such a mess, her lips so swollen, that Freya wasn't sure if she'd even be able to speak.

'It's you,' Echo said at last, her voice flat and clear. 'I thought . . . I don't know why, but I thought you were Dino. Is he here?'

'No, he's not,' Freya said, gently. 'I'm sorry. Cassie didn't think he should see you like this.'

'OK,' Echo said, her voice just a whisper now. 'She's right, I guess.'

'Listen, Echo, I'm so sorry about what happened to you.'

'I had it coming, I suppose.'

'What? No . . . No, you didn't, Echo. How could you think that?'

'I dunno. Karma, maybe. I should never have dragged you

into this. Lied to you. And now, knowing what really happened to Sam . . . ' Her voice cracked.

'Echo, what happened to Sam was nothing to do with you.'

'I didn't know she was dead, Freya. I would never have done this, if I'd known.'

Freya nodded. 'I know. I believe that. And *you* have to believe *me* – this isn't some punishment you were due.'

'I don't know. I'm not sure I deserve any better. Cassie told you, right? I haven't even been able to look after Dino, since he came back. He doesn't like Neil.'

'Is Neil the one who did this to you?'

Echo nodded.

'Well, Dino's a good judge of character, in that case.'

'Neil's not all bad,' Echo said, weakly.

'He doesn't seem all that good, either.'

'I'm not a fool, Freya, even if I look like one. Neil's the one helping me to get clean. He's with me on this. He just gets . . . he has trouble controlling himself sometimes.'

'Are you going to talk to the police?'

'I don't know. I've barely had time to think.'

'I know you're in a bad way, so I'm sorry to bring this up right away, but I think we need to make some decisions about your son. Cassie says she's struggling, and that she doesn't know how much longer she can do it. What do you want to do?'

'I can't really take him back myself, can I? Not like this,' Echo said.

'So what do you think would be best for him?'

'I just want rid of this – this feeling that I'm always getting it wrong.' She tugged at her hair as if there was an itch somewhere on her that she couldn't scratch. 'I'm not good with responsibility. I can barely look after myself. How am I supposed to get him to where he needs to be? I'll never be enough.'

'You can be enough. But you need support,' Freya said, gently.

'I don't want them round – like they were when he was young, all the health visitors preaching at me about how to raise my baby. I don't want social workers looking at me and how I'm doing things . . . '

'I'm sure they weren't—'

Echo seemed to snap, then. 'And what would you know, Freya? What, really, would you know about being judged?'

Freya went quiet. Maybe it had been easier for her, in some ways.

'That's one of the reasons why I picked you. Why I sought you out to look after my kid. Precisely because you've never been looked at the way I have. When you have a house like yours, it's different.'

'You think that?' Freya said.

'I don't know. Maybe. Maybe not. I'm exhausted, Freya. I can't do it any more,' she said. 'Please take him in. Care for him for me.'

Freya pictured Dino. Her heart ached for him.

The love she felt for him was there for good.

'OK,' she said. 'But if we're going to do this, we're doing it properly this time.'

At Cassie's flat, Dino came over and gave Freya a gentle hug, putting his arms around her waist.

It felt so good. Their greeting, like so many of their interactions that year, was silent, but filled with emotion. Today that emotion was pure, and warm, and Freya wanted to hold him for ever. She would never give him up. She would never give up on him.

That day had taught her a lot about what people were capable of giving. She didn't judge Echo for any of what had happened, how could she? She'd seen the pain etched into her face, the damage done to her in a before-time that Freya would never be able to access or understand. She didn't know much about Echo, she didn't need to – she knew that Dino needed a home, and that she could offer him one.

'Did you see her?' he asked.

'I did,' Freya said.

'Can I go in and see her too now?'

Freya felt deeply sad – for him, and for the loss of the hope she'd had that she could fix this for him. Cassie looked at Freya and shook her head. Freya bent to Dino's level, so that she could look him squarely in the eye. 'She's still not well, Dino. She loves you – so much. But she's not well enough to look after you.'

'When will she be?' he asked.

Some truths were hard truths, however you looked at them.

'I don't know, Dino. I know she misses you, but I don't know when she'll be well enough.'

His eyes reddened. She'd seen that expression too many times in him. The sting of a disappointment that he had tried so hard to make himself numb to. He wasn't numb yet, and she hoped she could help make sure he never became so.

'So for now, me and your mum, and Cassie, have agreed that the best thing is for you to come back with me. Is that OK with you?'

That evening, back at the house, Freya made hot chocolate for Dino and Jessie, and they all curled up together on the sofa watching a film. She and Echo had agreed – Freya would apply to be a temporary foster carer for Dino, and, if she was approved, they would take it from there.

She wanted to fill this boy's life with light and it felt as if darkness was crowding in from every angle. She wanted him to wake up to sunshine, just once, but every day there was more rain.

The doctors had said that Echo would make a full recovery. That, while it looked bad, and they needed to monitor for concussion, the damage was largely superficial.

Largely superficial.

Was it, though? she thought. She'd overheard the police talking in the corridor. 'A domestic,' they'd said. 'She'll go back. They always do.' Anger had flared in her, but that didn't make it untrue. She knew that Echo would go back to the man who had done this to her. And that there was still a chance that the next time might be the last time.

She held Dino a little closer to her. Had he ever been able to be a child, really? Not there, maybe not even here. He'd been brought into contact with more sadness than she ever would have wanted for him.

And yet here he was, close to Jessie, and making her smile. What he'd lived through, and on the edges of, had affected him deeply but it hadn't broken him. It was Freya's job now, to make sure that it never did.

She still couldn't make sense of how he'd landed in their lives. But he was here, and she was grateful to have him. She'd seen how much Echo loved him, but also how clear it was that he couldn't go back. Not now. Not for a long time.

Dino went up to set the bath running, and Jessie snuggled up to her mum on the sofa. They watched the end of *Shopkins* together. The neon-bright colours and cheery voices jarred, but they also distracted Freya, and she welcomed that.

'Will Dino stay this time? Jessie asked.

Freya looked at her daughter. 'Yes, he's going to stay. I'm going to talk to some people about becoming his carer. Is that OK with you?'

'Yes,' Jessie said. 'I want him to stay. I don't care if he's not my cousin. I don't care about that at all.'

293

'He's got his own family, and nothing's going to change that. But he's also part of our family now, I think. Don't you?'

Jessie nodded.

'And we don't let go of family easily.'

That night, Dino came and sat on the end of Freya's bed, and Freya put her book on the night-table and smiled at him.

'Hello,' she said, softly. 'I'm fairly sure you should be in bed, Dino.'

He shrugged. 'I'm not sleepy.'

She brought him in towards her for a hug. She noticed he had something clasped in his hand.

'I brought you this,' he said, handing her the dreamcatcher. 'Just in case you're having bad dreams.'

'Thank you,' she said. A lump came to her throat. She hadn't mentioned a thing to him, but her last few nights had been restless, a return to the broken sleep she'd had when Sam first left.

'Because I know you're sad,' he said, holding on to her arm gently. 'Jessie told me about your sister. And about how it was Adriana who did it, in an accident. I don't want you to be sad.'

She tried to keep back her tears, but they spilled over.

'Now I'm making you sadder,' he said.

'No,' she told him, gently. 'You're not, Dino. You're making me feel better. I loved my sister a lot. And when she was gone I kept hoping that she might come back.'

He knew, and she knew, about the messy part of all this. The false hope Echo had given her. And it was there, when they talked, even though Freya didn't want it to be.

Freya got another flash of her sister, walking down that A-road, alone. She wished that the thoughts, the images, weren't in her head, and that they wouldn't always be there. That she wouldn't hurt this way for ever.

'But now I know for sure, you see, that she's not going to. That she died, and that it's just me now.'

Dino hugged her a bit closer.

'I want to soak it all up, the lonely feeling, and put it away.' He said it so quietly, barely above a whisper.

She smiled at him. 'You don't need to do that, Dino. It isn't your job. My brain and my heart are just doing what they need to, so that I can let Sam go. Sadness doesn't have to be got rid of, it's there for a reason, and it needs space just to be there first, before it can go.'

'She must have been a nice sister.'

Freya laughed, through the tears. She was crying. At last, the tears were really coming.

'Sometimes,' she said. 'Sometimes she was awful. Sometimes she was brilliant. But she was always my sister.'

Dino gave a little smile. 'I never used to have any sisters at all. Now I have two. And I think I know a little bit now what you mean.'

They sat there for a while, in the half-light, holding hands, until she got up and took him over to his own bed.

The next day, Sunday, Freya met with Joe, and told him about the process she was starting.

'I've thought about it a lot,' she said. She'd barely stopped thinking about it, since she'd had the idea.

'You know, though ... he's a stranger, Freya. You don't have any obligation—'

'It's not about obligation,' Freya said. 'And he's not a stranger. Not any more. He's a child who needs a home.'

'But wasn't all this about Sam – at least at the start?'

'Yes, it was. But that was before I got to know Dino. I was desperate to find Sam – you know that better than anyone, Joe.

But the paths we take don't always lead us where we're expecting to go. Look at us,' Freya said, motioning towards Joe. 'This isn't about me trying to make something right with my sister any more. I'm not trying to build bridges with her, or with anyone else. I've come to love Dino. And I know that isn't easy for you to understand – Christ, it's not even that easy for me to understand. But it's happened, and it's not going to unhappen just because we don't have the same blood running in our veins.'

'I think I get it,' Joe said. 'Or at least I'm trying to understand. I know Dino's a good kid. But is that enough to make you want to do this? He's got his own mum and I know she's got problems, but—'

She'd explained, and she'd explained again, but he just didn't see it the way that she did.

'Joe. His home isn't safe – I'm sure about that. Echo will always be his mum, and I hope she'll be stronger soon, and capable of looking after him properly. But, right now, there's no way he can go back there.'

Chapter 37

Freya calls to update me, just like she promised she would. I like hearing her voice when she calls, like she's phoning from another world. She says she's going through the process of being assessed to look after Dino, and that so far it seems to be going well. She asks me how I am and I tell her some of it. I'm out of hospital now, and I'm home. I don't say which home. I talk to Dino, and we just chat about stupid stuff. He says he wants to come up and see me in a few weeks. I tell him we can go to Dreamland. He's always wanted to go there.

Neil's looking after me really well, making me proper home-cooked food, and lending me his iPad so I can watch Netflix. He says he's sorry. That he doesn't know how things got so bad – he does trust me. He'll trust me more this time, especially since I proved I cared about him, and our relationship, by choosing not to press charges.

Dino sat next to Freya on the sofa and nestled into the crook of her arm. Freya's attention drifted and she found her gaze resting on the pot on the mantel that held her sister's ashes.

'Your mum said something funny when we met,' she said.

'Mum says a lot of funny stuff,' Dino said. He wrinkled his nose. He looked so cute when he wrinkled his nose.

'What was it?'

'She said that maybe the only thing Sam was really in love with was the wind.'

'What does that mean?'

'Some people aren't built to stay tethered. They want to be free. They want to go on adventures. They want to fly to other places, and meet people, see things. And no matter if they have the best thing in the world right here, they're still going to want to fly.'

'And did your sister do that? Did she climb mountains and swim in the sea, and fight bandits?' Dino's eyes were wide.

Freya thought of Sam, and a lump came to her throat. That A-road on the way out of town where all of her dreams got cut short. The circuit of Fern Bay that she'd run for years, the school and Saturday job and family Sunday lunches that had never been nearly enough for her.

'Did she do that ...?' Freya said. The excitement in Dino's eyes. The lie she wanted to tell him. So that he would know that a life like that was possible. So that he'd know he could have it, just as much as the next person, if he wanted. But enough – there had been enough lies.

'You know what, Dino? She had a lot of dreams, and a lot of things she wanted to do. But her time ran out.' Freya shrugged. She felt heavy with the sadness of it. But she couldn't change it. A truth was just that. 'She had a good life, and we all loved her a lot. But she didn't get to go to the places that she wanted to.'

Dino looked at the urn, and then walked across to the mantelpiece. He touched it gently, running a hand over the pottery, taking in the detail of the texture.

'Maybe you could help her.'

*

Freya got into the car, with Louisa in the passenger seat beside her. In the back was a box that held the pot with her sister's ashes. Dino had had the right idea. It was time to set Sam free.

'You're sure you want to do this with me?' Freya said. 'I don't want you to feel you have to. I know this is pretty heavy stuff.'

Louisa shook her head. 'I want to do it with you. It doesn't upset me. We're helping her.'

'OK.' Freya placed her hands on the steering wheel and took a deep breath, composing herself. 'Let's do this.'

Louisa took her mother's hand and squeezed it. 'Granny didn't want to come?'

Freya shook her head. 'She's said goodbye already,' she said. She wanted to take the others out instead, take her mind off Sam.'

'She's been depressed a lot,' Louisa said.

'For years,' Freya said. 'I think we've all done a lot of grieving, in our own way, over the past years.'

'What were Sam's favourite songs?' Louisa asked.

'She liked the White Stripes,' Freya said. She got out and flicked through her iPod until she landed on a summer playlist.

The car filled with music. The music that had been the soundtrack to Sam's last few months on earth. The music that had given colour to the days she had. Freya pressed the button so that both of their windows went down, and fresh air filled the car. This was it. This was life. And they were living it for Sam now.

They drove up to the cliff car park, and got out of the car. Freya carried the urn carefully, in both her hands. It flickered across her mind, the people who should be there.

They stood near the cliff edge.

'You're ready?' asked Louisa.

'I think so.' Freya held the urn close to her. One last time. She and Sam were together. But even in that moment she knew it could never last, that it was not meant to last. Sam was born to fly free, and now she would finally be able to do that.

Freya took a couple of steps towards the cliff edge. She glanced back, and Louisa motioned for her to go on.

Sam could now go wherever she wanted. Freya might not have been the perfect sister, and she still felt that she hadn't found out the truth soon enough – but she could do something for her now. She opened the pot, tipped it out and let the wind take the ashes, the tiny traces of the vibrant person her sister had once been.

Freya stood there for a long while, looking out at the sea. Louisa came over and took her by the hand. 'You OK?'

'Yes,' she said. She felt as if something else had been carried away on the breeze, something that she'd been carrying that wasn't hers to carry. 'I think I am.'

'Maybe you can start living now,' Louisa said.

Freya looked at her elder daughter, who looked so grown up all of a sudden. The wiser of the two of them. 'I am living, Lou. This – you guys – this is my life. It's a good life and I'm lucky to have it.'

'I know,' Louisa said. 'But, while you've given us freedom, I don't know if you've ever let yourself have it.'

Freya thought of how it had been. Thinking of Sam each day – running the scenarios through her head, again and again. Sure that if she just pushed her search that bit further, thought harder to locate a memory or a clue, she would find the answer that would lead to Sam. The time she'd spent thinking that if only she could undo what had happened with Eliot, things could have turned out differently. Eliot was the person who'd made her feel most alive, and that had always felt like something she needed to rein in, control.

Louisa spoke again, her voice softer now. 'You can let it go.'

Freya felt a weight lift. The past was the past. It couldn't be unstitched and resewn. What she had was the moment. The days with her children. The wind whipped her hair across her face, bracing and cold, and she put her arm around Louisa, drawing her closer. Her feet were solid on the ground, and she felt strong. Strong enough to be there for her family, for Dino. Strong enough to be there for herself.

Chapter 38

Freya calls me to let me know he's been approved as a temporary foster carer, and I have to stop myself from crying with relief. I know some people might judge me, but believe me, I'm still sitting here with a hole in my heart. I don't care what they might think, because nothing could hurt me like all of this has already.

I'll miss Dino. I'll miss him like my heart's gone. But giving him away for now might be the only good thing I've ever done in my life.

Freya looked at Dino and Jessie sitting together on the sofa in their living room, giggling over a book. The phone call that morning had meant everything to her – she was now able to be Dino's carer, officially. She could offer him continuity, security. And he was already settled in other ways – he'd been going to the same school as Jessie since term started. It would be hard for Echo, she knew that, but from the way Echo had thanked her tearfully on the phone she'd been reassured that this was what needed to happen, for all of them. It wasn't for ever – it was for now. But now could be a long, important time, and none of them could afford to make any more mistakes.

Each child had their beginning, Jessie's was one that Freya had been instrumental in – while Dino's was largely a mystery to her. She was powerless to change any detail of either history. Did where they'd come from matter? Yes, it did. But did it matter more than where they were now? She didn't think so. Dino had strength in all the broken places.

Dino had changed their family – he'd helped Jessie to open up, and he brought out a softer side in Louisa, just as her teenage harder edges were forming. What they all had was love, and the motivation to keep trying. They saw now – as they had when she and Joe had first separated – that the shape of a family could change, and the new shape could be far more beautiful, and stronger, than the way it had been before. Their life without Dino would be like dawn breaking with no birdsong. He had taught Freya that deep within her there was a well of love she didn't know she had. It didn't care about blood ties.

Freya might once have aspired to a tidy, ordered life, but now, she wanted to live every minute, no matter how chaotic. Each child had unspooled a ball of wool in her life, in their lives, and now she was living in a room full of colourful, tangled threads. She wasn't going to sit there and spend her days untangling those small twisted sections. Life was too short for that. She'd lift that wool up, and spin around in it, watching as the colours rained down around her.

I'm in town today. Are you around?

The message sat on Freya's phone, staring at her. Eliot. Not in the past, not a memory that she was trying to push aside. Right here in her present – Eliot was back in her life again.

See you by the bay in half an hour? she texted. She bit her lip as she waited for a reply.

Sounds good.

They met in a café near the beach. It still felt strange to Freya, these pieces of her life coming to fit together in a new time, in a new way. But as she sat opposite Eliot she knew it was the only place that she wanted to be.

'How're things?' he asked.

'Good,' Freya said. 'I think I'm finally starting to move on.'

'In what way?'

'Being Dino's foster carer is really helping me. It's giving me direction, as well as giving him the security he needs.'

'He's lucky to have you.'

She smiled. 'I'm lucky to have him.'

Eliot nodded. 'I can get that.'

'It never happened for you – kids?'

He shook his head. 'I would have liked it to. But things didn't pan out. I travelled a lot, so perhaps that was part of it. You sound like you're a really good parent. To all of them.'

'Thank you,' Freya said. She thought of Louisa, Jessie and Dino, and how things had changed for them all over the past few months. 'I do the best I can.'

'I wouldn't ever want to get in the way of that,' Eliot said.

She looked at him, and there was a moment of unspoken understanding.

'I know,' she said.

There was space. She'd opened her heart to expanding her family, and now she felt ready to open her heart to caring about someone else.

'I never stopped wanting to be with you, Freya.'

She reached out and touched his hand, and their eyes met. That rush, of desire, of needing his touch, his hands on her – it was there, as strong as it had ever been. She kissed him, and he kissed her back, urgently, searching, wanting. Everything had changed, and nothing at all.

Chapter 39

February 2020

When Freya woke up she could hear the children playing together downstairs. She cherished for a moment the calm silence. She could wake slowly today, wiggling her toes until the feeling came in, and moving her fingers against the cotton sheets until her arms and hands were warm. Her focus came gradually. She turned to her bedside table to check the time on her alarm clock. She put the radio on to listen to the headlines. Northern Italy was shutting down. The news unsettled her, and she switched it off. As she did, she noticed two red envelopes, and they brought a smile to her face.

She opened Jessie's pink card and smiled at the message and the purple flowers she'd drawn inside. She opened the other.

To Freya,
Happy Valentine's Day.
I love you.
Dino

Freya smiled, and held it close to her chest. It was almost a year since she'd first met him, and now she couldn't imagine ever being without him.

'All set?' Freya asked.

They were standing outside the address Echo had given her. Her friend Cassie's flat. She'd seen Echo a dozen or so times since becoming Dino's carer. Each time she hoped that things would go smoothly, for his sake. Sometimes they did, and sometimes they didn't.

Standing there on the pavement, in his shorts and sandals, holding a bunch of flowers for his mum, Dino looked so small and young all of a sudden. He looked up at her, his eyes as wide as the day she'd first met him, and he nodded.

'I want to see Mum.'

'And you understand that, just like all the other times, we'll need to say goodbye to her at the end,' Freya said.

'I know.'

'OK. Let's go in, then.'

Dino nodded. His eyes were shiny, and the unshed tears caught at Freya's heart. But he didn't need her comfort, he needed her strength.

She took his hand, and unhooked the black metal gate. They walked together up the tiled path. Dino went over to the flat buzzers and got up on tiptoes. 'I know which one it is. It's this one.'

He pressed the buzzer for Flat C, and Echo's voice came over the intercom. 'Is that you, Dino?'

'Yes, Mum,' he said. His mouth creased into a smile. His eyes sparkled, and his whole face changed – filled with light. Freya gave his hand a squeeze and together they pushed the front door open.

The flat was on the first floor, and Echo and her friend Cassie

306

were waiting at the open door. Dino picked up pace and ran into his mother's outstretched arms. She pulled him in close to her, and held him tightly.

Freya stood back. Eventually Echo looked up at Freya and smiled. 'Come in,' she said. 'I got you custard creams,' she said to her son. 'Your favourite.'

Dino smiled at her. 'Thanks,' he said, quietly.

He went into the living room, took a biscuit from the plate, and hopped up on to the sofa. He cupped one hand to catch the crumbs.

Echo whispered to Freya, 'Thank you for bringing him.'

Freya shook her head. 'It's nothing. Of course he wanted to come. Listen – I'll go, give you some time on your own with him.'

Echo touched her arm. 'Don't. Please don't. Stay.'

'OK,' Freya said.

They sat together. Freya accepted the tea that Cassie made her.

'Sorry there are no toys here, D,' Echo said. 'I've still got them boxed up in our old place. Next time.'

'That's OK,' Dino said, looking down.

She gave him a cuddle, and he smiled again, shyly.

'So how've you been, champion?'

He shrugged. 'Good.'

'You like it down in Dorset?'

He looked at Freya, and she saw he was anxious to give the right answer. 'I like some things about it.'

'He's been doing really well. I mean, he misses you, of course, but he's settling well, and you and Jessie are thick as thieves, right?' Freya said.

'It's kind of fun having sisters,' he said.

'I miss you too, you know,' Echo said.

He nodded. 'I know, Mum.'

Echo smiled. Hugged him again.

Then she sat back on the sofa and closed her eyes, as if a profound fatigue was taking her over.

'Echo,' Cassie said, nudging her.

She mumbled, shifting slightly so that her face was resting on the sofa cushion.

'Mum,' Dino said, concerned.

'She's all right,' Cassie said, too quickly. She gave her friend another nudge. 'Wake up.'

Her eyelids flickered, but her eyes rolled back, as if she wasn't fully there.

The room fell silent. Freya felt every moment as an eternity. Cassie caught her eye, and Freya nodded reluctantly, in shared understanding. Dino glanced up at Freya, searching for an answer.

Cassie pushed at Echo again, and this time it roused her. She sat up, and rubbed her eyes brusquely. 'Sorry, sorry, guys. Don't know what happened there. I was miles away.'

Dino smiled faintly, in a way that didn't quite reach his eyes.

'Dude,' Echo said, putting a hand on his knee. 'Listen. I'm sorry. I'm feeling rough today. I know I promised we could go to Dreamland. But—'

'That's OK,' Dino said, quietly.

'Can I talk to you for a second, Echo?' Freya said. 'In private?'

Echo nodded, and got slowly to her feet. The two of them went out into the hallway.

'I can see you've got a lot going on,' Freya said.

'That's it,' Echo said, holding her head and pulling her hair up. 'My head's like this. Exploding. I can't take him over there today.'

'I get that,' Freya said. 'It's not just about today, though, is it? Are you using again?'

'No,' Echo said, but Freya could see the lie in her eyes. The lack of focus, the way they drifted.

'I don't believe you.'

Echo fell silent for a moment. 'I've tried to stop, Freya. It's really hard.'

'It must be,' Freya said. 'I'm not disputing that. But I need you to be honest with me.'

'Neil and I hit that bad patch. I needed something to get me through it. I've tried staying on the meds they put me on but they just make me feel numb. I'm done with that. I miss the ups. I can't handle not knowing who I am.'

'And that's more important than Dino?' Freya said.

She heard the judgement in her own words – she couldn't help it. Dino seemed to be the one getting lost in all this.

'What, me feeling like me?' Echo snapped back. 'In a way, yes. Or at least *as* important. Call it what you like. Judge me all you like. I don't blame you. But waking up, feeling like I know who I am? Not feeling like a robot? It's important. I'm still trying to kick this. I don't want to live this way. But it's not easy.'

'I need to know that you're trying,' Freya said.

'I am.'

'Really?'

'Yes.'

Freya wanted to believe her.

'I want you to think about Neil. About whether he's really helping you in all this.'

Echo went quiet, and looked down. 'It's complicated,' she said.

'I know. But there are people who can help you. Women's Aid, would you call them? I'll text you the number.'

'It's not that easy,' Echo said, flatly.

'I know it's not easy. But do you want to go on like this?'

Echo looked down at the floor, and shook her head.

'You can take that first step.'

'I don't know,' she said, looking up, her eyes glazed. 'I keep messing up. Again and again.'

'It only takes one time, one time that you keep on going.'

Freya had a new sense of urgency. Things were changing. Something bigger than them was happening, she could feel it. She didn't want Echo to stay stuck – not now.

They fell silent for a moment.

'So Dino's pretty crushed, right?' Echo said.

'It's tough on him, yes. He's been looking forward to going.'

Echo looked at her, searchingly. 'Maybe you could take him there?'

'You're sure?'

'Yes,' Echo said. 'You'd be doing me a favour. He shouldn't miss out.'

They went back into the living room, and spoke with Dino. He looked at Freya and smiled.

'If that's OK with you, Dino?' Freya asked.

He nodded.

'You can tell me all about it,' Echo said. 'Call me up tonight and tell me.'

'I will, Mum.'

'I just ... you know. I'm sorry,' Echo said. 'It's just ... I'm not great today. I need to get my shit together. Oh, man. Now I'm swearing in front of you.' She shook her head and she and Dino both laughed. 'Sorry, dude.'

'I know that bad word already,' he said. 'But I'm not going to use it.'

'Good boy,' Echo said, kissing the top of his head. 'You're a really good kid. And I'm sorry I've messed up a lot lately. But I love you. I want you to know that I love you.'

'I know, Mum,' Dino said, hugging her. 'I love you too.'

He's gone. I've still got the feeling of him in my arms. His warm sweet body. The love between us was all still there, nothing had changed. But it was all ...

I don't know. It was too much. I wanted to keep it, just like that. A hug. A perfect moment. I didn't want to take him out and mess it up and have it all go wrong, so he'd remember what a failure I am. I feel rough after last night still. But this is the last day I'm going to feel that way. The very last day.

I'm going to earn that love back. I'm going to make myself worthy of it. I'm going to strip my life back until all it's got in it is good things.

I pick up my phone and stare at the number Freya gave me.

One step. One small step.

Freya held Dino's hand in hers, just tightly enough that he'd know she wasn't about to let him go. The winter sun was bright, glinting off the Dreamland sign. A crowd of children passed them, jostling their way into the amusement park, their chatter and excited voices merging with the clamour of the rides.

'Can we really go in?' Dino asked. She saw that even now he didn't trust it – he was waiting for his hopes to be dashed.

She smiled at him, and squeezed his hand gently. 'Yes. Yes, we can.'

'And when we're in there, can I go on things?'

'Yes, we can go on the rides,' she said, gently. 'You can go on whatever you want to.'

He looked incredulous. 'Really?'

'Yes,' she laughed. 'That's why we're here, Dino.'

He wrinkled his nose a little, then smiled.

'You're ready?' she asked.

He nodded. 'Definitely.'

They walked together into the whirl of it all: the gleeful screams, the spinning teacups, the smell of candyfloss. 'That one.' He pointed at the rollercoaster, the carriages hurtling along the track under a brilliant blue sky. 'I want to go on that one first.'

'Sure,' she said. She reached into her purse to give him the money.

His gaze was steady. 'With you, Freya.'

She glanced up at the highest point of the ride, and a flutter of vertigo caught her stomach. She did not want to go up there. No part of her wanted to go up there.

'Come up with me, Freya,' he said.

She'd once thought she needed to make space for Dino in her life – but in the end it wasn't him, but her own self. Who she could be if she wasn't scared any more.

Keeping her feelings pushed down hadn't ever stopped them existing. The more she'd tried to ignore them, the more they had found a way to trip her up. She'd gone too long not being brave, and now she wanted to be braver. It didn't feel like a choice any more.

In Dreamland, in that blur of colour and light and laughter, she was becoming someone new. The past was heavy with pain and loss, and she'd kept herself tied there for too long. The road ahead had to be different, brighter. She'd make it that way.

'Let's go,' she said.

There were goosebumps on Freya's skin. Today was the start of something.

She was alive.

Acknowledgements

Thank you to my agent, Madeleine Milburn, and my editors, Viola Hayden and Rebecca Farrell, for your invaluable editorial insights, support and guidance. Thanks to all at Sphere, especially Lucy Malagoni and Darcy Nicholson. Thanks also to Thalia Proctor and Linda McQueen, who helped me pull the details of this story into line.

To James, my other half, and to my children, Finn and Marlena, who inspire me daily.

To Caroline Hogg and Emma Stonex, for being who you are, and for riding this rollercoaster with me.

One of the Family
Reading Group Questions:

1. Did you guess Dino's secret before it was revealed? Why, or why not?

2. How does your view of Dino change as the story progresses? Do the chapters from his perspective change how you view his behaviour?

3. How is Dino seen by those around him, and how does that work for them? In what ways is the idea of 'the other' relevant to this story?

4. How do you feel about Echo's actions throughout the story? Was Freya right to forgive her? Do you think she will ever be able to change?

5. Freya is protective over Louisa, but do you think she ever goes too far? How do you think what happened to Sam affects her relationships with her daughters?

6. 'She loved him, but that love began to feel like a habit, something she did because she couldn't remember how to do anything else.' What do you think about how Freya and Joe's relationship changes in the book? Could loving someone as a habit describe any other character's relationships in the story?

7. Discuss Sam's reasons for running away. How did your perceptions of her and her relationship with Freya change throughout the book?

8. A lot of characters experience significant loss in different ways in the book. Who did you empathise most with and why?

9. There are many different family dynamics shown in the book – how would you define family? Which characters, who aren't related, would you say behave as family?

10. 'She was alive.' How are these final words significant to Freya's journey? In what ways do you think she has changed?